MURDER UNDONE
Gripping Psychological Suspense

ROBIN STOREY

This book is a work of fiction. Any resemblance to any person alive or dead is purely coincidental.

Storey-Lines

Cover design by Judy Bullard

Proofreading by Jo Robinson

DEDICATION

For Aaron

TABLE OF CONTENTS

PROLOGUE

April 1995

THE horizon over the harbour was pink, blending into gold and purple, the boats bobbing gently on the water. They'd done this often after they were first married, sitting on the deck with a drink watching the daylight fade to evening over inconsequential chatter and comfortable silences.

Eva glanced at Charlie as he stared into the distance. He hadn't touched his champagne. Was he thinking about those early days? Even if he was, he'd feel no guilt. Maybe he was planning his exit strategy, preparing for the right circumstances to tell her he was leaving. Even in profile his face was drawn and weary. Having an affair was hard work–juggling the urgent passion of new love with the pretence of being a loving and devoted husband.

He turned his head and smiled. Despite herself, her stomach flipped. After sixteen years of marriage she could still appreciate, as if seeing him anew, how attractive he was when he smiled. His golden-brown eyes twinkled under his caterpillar eyebrows, warming and softening his face, so you felt good just looking at him and you wanted to succumb to his charm. It had taken her many years to realise that the warmth was only skin deep.

'It was so good of you to do this, sweet pea,' he said. 'I could have taken you out to dinner if you'd wanted.'

'I like cooking for you. I thought it would be more romantic to spend our anniversary at home, just the two of us.'

Especially as it would be their last night together. In less than three hours, he'd be dead.

'What delectable dish are you cooking? '

She smiled. 'You'll have to wait and see. I'll go and check on the progress.'

She felt his eyes on her as she walked across the deck and through the open doorway into the kitchen. She'd bought a new cocktail dress for the occasion, Lisa Ho, royal blue with a plunging neckline, draped over her curves as if it was designed for her. Not that she didn't already have a wardrobe full of designer dresses, but she never passed up an opportunity to buy another one.

Two saucepans simmered on the huge stainless steel stovetop. The aroma of curry filled the kitchen—beef vindaloo, Charlie's favourite. She took the lids off both the saucepans and peered inside. They both looked and smelled identical, but only the rear saucepan contained chopped up aconite root, one of the most poisonous plants known to man.

She'd done a lot of research to find the right one—aconite was fast acting, undetectable in routine observation, and the symptoms mimicked those of a heart attack. It was pure good fortune that Charlie liked curry, which masked the taste, and that he never ventured into the kitchen, so he wasn't likely to ask why she was cooking two separate meals.

The coconut rice in the rice cooker was almost cooked to fluffy perfection, and the naan bread was warming in the oven. All was going as planned. In the fridge were two creme caramels she'd made earlier for dessert. Of course they wouldn't get to dessert, but she had to make everything look as authentic as possible.

Her insides were trembling and she felt light-headed, as if she were about to faint. She took hold of the kitchen bench to steady herself. *Do you really want to do this?* She loved and hated Charlie with equal intensity. Much as she couldn't bear to think of life without him, to think of him with *her,* the two of them living in this very house, was like having her heart ripped out of her chest.

She took a few deep breaths until she felt calm and steady and her resolve had hardened again. She'd made the decision and she had to go through with it.

•••

They ate their entree of sauteed prawns and watercress salad sitting at the dining table, candles flickering in their antique brass holders next to a vase of fresh roses the gardener had picked from the garden. Natalie Cole's sweet, mellow tones serenaded them from the CD stereo. Through the glass French doors the harbour was a shining, velvet expanse with the majestic rise of the Sydney Harbour Bridge arching against the dark sky.

'There's no mistaking that aroma of beef vindaloo,' Charlie said. He reached across the table and laid her hand in both of his. 'You're a good wife to me, much better than I deserve. I know I haven't been around much lately. Getting that new mine in Western Australia operational has just been one headache after another.'

The humble pie act didn't fool her for one minute. 'I understand, darling.' She gently slid her hand out of his and rose to get the main course.

She returned with bowls of sides—cucumber and yoghurt, and banana with coconut, then two plates of steaming curry and rice and a basket of naan bread.

She watched Charlie as he picked up his knife and fork, stabbed a large hunk of beef and piled some rice on top. Her heart was hammering, and sweat was pooling in her armpits and trickling into her cleavage. There was still time to stop it—she saw herself yelling, 'Don't eat it!' springing up and whipping the knife and fork out of his hands.

But she didn't. She sat there, unable to move, watching him shovel the forkful of food into his mouth. The moment was over. There was no turning back.

'Superb, as usual,' Charlie said, taking a piece of naan bread from the basket.

Eva forced a smile. 'I'm glad you like it.'

She picked at her food, willing her hands to stop shaking; fortunately Charlie was enjoying his meal too much to notice. She watched him out of the corner of her eye. At sixty-one he was twenty one years older than she was, and even his regular exercise regime had failed to prevent the beginnings of a paunch, the legacy of a love of fine cuisine.

But women didn't care about a man's looks if he had money, and when you combined that with old school charm and an undercurrent of raw sexual energy it was an irresistible force. No doubt that was what had attracted *her* to Charlie, and many others before her.

Charlie put down his knife and fork with a sigh of satisfaction. 'That was the best curry yet.' He looked at Eva's plate. 'You've hardly eaten anything.'

'I'm not really hungry after all that cooking. Come and relax until it's time for dessert.'

Charlie refilled their glasses and they settled on the couch in the living room. 'Cry me a river,' Natalie crooned. Charlie seemed more at ease; the champagne had worked its magic. He put his arm around Eva, his hand warm on her shoulder. The sweat had dried on her body, leaving her chilled. A sense of fatalism had overtaken her and calmed her, and she had the sensation of standing outside herself, watching the events she had set in motion unfold.

'I haven't told you how beautiful you look,' Charlie said. 'Is that a new dress?'

'Yes.' Eva smiled. 'It's my anniversary present to you.'

'Lucky it looks so good on you, it wouldn't suit me at all.'

His hand dropped from her shoulder to her breast and he ran his fingers lightly over the soft material of her dress. Her nipples hardened. He put his mouth to her ear. 'I have something for you, too.'

He got up, went inside and came back with a small box. 'Happy anniversary, darling.'

Eva opened it and took out a delicate necklace, diamonds glittering in the lamplight.

'Oh darling, it's beautiful!'

'Let me put it on for you.'

As she held out the necklace, he groaned. His face was gray and beaded with sweat. He lurched off the couch, clutching his stomach and raced down the hallway.

Eva followed him to the bedroom. She could hear him in the ensuite, coughing and retching.

'What's happened, Charlie?' she called to him from the doorway.

'I don't know,' he gasped. 'What did you put in the curry?'

'It can't be the curry, I'm fine. Maybe you've caught a stomach bug.'

This was where she had to make a judgment call. She didn't want to call the ambulance too soon, in case he survived. If she called them too late, it would look suspicious.

'Should I call an ambulance?' she asked, knowing what his answer would be.

He staggered out of the ensuite, wiping his mouth. 'No, probably just a stomach bug, as you say. I'll lie down for a while.'

Eva hovered around as a concerned wife would, at the same time refusing to allow her mind to focus on Charlie's distress. After half an hour of trips to the toilet, Charlie's breathing became laboured.

'I'm burning up, I feel as if I'm on fire,' he gasped. He gazed up at her from the bed, his eyes filmy with confusion. 'What's happening to me?'

Once other symptoms besides vomiting and diarrhea kicked in, the end was near. She took his hand. It was cold and clammy. 'I don't know, but this is more than a stomach bug. I'm calling an ambulance.'

She did so and it arrived within five minutes, sirens blaring. She described the symptoms to the paramedics as they placed him on a stretcher and hooked him up to an oxygen mask. By now he was unconscious. She fluttered around him, wringing her hands.

'We thought it was just a stomach bug, but I got worried when he became breathless. Will he be all right?'

'Can't tell you at this stage. We'll take him to St Vincent's. You can drive there and park in the emergency visitors' car park.'

As she negotiated her way through the traffic in her Mercedes, there was only one thought churning around her mind. *Please don't let him live.* She parked and rushed into the emergency department at St Vincent's hospital.

She'd only been in the waiting room for fifteen minutes when a doctor came out. From the look on his face, she knew what he was going to say.

'I'm sorry, Mrs Dennehy, we couldn't save him.'

CHAPTER ONE

April 2015

IT was the snoring that woke her, bouncing off the walls of the bedroom. Eva half sat up and looked at the man lying on his back beside her. Her heart skipped a beat. For just a moment–the shape of his bald head, the contours of his cheeks–he looked like Charlie. But in the creeping dawn light it was easy to see the man was nothing like him. Jowly, a thick pelt of hair on his chest and arms, bloated belly that rose and fell in rhythm with the snores. And oozing stale alcohol.

She grimaced. She supposed she smelled the same. Certainly her dry, gritty mouth and gathering headache was testament to that. She checked the bedside clock. Five am. She was getting soft–she usually kicked them out straight after sex.

She shook his shoulder. 'Hey, time to get up.'

No response. What the hell was his name? Last night was hazy–she thought back to when he'd sidled up to her at the bar and bought her a drink. They did the usual introductions, as if names really mattered, as if they weren't going to end up in bed together, strangers grasping at each other for whatever temporary comfort they could find.

'Frank!' A thunderous snore almost deafened her. 'Eddie! George!'

His eyes flew open. George, that was it. He turned his head and stared at her, frowning.

'You have to leave! Now!'

Comprehension slowly dawned. 'You're not even going to cook me breakfast?'

'Do I look like the chef at The Sheraton?'

'Jesus, you're a hard woman.'

He sat up and hauled himself out of bed. She watched him as he retrieved his jeans, underpants and shirt from the floor and put them on. Her memory was waking up and she saw his thick, hairy hands exploring her body as his mouth clamped down on hers, moving down to bite her nipples, which made her yell. A couple of rough finger pokes to make sure she was wet enough, a few minutes of humping, it was all over. She'd made the mistake of allowing herself to drift off to sleep instead of getting rid of him.

Not a lot of sexual pleasure, about as much as she'd got with Edgar before he lost interest completely, but it was the closeness, bare flesh melded together, need and want and desire mingling in the illusion that she mattered to someone, if only for a few hours.

She got up, wrapped a robe around herself and escorted him through the living room to the front door. She always used the guest wing when she brought men home, it helped to keep that part of her life separate from her normal life. George turned to her and grinned.

'I like a bossy woman. Reminds me of my wife. She died last year of cancer. But I told you that last night, didn't I?'

She had no recollection of that. 'Yes, you did.'

Looking at him now, she couldn't imagine what had attracted her to him. That's what double whisky shots and dim lighting in bars did to you.

George took his mobile phone out of his pocket. 'What's your number, honey? I'll take you out to dinner one night.'

For God's sake, let's not pretend this was anything but a one night stand. She'd told him she was widowed and he obviously thought he was on to a good thing when the taxi dropped them off the night before.

'Wow! This is some joint!' he'd exclaimed, staring up at the three-storey mansion set into the cliffside with its views of Tamarama beach.

'Sorry, I'm not interested,' Eva said.

He gave her a hard look before slipping his phone back in his pocket. 'I see. One of those love 'em and leave 'em types. Good luck, might see you again, picking up some other poor sucker.'

He slammed the door shut behind him, and she watched him through the window as he strode down the front path, wearing his injured pride like a mantle.

•••

She was too wide awake to go back to sleep, so she locked the guest wing and went back into the main house. She'd tidy up and wash the sheets later—Edgar wasn't due back till tomorrow. Not that he ever went into the guest wing.

After showering and dressing in her designer sweat pants, T-shirt, hooded jacket and Nikes, she slipped out the front door and down the sloping front path that was bordered by a lush lawn and well-behaved garden. On either side stood two large identical fountains, with cherubic angels peeing water. She shuddered every time she passed them; Edgar's taste was in direct proportion to his wealth. She'd tried to persuade him to replace them with something more tasteful, but although he let her have her way on most occasions, he remained steadfast about the angels.

Locking the security gate behind her, she crossed the road to the path that wound along the coastline, snuggling into her jacket against the crisp autumn breeze. The sea was blue-grey, the sun a glowing orb poised at the edge of the horizon, as if waiting for the curtain call to come out from the wings. Apart from the occasional jogger on the beach, she could almost believe she was the only person in the world. The path was part of the popular Bondi to Coogee Beach Coastal Walk, but it was still too early on a Sunday morning for the recreational walkers.

Her steps marked out a soothing rhythm, in time to the throbbing in her head. She swallowed her hangover nausea. If she walked fast enough, maybe she could walk off the memories of last night. Because she'd had them again. The visions. They haunted her almost every night now, though she'd hesitated to call them visions when they started six months ago, because it made her sound like a psychic or a religious maniac.

But they were more than dreams. Larger, clearer, sharper. And always of Charlie. Right there in front of her—she could touch his skin, feel his pulse, the warmth and aliveness of him, resurrected from the still, wax-skinned body that was her last memory of him. And always the same expression on his face, asking the same question. Why?

'You were going to leave me,' Eva had said. 'There was no other way.' Her cheeks were wet with tears. 'Can you forgive me?' she whispered.

He didn't answer, his eyes cold, a look she knew well. She shouted, sobbed, begged, pummelled his unyielding chest. No matter what the vision, it always ended the same way, with her sitting bolt upright in bed, hair damp with perspiration, staring wide-eyed into the darkness where Charlie had stood before her just seconds ago.

Sometimes Edgar woke and insisted on making her a cup of cocoa, even though she reassured him it was only a bad dream. Last night, thank God, George had slept through it all and she eventually drifted off to sleep again. The visions always exhausted her, leaving her feeling wrung out the next day.

After an hour the sun had risen, taking the edge off the breeze and promising a clear morning. Eva took off her jacket and wrapped it around her waist. The world was awakening; people were cycling, walking their dogs, striding out while bellowing into their mobile phones, heading to the beach with towels and surfboards.

She left the path and crossed to a small bunch of shops overlooking Coogee Beach. She bought a couple of bananas from a fruit shop, then found an outside table at the Coogee Cafe and ordered a double strength latte. While her stomach revolted at the thought of eating, she forced herself to eat both bananas. She'd been given that tip from an old drunk she'd met in some bar—apparently it was the potassium in the bananas that got rid of the nausea. Whatever the reason, it always worked. Within minutes her stomach had settled, just in time to drink her coffee.

The breakfast crowd buzzed around her. A balding man in slacks and sports jacket strode past. Eva held her breath. Of course it wasn't Charlie, but the spring in his step reminded her of him, how Charlie seemed to bounce up from the balls of his feet when he walked. She was seeing him everywhere during the day as well. What was happening? It had been almost twenty years—why now? *He's haunting me. He's doing it for revenge. He's waited this long so he could catch me unawares*. Though she had no belief in psychic phenomena and her rational mind told her it was bullshit, it was the only explanation she could think of.

She finished her coffee and got up, feeling half-human again. As she was about to cross the road to retrace her steps home, the sound of voices singing floated towards her. Angel voices, clear and pure. She turned and walked in their direction and found herself in a leafy side street shaded by trees on either side, crammed with parked cars. A pink sandstone church stood in front of her. St Gabriel's Catholic Church. The voices faded away to an 'Amen.'

She went to the front door and peered in. The church was about three-quarters full—religion was still alive and well in this part of town. Perhaps the well-off were the only ones who could afford the luxury of believing. The priest, a tall man with unruly grey hair brushed back from his forehead and a bushy beard, reminded her of a folk musician she'd picked up at a bar a couple of months ago. His tone of voice was warm and conversational, a far cry from the fire and brimstone booming she remembered from her youth. The all-female choir sat in the side gallery, heads all turned towards her as one.

She either had to come in or leave, to avoid further attention. She slipped in and sat in the back row next to an elderly woman with purple hair. The woman gave her a curious sideways glance.

'Blessed are you, Lord, God of all creation. Through your goodness we have this bread to offer, which earth has given and human hands have made. It will become for us the bread of life,' the priest proclaimed.

'Blessed be God for ever,' the congregation replied.

The Eucharist, leading up to communion. Eva was amazed that she remembered it—she hadn't been to Mass since she was fourteen, having plucked up the courage to announce one Sunday morning to her mother that she was an atheist (pronouncing the word with pride) and would no longer be accompanying her to Mass. She never forgot the look on her mother's face, as if it was her own fault that her daughter had eschewed her beloved God.

Cora Stewart had made a career out of suffering, and Eva, determining that religion was to blame, had decided to throw off its yoke before it dragged her down. No way was she going to live her life apologising for being alive, and at that moment, she made a commitment to herself that she would carve out her own destiny.

The words of the priest and the responses of the congregation flowed over her like the ripples of sun through the stained glass windows. The aroma of wood polish mingled with the lavender scent of the woman next to her. It was comforting enfolded within the womb of the church and its rituals, a solid and unchanging sanctuary in an uncertain world.

Eva looked up at the slice of blue sky visible through the top of the nearest window, imagining her mother looking down on her from heaven, her face as Eva last saw it, caving in on itself, her eyes huge, skin as fragile as tissue paper. *You'd be proud of me, Ma, at Mass for the first time in forty-six years.*

'The peace of the Lord be with you always,' the priest said. He was looking straight at her. She shivered and looked away.

'And also with you,' chanted the congregation.

'Let us offer each other a sign of peace.'

The purple hair nodded towards her. 'Peace be with you."

'Peace be with you,' Eva said, and again to the couple in front who turned around and smiled. This was the part that had always embarrassed her when she attended church as a teenager. Some people just nodded, others shook your hand, one time an old man with wet rubbery lips kissed her on the cheek. After the breaking of the bread came communion. She watched as the congregation lined up, pew by pew to receive their wafer and sip of wine.

Her mind flashed back to the age of ten when she'd had her best friend Sally sleep over on a Saturday night. Eva's mother had insisted on them both accompanying her to church the next morning. When Eva went up to receive communion, Sally followed her.

'You can't take communion, you weren't baptized!' Eva hissed at her.

'Who's going to know?' Sally whispered back, with a mischievous grin.

When they sat back down again, Sally said, 'That bread's disgusting, it tastes like cardboard!' All the heads in the row in front of them swivelled around in unison. Eva glared at her and spent the rest of the service in a sweat, waiting for God to rain down his anger on her, for allowing an 'unblessed' to receive communion.

As her neighbour returned to her seat, she gave Eva a quizzical glance. What good Catholic went to church and didn't take communion?

Then they were standing, singing the closing hymn, led by the choir. The women in the choir were a range of ages, but they all had one thing in common—

their faces shone with a guileless enthusiasm, a smile hovering around their lips as if they all shared a divine secret. How much easier would life be if she believed? If she woke up each morning lit up from inside with that unswerving devotion, that certainty? God supposedly forgave you all your sins, even if people didn't. For a few moments, Eva's heart ached for what those women had. But even if she did believe, it wouldn't change anything.

After a couple of community announcements and a closing prayer, it was over. It was Eva's intention to make a quick getaway, but somehow the priest—perhaps he had angel wings—had made it to the front door just as she was walking out.

He held out his hand. 'I'm Father O'Halloran. Are you new to the area?' His handshake was firm.

'I'm Eva. I live in Tamarama—I'm just here for the day.'

Up close he looked older, easily in his sixties. His profession was portrayed in the planes and gullies of his face; he'd seen suffering and the worst of humanity, yet a sheen of compassion overlaid it all.

'Nice to meet you,' he said. 'Feel free to drop by at any time.'

He smiled, his eyes meeting hers briefly before he turned to greet the person behind her. The look was so intense it stopped her in her tracks. It was as if he knew what she'd been thinking in church, knew everything about her, that she had secrets she'd never told another living soul. *You're getting paranoid now.*

Her arms had broken out in goosebumps. She put on her jacket and walked away without a backward glance.

CHAPTER TWO

'I WON'T be coming home tonight.' Edgar's voice boomed down the phone. 'Mum's just gone into palliative care. They think...' he faltered, 'it will only be a few days.'

He was on a business trip to Melbourne and as he always did, he'd called into see his mother, who was in a nursing home with dementia.

'Oh, honey, I'm so sorry,' Eva said. 'Do you want me to fly down?'

'Not unless you really want to. She won't know who you are. She doesn't even recognise me. Lynn's here now and Roderick's flying in tomorrow.'

'In that case, I'll stay here, if you don't mind. I'm sure you'd rather not have a crowd in there in her last days. But I'll be thinking of you. Phone me tomorrow.'

She sighed with relief as she put down her phone. She could think of nothing worse than keeping a bedside vigil for her mother-in-law, nice old lady that she was, and watching her fade away. The last thing she wanted to be reminded of right now was death. Of course now that she tried not to think about it, death was all that came to mind. She saw her mother in the hospice during her final days with cancer, shrinking into her bones until she became a stranger; her tiny room thick with the suffocating stench of death.

Yvonne Rawlings was ninety-five. She'd lived well above her allotted life span, whereas Cora Stewart had been only forty-five when she died.

'A life cut too tragically short,' the priest had said at the funeral.

'It was her own fault!' Eva wanted to shout. 'She loved being the martyr. Never thought she was good enough to do anything but clean school toilets. After my father left it gave her even more reason to be a victim. It was inevitable she'd get cancer.'

She got up from the recliner lounge by the swimming pool and went inside to the bar in the entertainment area. It was just after three pm, too early to start drinking, but what the hell. She'd have a couple now just to soothe the crawling itch inside her, then she'd go to the bar later. She was not going to allow herself to think about Charlie's death.

●●●

'Same again?' Gerry asked.

He was only asking out of courtesy. Her answer was always 'yes'.

He poured another champagne and slid it over. She liked sitting at the bar—she was in control. She could talk to Gerry in between customers when she was in the mood, and when she wasn't he sensed it and left her alone. Men eyed her when they came to order a drink, and if she liked the look of them and felt like some company, she made eye contact and let it go from there. If she didn't, she ignored them.

The Red Door was her favourite hotel; she liked the ambience of discreet cosiness. This was not a place where people came to party; the clientele were mainly couples who ate and went home, or businessmen meeting for an after-work drink. No-one knew her here. Though she and Edgar lived in luxury and he had his share of wealthy men's toys, he preferred a quiet, low profile life. Once that would have frustrated her; now it suited her.

'You okay, Eva?' Gerry said, whipping out the cloth from the back of his pants and wiping down the counter.

'Yes, why do you ask?'

'You look upset.'

'Do I?'

She gulped her champagne. The effect of the drinks she'd had at home had worn off and it always took a couple of glasses of pub champagne to feel that warm buzz in her head. 'It's twenty years today since my husband died.'

It slipped out before she could stop it. Gerry regarded her for a moment. It was the first piece of personal information she'd offered him. 'I'm sorry to hear that. No wonder you're upset.'

He pulled a beer for a customer then turned back to her. 'So how did he die?'

'Heart attack.'

It came out so glibly she could almost believe it herself. Well, the doctors believed it. Not even an autopsy ordered. It was a stroke of luck that Charlie had had a heart scare a year prior and was on medication for high blood pressure.

Gerry gave a sympathetic nod. 'My Mum died ten years ago. It's true what they say—you never get over it. Sometimes I still cry when I think of her.'

It was hard to think of Gerry, a big, hairy bear of a man, crying. He picked up a big bag of peanuts and started refilling the snack bowls on the bar.

'Do you believe in God?' Eva asked.

He stopped in mid-refill. 'Geez, you're getting deep and meaningful now. And so early in the night.'

He emptied the bag and threw it in the bin. 'Yeah, I do. It's like an insurance policy. If there is life after death, then I'm a shoo-in. If there's no life after death, so what? It hasn't cost me anything, except a few prayers occasionally.' He grinned. 'When my footy team's losing.'

There was a rush at the bar, which kept him busy, then he came back over and said, 'What about you? Do you believe in God?'

'No. I was brought up as a Catholic, but I'm not a believer.'

He pursed his lips. 'I've got a mate who's Catholic—cattle ticks we called them when I was a kid—and he says it's harder to shake off than a dose of the clap. They've got you by the balls as soon as you're born—all that guilt and suffering and reward in heaven crap, it's pumped into you in your mother's milk.'

Eva said nothing, thinking of her mother and the sternly religious upbringing she'd had.

'Sorry if I've offended you,' Gerry said, 'but you asked.'

'You didn't offend me. There could be some truth in what you say.'

He grinned. 'It'd be the first time ever. Another one?"

Eva nodded. She felt a presence beside her and turned to see a sleek, silver-haired man in a business suit smiling at her.

'Can I buy you this one?'

In her mind's eye she saw herself in the taxi going home—light-headed, loose-limbed, the man's hand travelling up her thigh, the ache of desire, knowing the sex would never satisfy her but not caring, the rough passion, tangled limbs in sweaty sheets. Then getting up to show him out and collapsing back into bed, where she would drift into an uneasy sleep—until Charlie's apparition appeared.

An intense weariness was seeping into her bones. 'I'll give it a miss,' she said to Gerry.

'Thanks, anyway,' she said to Silver Hair, slid off her stool and walked out. She could feel their stares burning into her back.

CHAPTER THREE

A BRISK wind swirled the leaves around her feet as Eva approached St Gabriel's Church. Grey clouds bunched up, allowing only a few weak rays of sun through the sentinel of trees along the road. They'd been threatening rain all day and she'd brought her umbrella just in case.

The walk was invigorating—the crisp air biting at her face made her feel alive and helped to dispel the last vestiges of her hangover. She'd vowed to herself last night that she wouldn't drink, but she was so terrified of what she was about to do that she drank herself to sleep in front of the TV. Edgar was still in Melbourne; his mother had taken her sweet time to die, and he was now organising the funeral.

The front door of the church was open. Eva stood in the doorway. It was empty. Being Saturday, there was no service till seven o'clock. Her appointment for an anonymous reconciliation was for four o'clock. *If you turn and run now, no-one will be any the wiser. Go home and forget you ever wanted to do this.*

Shutting out the voice in her head, she walked to the confessional booth and slipped inside. The grille in the wall through which you talked to the priest reminded her of a prison. Not that she'd been to one. Or intended to go. The priest was bound not to disclose confidential information to anyone, not even the police.

She knelt on the bench in front of the grille and took a deep breath. It had been so long. Should she say something, or wait?

'In the name of the Father, and of the Son and of the Holy Spirit, Amen,' a voice said through the grille. She recognised the gentle tones of Father O'Halloran.

Then it came to her in a flash. Maybe Gerry was right, you never forgot. 'Forgive me Father for I have sinned.' Her voice was hoarse, she cleared her throat. 'It's been forty-six years since my last confession.'

She was a child again, waiting for a thunderclap from heaven to strike her down.

'What sins do you accuse yourself of?'

'Murder.'

It was out, the word she'd never said out loud, lingering in the air with a sinister resonance. Still no thunderclap. Like a boil that had been pricked, it was easier now to let the rest out.

'I killed my husband. Twenty years and two weeks ago. I found out he was planning to leave me for his mistress, so I poisoned him. I deliberately chose a poison that mimicked heart attack symptoms, so I was never suspected. You're the first person I've told.'

Her tone of voice was matter of fact, but her heart was racing. What was he thinking? Priests are not supposed to judge, but they're also human. Was that the worst sin he'd heard? Surely not.

'You've carried a heavy burden over the last twenty years,' Father O'Halloran said.

'Yes.' Her voice wavered. 'I loved him so much.' Then the words poured out. *This is not what you do at confession. He's not your therapist.*

But she couldn't stop herself.

CHAPTER FOUR

'IT'S a long story, Father, and I have to start it way back when Charlie and I first met. I was twenty-three and at a bit of a loose end as my mother had recently died of cancer. I'd returned to Bindaboon, my home town, to look after her for the last eighteen months of her life. My father left when I was six, so she was my only family. After she died, I moved back to Sydney and got a job as a secretary, as we called it then, with a firm of architects. I hated it; the work was tedious and the pay was pitiful.'

'One day my boss asked me to take some plans over to a client as they needed them urgently. I took them over in my car, and on the way back, the traffic was stopped at a red light, but I wasn't concentrating and ploughed straight into the rear of a shiny red Mercedes. I was in tears even before the driver got out and started abusing me. Then I saw a man get out of the back seat and he came over and said, "That's enough, Robert, she's upset enough already." '

'The Mercedes had a few dents, but my car, being an old Toyota, was a lot worse off. The bonnet was all crumpled in and it was undriveable. After the police had arrived and done their report, the man, who turned out to be Charlie, arranged for my car to be towed to the mechanic's, rang my boss and explained what had happened, and took me to the nearest cafe for a cup of coffee. '

She paused. 'And that was it. I wouldn't say it was love at first sight, but there was definitely a spark there. Charlie was older than me by twenty one years, but I certainly didn't feel the age gap. There was something about him, the way he looked at me and listened to what I said, that by the time I got back to the office I was walking on air and I didn't even care about my car. '

'I know it sounds corny, but we had a whirlwind courtship—he took me to restaurants I'd only read about in the social pages, to concerts and the ballet and opera, and bought me beautiful clothes to wear on such occasions. '

And made love to me like I'd never been made love to before. And when I thought it couldn't get any better, it did.

'And eighteen months later we were married—I'll never forget the day he proposed to me. We were snorkelling off one of the secluded islands in the Bahamas and he dived down and came up with a small tin and when I opened it, it was a ring inlaid with twelve diamonds—one for each month we'd known each other.'

She was there now, the shimmering aqua water lapping around her body, behind her the postcard scene of palm trees and pristine beach. And the look on Charlie's face as she opened the box—hope, tinged with a little uncertainty. Because she wasn't a pushover by any means; she wasn't always available when he wanted to take her out, and she let him know she had another life, even though in reality she didn't. And there were things from her past she hinted at but didn't reveal, to cultivate an air of mystery. There was nothing more off-putting to a man than telling him your whole life story in the first few dates. Even though she was expecting it, she couldn't help the tears as she held the ring aloft.

She swallowed the sob rising in her throat. 'I know people wondered why Charlie married me. I could see it in their faces—what's she got that's so special? To them I was just a lowly secretary living a very ordinary, unglamorous life. After two marriages and divorces Charlie had been single for a few years and had a reputation as a playboy, never seen with the same woman more than once, according to the gossip columns. He had a smorgasbord of stunning women who would have done anything to be his wife. So of course our wedding made the headlines too—Third Time Round for Multi-millionaire. Along with the implicit assumption that I'd married him for money and he'd married me for my youth. But Charlie and I weren't the "rich older man marries young trophy wife" cliche.'

'You want to know why Charlie married me?'

There was no response. Eva shifted her position on the bench. 'Am I boring you, Father?'

'Not at all, I assumed it was a rhetorical question.'

'I know this is very long-winded but I want you to understand why I murdered him. The reason Charlie married me was because I was the woman he needed. He probably didn't realise it then, or if he did it was subconscious. But I knew. His previous two wives had been very high profile and attention seeking and there was a lot of publicity when they and Charlie divorced. He didn't need a woman who would try and take the limelight away from him, he needed someone who'd stand by his side and support him, someone he could show off and be proud of, but who also knew when to step aside and let him take centre stage. And I was that woman.

'And I soon showed those snobby bitches, sorry Father—that I had what it took to be Mrs Charles Dennehy. I had the figure to wear the latest designer clothes and I knew how to look classy without being tarty, which is more than I can say for some of them; I loved cooking and entertaining. "Eva's soirees" became legendary—I did my share of fundraising for charities which is expected of you in those circles, and I could hold a conversation on any topic from politics to art. So the women hated me because they were jealous of me and thought I wasn't worthy of Charlie, and the men loved me because I was young, beautiful and intelligent, and could charm the socks off them.'

She adjusted her position again. Kneeling on a hard wooden bench was presumably part of the penance.

'There was one major flaw in my happiness—Charlie was a womaniser. I know what you're thinking—didn't you know that when you married him? Especially with his playboy reputation. The short answer is yes I did, but I hoped, rather naively as it turned out, that he wouldn't need to see other women once we married. My friend Helga had a theory that all wealthy men have this need to constantly reassure themselves of their sexual potency; as their success is proof of their business acumen, so continual sexual conquests are proof of their virility. She'd say, "It comes with the territory, darling, it's the price you pay for your marriage. You can be the jealous wife and make things hard for yourself or you can just look the other way and enjoy your life."'

She could see Helga now, tapping her impossibly long fingernails on the table as she spoke, with her usual unshakable air of authority. It was easy for her to say, she and Sol had an open marriage and she declared she didn't have a jealous bone in her body.

'But I couldn't look the other way. I couldn't bear the thought of Charlie with another woman. Even though I knew he was unfaithful, I couldn't prove it. He had ample opportunity—he worked long hours and went away a lot on business. And he had no shortage of willing applicants, the same charisma that attracted me drew in other women too, and some of them weren't too subtle about it either, but he'd always laugh it off and make me feel as if I were being paranoid if I got upset about it.

'I admit, I was the classic jealous wife, I went through his pockets looking for incriminating evidence, I interrogated him when he got back from business trips. He'd laugh and tell me I was being silly, and he'd kiss me and all my doubts would evaporate in the steamy passion of our lovemaking. Other times, if he was fed up with me, he'd give me this look that made me shrivel up inside and he'd say, 'Eva, you're being totally unreasonable." '

She was hoarse from talking. She pulled a water bottle out of her handbag and had a couple of sips.

'Are you still there Father?'

She felt foolish as soon as she'd asked. Of course he'd still be there, even though he'd had ample time to wander out and make himself of a cup of tea with her being none the wiser.

'I'm still here,' he said reassuringly, as if to a child.

'The funny thing is that after sixteen years of suspicion and accusation, I finally got evidence of his infidelity by accident. It was a Monday night, normally my night for yoga, but I'd stayed home because I had a headache. I was in bed and Charlie was working in his home office. The phone rang and I picked up the bedroom extension and a woman said, "It's me."'

'I was about to say, "Who's me?" when Charlie said, 'I can't talk for long. Eva didn't go to yoga, she's got a headache.'

'And I realized that he'd picked up the office extension at exactly the same time and didn't know I was on the other end. So of course I kept listening. I won't repeat the conversation verbatim though I can remember every word, but it was obvious they were lovers. He called her Veronika and she said in a come-to-bed voice, "I can't wait until we're together for good. You know my biological clock is ticking, darling, I don't want to wait too much longer to have a baby." ' And he said, '"I know, sweet pea, just be patient, it will happen, I just have to wait for the right time." '

'Then they arranged to meet the next night at La Bella restaurant. I waited till he rang off, then I put my receiver down. I was in complete shock. Sweet pea was his pet name for me! Not only was he planning to leave me for this Veronika, he was going to have a baby with her. Charlie had told me right from the start that he didn't want children. "I'm too selfish," he said, as if it were something to be proud of, "and I don't want to share you with a child." '

'I would have enjoyed being a mother but I accepted that was part of the deal, and I had a pretty full life being Charlie's wife. I wanted for nothing. That was the part that hurt the most—in fact once the shock wore off, I was so furious I wanted to march into his office right then and confront him with it. But something stopped me. I wanted to see what she looked like, to see them together.

'There was a hotel next door to La Bella so the next night I went there at about six thirty, bought a drink and sat at a table at the front window where I could see people approaching the restaurant. Charlie's car pulled up and he got out, and then a woman got out of a car nearby. To say she was stunning was an understatement. She looked to be in her early thirties, tall with jet black hair in that sort of tousled bob that was all the rage then, and slanted eyes like a cat. Even her business suit didn't hide her curves. She had this exotic, untamed look about her. Maybe Charlie fancied himself as the hunter who could tame her. They walked into the restaurant together, and even though there was no physical contact between them, I could see the sexual sizzle practically steaming out of their ears.

'I must have sat there for ages staring into space because the bartender came over a couple of times to ask me if I wanted another drink. The phone conversation and seeing them together played on a continuous loop in my head, and then I realised that the reason they were both in business suits was that if word got back to me they'd been seen there, Charlie could say it was a business meeting.

'That had happened before—I'd heard gossip about Charlie being seen with certain women and his stock answer was always that it was a business meeting. And when I made further enquiries it was always the case that the woman ran a PR agency, or was in human resources or some such thing, so a professional relationship was conceivable. Only I knew it wasn't.

'What was so special about Veronika that he was going to leave me for her, aside from the fact that she was young enough to be his daughter? What set her apart from the scores of women he'd had before? Or was that what he said to all of them and he was just stringing her along? Somehow I doubted it—to promise a woman that you'd leave your wife and have a baby with her if you didn't intend to go ahead with it was asking for trouble. And there was something in

Charlie's voice on the phone to Veronika, a depth and a tenderness. Like he'd had with me.

'And that was when the seed of the idea was planted in my mind. To murder him.'

•••

Her face was damp—when had the tears started? They became rasping sobs. Twenty years' worth of sobbing that she'd smothered in alcohol.

'I'm sorry, Father.' She took a few deep breaths and made herself calm down. 'For these and all the sins of my past life especially for my sin of murder, I am truly sorry."

'There's something you need to know,' Father O'Halloran said. 'I know who you are.'

Her heart missed a beat. 'How?'

'I recognised your voice from when I met you a couple of weeks ago. I have a good ear for voices. Comes from years of listening to confessions. And I knew from just looking at you then that you were suffering—it was written all over your face.'

Was it so obvious? She knew Edgar was concerned about her. She'd often caught him giving her sideways glances. He'd even taken her away for a two week cruise around the Caribbean, even though he hated cruises. But it hadn't helped, the night visions of Charlie had found her there. She couldn't escape them.

'And as I'm sure you're aware, I'm bound by the sacramental seal not to disclose anything you've told me. To anyone.'

'Yes.'

That was the real reason she was there. Not to get absolution from her sins but to confess without judgment or consequence.

'Under normal circumstances, penance consists of prayer. But there is also the option for you to make amends. Are you willing to do that?'

'I'm not giving myself up to the police, if that's what you mean.'

'I'm talking about true redemption. I can give you the chance to go back to your life of twenty years ago and re-live it, to undo your crime.'

'You mean, as in a time machine?'

'Yes. Not literally a machine, but you will travel back in time. You'll have the chance to make amends by not murdering your husband. Your life, of course, will take an entirely different path. You must be prepared for that.'

'You can't be serious, that only happens in science fiction.'

'What was science fiction yesterday is reality today. I can assure you it's possible, but the only way I can prove it to you is to do it.'

He's obviously crazy. Perhaps I should just humour him and say yes.

'The decision is entirely yours. If you prefer, we can complete your confession in the usual way by prayer—penance, contrition and absolution. And you can walk out of here absolved of your sin of murder. Or you can choose to enact your penance by travelling back to the past. But if you choose that option, it's irrevocable. Once you're there, it's as if the past twenty years have never existed. But you will remember them, and you will have the chance to avoid every mistake and redeem every sin.'

He sounded so calm and reasonable, but maybe that was part of the craziness. What was the term? Grandiose delusions. Supposing he really could send her back twenty years, did she want to live her life all over again? Of course she regretted killing Charlie. Her grief had been overwhelming and she had missed him every day since, but how could she have lived with his being in love with another woman? How could she have held her head up high as the deserted wife? And to stand by and witness Veronika having the child that she, Eva, had wanted—that was more than she could bear.

'It's a very difficult decision, Father. And time travel—I don't know—'

'You don't believe it, do you? That I can send you back in time?'

'You have to admit, it's pretty far-fetched. Like something out of Doctor Who.'

'I don't have a Tardis.' She heard the smile in his voice. 'And I can assure you I'm as sane as the next person. But as I said earlier, there are no test runs. You just have to take my word for it. Think of it as a gift from God.'

She realised with an overwhelming sadness that despite all the questions bouncing around in her mind, living her life over again could be no worse than continuing with her present life. Her marriage to Edgar, while it provided her with the material comforts and lifestyle she wanted, was unsatisfying in every other respect. She had no close friends, she was spiralling into a vortex of drinking and promiscuity and though she hated herself for it, she couldn't stop. And to top it off, she knew that Charlie wasn't going to give up—he'd keep on haunting her until she went insane herself.

As for it being a gift from God, that would remain to be seen.

'I've made my decision, Father,' she heard herself say. 'I'm ready to go back.'

'A brave choice, Eva. Sit still and breathe deeply.'

She didn't feel brave; her heart was pounding so hard she was nauseous and she was shivering all over, from the inside out. She practised the abdominal breathing she'd learnt at yoga years ago. Her head started to spin. The lights went out and she was in complete darkness. A fierce wind filled the booth and she was lifted off her seat and catapulted backwards, like the sudden start of a rollercoaster ride.

Images flew past her—sitting in the living room of her home at Tamarama watching the sun rise through a bleary alcohol haze after another one night stand, her marriage to Edgar, a lavish affair in a floating function room on the harbour and the write up in the gossip mags—'Millionaire's Widow Marries Again,' the parade of wealthy but unsuitable men she'd dated before Edgar, reading the letter she'd received from Helga, whom she hadn't seen for years, with the news that she and Sol were sailing around the world, Charlie's funeral, mourners spilling out the door of the church, the priest lamenting the loss of a successful businessman, philanthropist and man of integrity, Veronika, pale-faced and kohl-eyed, like a modern day witch, not daring to meet her gaze, Charlie's face, ashen with pain as he hung on to the end of his life like a man on the edge of a cliff.

And then, nothing.

Robin Storey

CHAPTER FIVE

THE water bubbled around her body, deliciously warm and velvety. The tang of chlorine and vanilla essence permeated the air. Soft violin music burbled in the background. A hand shook her shoulder. 'Wake up, champagne's arrived.'

Eva opened her eyes. She was in a huge marble spa bath, petals floating on the churning water, looking straight out a window to a lush riot of garden, hanging baskets, and trellised vines. Candles flickered all around the room and a pile of fluffy towels waited on a nearby shelf. She knew this place, had been here many times.

A woman lolled a couple of feet away in the spa, blonde hair in a bun on the top of her head, a few damp strands that had escaped framing her long, high-boned face. Her breasts, straining out of her bikini top, bobbed on the water like two inflatable beach balls. The woman smiled. It was Helga. But it couldn't be, because Helga and Sol were sailing around the world.

'Did you have a late night?' The woman reached over and plucked a glass of champagne from a low table beside the spa. 'Bottoms up!' She took a sip and placed it back on the table.

'What's wrong? Do I look that bad?' She patted her hair and glanced down at her breasts with the complacency of someone who knows there's nothing further from the truth.

It was Helga, and not only that, it was Helga quite some years ago. As if time had stood still and she hadn't aged. Time. Something niggled at the back of her mind. She was in a church and there was a priest—

'Eva, are you okay?'

'Just tired.' She picked up her glass of champagne and took a long, slow sip to buy some time. The memory was coming back—the confession, Father O'Halloran's offer to transport her back in time, her acceptance, hoping yet not believing he could do it.

She looked down at her body submerged under the water; at her black and gold bikini, her flat, firm stomach, smooth, tanned thighs and perky breasts in their halter top. Not as arresting as Helga's but pretty damn good. This was not the body of a sixty year old.

And she remembered this bikini. She had a whole shelf of bikinis, but this was her favourite. She'd worn it here, the Eden Day Spa and Retreat, on the morning of Charlie's death.

•••

'You know, of course, about Derek's affair,' Helga said.

'Derek?' Eva racked her memory.

'Derek O'Connor, the coach from the tennis club. You know, looks like Dustin Hoffman. Only taller and not as weasly looking. He would have made a prettier Tootsie than Dustin.'

'Oh yes,' Eva said, though she couldn't remember at all.

'He's having an affair with his son's teacher and Angela is having a fling with her ski instructor.'

Eva assumed Angela was Derek's wife, though she couldn't remember her either. She and Helga were now in the nail salon adjoining the Jacuzzi, side by side in bathrobes in reclining chairs, enjoying a pedicure. The two young Asian girls who were attending to their feet ignored Helga's chatter and laughed and talked amongst themselves.

'The other night the four of them ended up at the same restaurant. Derek and his woman were there first when in walked Angela and her guy! What are the chances that they'd turn up at the same restaurant on the same night? And the hilarious thing is that Derek and Angela just pretended not to know each other and ignored each other for the whole night!'

'I'd love to have been a fly on the wall at their house that night. Or maybe they kept up the pretence when they got home. "Did you have a good night, dear?" She affected an upper class English accent. "Yes thanks, did you?" “Yes, super, thanks.” “Jolly good then, good night.”'

Eva laughed. *I've missed you, you were my only true friend.* She glanced sideways at Helga, then looked quickly away before she caught her staring. She'd always envied Helga's self-assurance, her ability to send herself and others up and not care a jot what anyone thought. *I can't believe I'm here, twenty years ago. Am I dreaming? Will I wake up and find myself a haggard, miserable sixty-year-old again?*

She looked around at the other women in the salon having their hands and feet beautified. The Eden Day Spa was a popular haunt for wealthy women to be pampered, and many, including Eva and Helga, were regular customers. Some of the women were reading magazines, others were laughing and gossiping, a couple were smoking cigarettes and no-one was staring at a mobile phone. Dreaming or not, she was definitely back in 1995.

Helga was asking her a question. 'You know what their big mistake was?'

'Who?'

'Derek and Angela. Their mistake was going out to dinner. Taking it out in public is always risky. Just keep it to the bedroom, I say. And preferably not your own.'

She reached over and gave Eva's hand a squeeze. 'Honey you're not on the planet today. You haven't been overdoing it on the mother's little helpers, have you?'

'Of course not, you know I don't take pills.'

'Whatever gets you through the day is okay, as far as I'm concerned. What are you and Charlie doing for your wedding anniversary?'

Eva's heart skipped a beat. Their anniversary was today. In her previous life she'd had the romantic dinner at home planned down to the last detail, even to the extent of arranging the morning at the day spa with Helga, because that was what she usually did before a special occasion, and it was important to keep to her normal routine to avert any suspicions. But of course now she wasn't going to kill Charlie.

'I was planning to cook him dinner, but now I'm thinking we might go out.' The prospect of spending a night at home with Charlie, the memories of his death hovering like an uninvited guest, was not a welcome prospect. It had been hard enough over those last few weeks, knowing that he was planning to leave her and not let on that she knew.

'Good idea if you're not up to it. I, on the other hand, am feeling rather horny.'

She nudged Eva and nodded in the direction of the doorway. A man strolled past in white cotton long pants and shirt, his lithe, muscular body evident even under his loose clothing. Eva caught a glimpse of olive skin and dark hair.

'Felippe, the new masseur,' Helga said. 'He's from Brazil. I've got an appointment with him after this and I don't think he'll be averse to providing a bit of extra service.'

'How do you know?'

'Just a hunch. And to make sure, I'll throw some cold water on my boobs before I go in to make my nipples stand up, and when I'm turning over on the table the towel will accidentally fall off to expose my newly waxed pussy.'

'In that case, the poor guy doesn't stand a chance.' It was true. Helga always got her man.

●●●

Eva unlocked the front door of her home and stepped into the hallway. She heard the clip of toenails on the polished wooden floor and a furry bundle flung itself at her. She bent down, put her arms around the neck of her poodle labrador cross and buried her face in her soft, woolly fur.

'Dodie, Dodie—oh , it's so wonderful to see you again.'

Dodie licked the tears from her face. Eva had found her on the side of a busy road three years ago, a shivering, frightened ball of fluff. She'd obviously been dumped by her owner. Eva had brought her home and nursed her back to health. Charlie, not being a dog lover, tolerated her presence as long as she slept in her kennel outside at night. Dodie had died of bone cancer just before Eva married Edgar.

She drew back and looked into Dodie's shaggy face and bright, all-knowing eyes. 'I get to enjoy you a second time around.'

She could swear Dodie was smiling.

She got up and with Dodie at her side, she walked slowly through her home. Looking, feeling, remembering. She ran her hands over the antique bookshelves in the living room, the finely woven silk quilt on their king size bed, the intricately embroidered Chinese wall hangings, she breathed in the scent of the fresh roses in the crystal vase on the dining table. Memories flooded her mind in every room. She and Charlie, talking, eating, drinking, laughing, making love.

She opened the living room doors and strolled out into the huge undercover entertainment area, looking out across Sydney Harbour. Dodie bounded out and headed straight for the lawn dotted with colourful gardens and native trees, rolling on her back on the lush grass. Eva and Charlie had loved entertaining, and held regular functions on the lawn under huge marquees, many of them fund-raisers for charity.

She saw the guests there now, dressed in their glittering finery, and heard the buzz of chatter and the clink of glasses, the waiters weaving their way through the crowd with trays of food and champagne. Charlie looking so handsome in his evening suit, exuding charm and bonhomie, Helga, voluptuous and dazzling, making people laugh at her snarky send-ups, and Sol hovering nearby with his usual enigmatic expression.

In front of the entertainment area a fifty metre swimming pool shimmered in the soft autumn sunshine, bordered by palm-tree gardens and lounge chairs. Their gardener, Harry, was standing beside the pool holding a long-handled net. She watched the muscles in his tattooed forearms flexing as he plunged the net into the water and scooped up a pile of leaves and debris. He looked up, saw her and waved.

'Hullo, Mrs D. Beautiful morning isn't it?'

‘It sure is.’ She smiled and waved back. He was always so exuberant. So he should be, they paid him well.

She called Dodie back in and went inside to the kitchen. She took out the plunger out of the coffee pot, scooped some granules into it and put water on to boil. It was such a strange feeling to be back in this house, a house she hadn't set foot in for almost twenty years. Strange and overwhelmingly sad. She'd loved this house; it was her house. Of course it was Charlie's as well. He'd bought it after they became engaged and given her carte blanche to do whatever she wanted with it.

The interior had been dated, so with the help of Helga, who ran her own interior decorating business, she'd given it a complete facelift—white kitchen, neutral walls, timber floors, lots of glass, and simple, clean-lined furniture, giving it an overall effect of airiness and spaciousness. She and Charlie had begun their married life in this home. Her hopes, dreams and expectations were contained within it, embedded in its walls and floorboards, woven within its fabrics.

And she'd lost it. The contents of Charlie's will had revealed that all his properties, including the house, belonged to the Dennehy Corporation and Eva had no claim to it. All she got was the money from his life insurance policy—not enough to live on over the long term in the way she'd become accustomed.

She was so consumed with anger and jealousy, so determined that Veronika wasn't going to become the next Mrs Charles Dennehy and live in her, Eva's home, it hadn't occurred to her that she might not be entitled to live in it herself. Even if it had, how could she have found out the contents of Charlie's will without arousing suspicion? As she packed her personal effects and arranged for the furniture to be transported to her new, modest home in Melbourne, she swore she could hear Charlie's laugh echoing through the house.

She poured her coffee, went out on to the deck and settled herself into a reclining deckchair with Dodie at her feet. The sparkling vista of the harbour stretched out before her, hugged by the cliffs on the western side, dotted with a never-ending variety of boats. The sailing boats mesmerised her, skimming majestically along the water; if the wind dropped, they seemed to bob up and down in the one spot. She never tired of the view, it changed every day. It calmed her, made her feel at one with the world. But towards the end, not even this could quell the turmoil inside her.

'I'm beginning to think this isn't a dream,' she told Dodie. 'It all feels too real. I mean, here I am, back in 1995! How did Father O'Halloran do that? Did God give him special powers? Maybe I should start believing again.'

Dodie looked up at her. 'I wonder if I can stop you from dying as well.'

Dodie cocked her head on one side, her eyes questioning. Eva sighed. 'I guess not. No dog is immortal. But I don't know how I'm going to make things any better with Charlie. I mean, he's already in love with Veronika, I can't make him unfall in love with her.'

Dodie whined in agreement.

'He told her he's waiting for the right moment to tell me he's leaving me. How does he know when it's the right moment? Is there an etiquette book that tells you? "The best time to leave your wife is on your wedding anniversary, so it will always have unhappy memories for her. And make sure you wear the right attire—a suit and tie and a crash helmet, to protect you from the flying crockery." '

Her insides went cold. Could that be Charlie's plan? To tell her tonight? Then she remembered. He'd bought her the necklace. Surely he wouldn't buy her an expensive gift and then tell her he was leaving her. She sipped her coffee. Goddammit, she needed something stronger.

She got up, went into the kitchen, opened the refrigerator and took out a bottle of Moet from the door. On the top shelf were the two creme caramels she'd made the night before for their dessert tonight. And the packet of chuck steak for the curry. She remembered with a lurch in her stomach the aconite plant in the garage. She had to get rid of it—no-one must have any inkling of what she'd planned to do.

She put the Moet back in the fridge and grabbed her car keys. 'Be back soon, Dodie.'

She locked the front door and went through the interior doorway to the garage. She took the plant out of its secret hiding place, under a pile of old rags where neither Robert, their chauffeur, or Harry would find it.

She'd tramped all over plant nurseries on the other side of the city, in a wig and sunglasses, ostensibly to find a different and colourful plant for her garden, and had eventually found a wolf's bane, the common name for aconite. Its purple, bell-shaped flowers were a bright, innocuous contrast to its deadly roots. She shoved it in a garbage bag, put it in the boot of the car and drove off.

CHAPTER SIX

'AINSLEY, it's Eva here. May I speak to Charlie, please?'

'I'll just see if he's available,' Ainsley said, her tone cool and measured. She always let Eva know, in a multitude of subtle ways, that she had no special privileges over and above all the other people clamoring for a piece of Charlie's attention.

'Hullo, darling.' He was alive, it was really him. She opened her mouth. Nothing came out.

'Eva?'

She swallowed the lump in her throat. 'About tonight. I'm not up to cooking so I wondered if you'd mind if we went out for dinner instead.'

'Not at all.' She thought she detected a note of relief. Perhaps he didn't relish the idea of being at home, just the two of them, when he'd rather be with *her*. 'Where did you have in mind?'

'I don't know yet.' Then the idea occurred to her in a flash. 'How about I make a booking and come and meet you at the office?'

'Great idea. I'll send Robert over to pick you up at seven.'

•••

Robert pulled up outside the office block in North Sydney at seven-twenty. The many windows still alight in the ten storeys were evidence of the long hours required to earn the privilege of a business in this building. Eva took the lift to the fourth floor and opened the door to the Dennehy Corporation. The muted tones and sumptuous furnishings of the waiting room gave it the desired ambience of restrained opulence.

Ainsley was standing behind the reception desk, her handbag over her shoulder, ready to go home. She often worked late, considering it not an imposition but a privilege. She had the ability to size you up thoroughly in a brief glance, and Eva knew she'd taken in everything—the cocktail dress that showed off her cleavage and rounded hips, her hair up in an elegant chignon to highlight her cheekbones, the high heels that accentuated her well-shaped legs.

One of the gossip mags had described Eva as the reincarnation of Ingrid Bergman, albeit an Ingrid Bergman with chestnut brown hair, and indeed Charlie had told her that it was her dewy-eyed, radiant beauty that had instantly attracted him to her. Now at forty it took time and money to maintain those looks—it was fortunate she had plenty of both. Not that it was doing her any good.

'Mr Dennehy is in a meeting with Mr Berman,' Ainsley said. 'He won't be long if you'd like to take a seat.'

'I'll wait here,' Eva said, standing by the window.

Ainsley narrowed her eyes slightly. It gave her a feline look, but not in an attractive sense. With her pale complexion and mass of ginger hair, she reminded Eva of a tabby cat.

'Good night. Have a lovely evening.'

Eva watched her walk out, her ample hips swaying. A fat tabby cat. Eva had overheard someone at a cocktail party say that the reason Charlie had hired Ainsley was because she was not likely to become a temptation. There was probably more than a grain of truth in that, the bonus being that Ainsley was also supremely efficient.

As she opened the door, Ainsley turned as if it was an afterthought and said, 'Congratulations on your wedding anniversary.' The undertone was unmistakable: 'Congratulations on making it this far, when we all thought it wouldn't happen.'

Fuck you, you snooty bitch, you and your smarmy sales manager husband and spoilt private school kids and your suburban middle-class narrow-mindedness—just because you see more of my husband than I do doesn't give you the right to treat me like some gold-digger who got lucky. I worked hard for this marriage.

'I'll get those documents to you tomorrow to sign,' a familiar voice said. Sol came striding out from the direction of Charlie's office. She'd forgotten what a striking figure he was in his bespoke suit, tailored perfectly for his tall, slender frame and face as smooth and pale as alabaster, his nose just Roman enough to offset his finely wrought features.

He nodded to Eva with a slight upturn of his mouth. 'Happy anniversary. Enjoy your dinner.'

Another person who thought she wasn't good enough for Charlie, though Sol's disapproval was more subtle—a sideways glance, a tilt of the head. He kept himself tightly contained, which gave him an air of arrogance. Helga maintained that it masked his shyness, but Eva wasn't so sure. Sol was born into wealth, and like many in that situation, grew up considering success, prosperity and status his due. He could never conceive what it was like to live from one day to the next, despair and hopelessness hanging over him like the odour of tinned stew and two minute noodles. That's what she and Charlie had in common, why they understood each other.

She heard a door close down the hallway. Her heart beat quickened. Charlie appeared. He looked weary, his top shirt button was undone and his tie was loose. He was shorter than she remembered, with less hair, his face was craggier. How memory played tricks on you, erased things and superimposed others, even someone whose body you knew as well as your own.

'Hullo, sweet pea.' She tensed as he came towards her. He kissed her on the cheek and slid his arm around her waist. 'You look stunning.'

The warmth of his arm on her body released something within her, and then she had her arms around his neck and was holding him tightly to her, inhaling the aroma of his skin and trying to hold back the tears. 'I've missed you so much,' she whispered.

'You saw me this morning.' He drew back. 'What's going on?'

She smiled. 'Can't I miss my own husband when he goes to work and I don't see him for a whole day?'

'Of course you can, but you seem upset.'

'I'm just happy to see you again and that we're going out to dinner. Just the two of us.'

Charlie straightened his tie and buttoned up his shirt. 'Where are we going?'

'Helga was telling me about this fantastic Italian restaurant she went to recently and it sounded ideal, so I booked it. It's in Mosman, La Bella.'

The signs were minute; a momentary blanching, the merest flicker of his eyes. If she wasn't watching for them she would have missed them.

'Sounds wonderful. I'll just go to the bathroom and I'll be with you.'

●●●

Eva tried hard not to let the memory of seeing Charlie and Veronika entering La Bella spoil the evening. She pretended it was like their wedding anniversaries used to be; the two of them chatting and laughing, revelling in their intimacy, the spectre of Charlie's dalliances pushed to the back of her mind. She'd become good at that, sometimes made herself believe there'd never been any other women. The problem was she could never sustain it for very long.

After the waiter had delivered their aperitifs, Charlie clinked his glass against hers. 'To my beautiful wife.'

He still had that way of looking at her as if she were an object of beauty he'd worshipped all his life and couldn't believe his luck in finally winning. Despite her resolve not to fall under his spell, she felt herself soften.

She clinked back. 'To sixteen happy years. And many more to come.'

The way he smiled, she could almost believe he wanted that too. He reached into his coat pocket and pulled out a small, gift wrapped package.

'Happy anniversary, sweet pea.'

Eva unwrapped it, opened the box and took out a necklace with a single diamond pendant, surrounded by a cluster of diamonds. They sparkled in the candlelight.

Even though she knew it was going to be the same necklace he'd given her in her previous life on the night he died, its luminous beauty still overwhelmed her. As a teenager, she'd often hovered outside the windows of jewellery shops, gazing at their glittering array, as far out of her reach as the moon. Charlie had given her numerous pieces of jewellery over the years, and each one had filled her anew with the same pleasure as the first.

'It's beautiful,' she breathed.

'Let me put it on for you.' Charlie got up and went behind her. He took the necklace and placed it carefully around her neck. His hands brushed the back of her neck as he fixed the clasp. She shivered. He let his hand linger there, warm, possessive, full of promise.

As he sat down again, Eva noticed that the couple at the next table were watching them; the woman was gaping.

The waiter appeared to take their order. 'The necklace looks fabulous on you, Signora,' he said, giving a little bow. He was too well-trained to stare, but she knew he was taking in her cleavage in his peripheral vision.

They ordered an antipasto platter to share, prawn linguine for Eva, pork pappardelle for Charlie, and a bottle of Veuve Clicquot.

When he left, Eva said, 'I didn't get a present for you.'

Charlie took her hand. 'I don't want one, you're the one who deserves it. You've been very patient. I know I haven't been home a lot. This new mine in Western Australia has just been one headache after another.'

The only time Charlie ever discussed business with her was when it provided a handy excuse for being away from home. 'But I don't want to think about business tonight. I want to enjoy being with you.'

But you haven't told me you loved me. Not for a long time.

'Do you love me, Charlie?'

She was tense, watching him. The restaurant noises receded, the world was standing still, waiting for his answer.

'You know I do, sweet pea.' Words. Tender, honeyed, so easy.

You fucking liar, I hate you.

•••

She let him seduce her. *Have some self-respect, for God's sake, he's in love with someone else*, her mind told her. Her body took no notice. The moment his hands touched her bare shoulder she felt herself loosening. He eased her breasts out of her dress and flicked his tongue over her nipples. By the time he gathered her up in his arms as if she were a child and carried her into the bedroom there was no turning back. She'd had no lover like him, before or since—he made her ache, shiver, beg, cry out, shudder, moan and buck with a pleasure so intense she couldn't bear it. And at the end, so sated, so drained of energy she could hardly move.

She lay listening to his steady breathing, then slid out from under his arm, slipped on her robe and padded out to the kitchen. She turned on the jug, spooned some tea leaves into the teapot, then went into the living room, opened the curtains and stood looking out to the harbour. The water shimmered, reflecting all shades of light, the harbour bridge glittering like a silver rainbow.

Her thighs were sticky, the smell of sex strong. Did he make love like that, like it was the last time he'd ever have sex, to all his women? To Veronika? She could bear it, perhaps, if the sex with them was perfunctory, 'wham bam thank-you ma'am, goodbye.' If he kept the passion, the emotion, just for her. But Charlie wasn't like that. Whatever drove him to be at the top, to be better than everyone else, drove him in every part of his life. And on second thoughts, she couldn't bear it, no matter how he treated those other women.

Helga had teased her about her small town morality, as she called it. But at least it was straightforward. And honest. When you love each other you don't sleep around. Boundaries, not up for negotiation or dispute. Helga and Sol had an arrangement that each could sleep with whomever they wanted, no questions asked.

'People think that in an open marriage, both parties are out every night screwing themselves senseless,' Helga said. 'But it isn't like that at all. When you have the freedom to do something, it loses its urgency and you can be choosy; it simply means that if either of us meets someone we're attracted to, we can follow up on it if we want to. And I can guarantee, honey, that a bit of extra-marital frolicking does wonders for your sex life at home.'

It seemed to work for her and Sol; they appeared genuinely devoted to each other, but Eva was not convinced of the philosophy behind it and had no desire to try it out herself.

Once she had confronted Charlie, well before she found out about Veronika, hoping to force him to admit the truth about his behaviour. She cornered him at a cocktail party, so he'd be forced to answer her and couldn't take the option of walking out.

'Why don't you come right out and admit you're fucking other women?'

He looked puzzled. 'What brought this on?'

'I just want you to tell the truth. Because everyone in this room, including me, knows that you can't keep your dick in your pants to save yourself.'

'Language, Eva, for God's sake. I hate it when you swear.'

'Because I'm not the sweet, demure, girl you thought I was?'

'Is this because of Babs?'

Babs was the hostess of the cocktail party, who'd greeted Charlie on their arrival with a kiss that was far too long to be friendly and a good look down her cavernous cleavage.

'Of course it isn't.' Although Eva had given Babs a filthy look and steered Charlie away to another acquaintance. 'Though I wouldn't be surprised if you've fucked her as well, if she stayed sober long enough.'

He took the empty champagne glass out of her hand. 'I think you've had too much to drink.'

'Don't fucking tell me how much I can drink.' She hailed a passing waiter and swiped another glass of champagne from his tray. 'All I want you to do is to admit the truth. Your dalliances are the worst kept secret in this city.'

He looked at her with a pained expression. 'Eva, I thought you of all people would know not to take any notice of gossip. I assure you I am not sleeping with other women. If you can't take me at my word, there's nothing more I can say.'

He looked around and spotted someone waving to him from across the other side of the room. 'I have to go and talk to Frank. And if you keep drinking like that you're only going to embarrass yourself.'

He disappeared into the crowd. *Embarrass you, you mean.* Eva downed her champagne and got another.

She knew why he wouldn't admit it. Having affairs was de rigueur for most of the successful men in their social circle, but to acknowledge it would be business suicide. With the tabloid media always sniffing around, an admission would soon become headlines. Despite Sydney's reputation as a progressive and sophisticated city, its upper echelon of wealth and power was a conservative, old school bunch, including many Roman Catholics who wouldn't want to be seen doing business with a philanderer. And the wives turned a blind eye, so they could hold on to their money and the life that went with it.

That was her mistake. Thinking, hoping that she would be all Charlie would need. Her second mistake. The first was falling in love with him.

'Okay, Father, you sent me back here,' she said out loud. 'Now what the fuck am I supposed to do?'

CHAPTER SEVEN

THE cameras flashed as Charlie and Eva stepped out of their limousine into the lushly carpeted foyer of the lean, forty-storey high rise building overlooking Darling Harbour. Dennehy Towers, the latest construction project of the Dennehy Corporation, twinkled with coloured lights, resembling a multi-coloured rocket.

A reporter stepped forward, blocking their way. Eva recognised his well-fed, obsequious face as the gossip columnist from one of the Sunday rags.

'How much are you hoping to raise tonight, Mr Dennehy?' he asked.

'We're on target to raise a quarter of a million dollars,' Charlie replied. 'And that will be distributed equally amongst the six charities who have their offices here.'

Charlie had donated six offices in the block to hand-picked charities to use rent-free, and when officially opening the building that morning, the Lord Mayor had made reference to Charlie's 'legendary philanthropic spirit'.

'Fabulous!' the columnist said. 'You must be very proud of your husband, Mrs Dennehy.'

Eva smiled at Charlie and squeezed his arm. 'Indeed I am.'

A young female reporter with a TV camera close behind her shoved a microphone in Charlie's face. 'What do you say to the allegations of bribery and corruption made by Councillor O'Brien yesterday?'

Charlie's eyes hardened. 'I will not dignify that with a response.'

He quickened his pace. 'So you deny the allegations?' the reporter called out, trotting after him. A security guard stopped her at the roped off barrier. Charlie swept Eva into the lift.

'What about the allegations of under the table business at The Waterfront?' the reporter called out as the lift doors closed.

'What was that all about?' Eva asked.

'Tim O'Brien insinuated at a council meeting yesterday that there was something underhand in the approval process for the construction of this building. It wasn't an allegation, he's too cowardly to come right out and say it because he knows there's not a shred of proof.'

'He's got it in for you,' Eva said. 'I seem to remember he's said similar things before.'

'That's all it's been, just spurious claims with no evidence.'

'What did she mean about under the table business at The Waterfront?'

'I have no idea. It's bullshit, of course. Women get narky about The Waterfront because it's a men's club. Don't let it concern you.'

He adjusted his bow tie and smiled at her, the smile that always made her glow right down to her feet. 'It's going to be a wonderful night, thanks to you. I'm proud of you, you've worked so hard.'

Being in charge of the organising committee for tonight's gala ball, Eva had worked non-stop to finalise all the details in the two weeks since her arrival in the past.

'I'll be glad to put my feet up tomorrow, that's for sure.'

The lift door opened out into the grand ballroom, 1920s style with parquet floor, elaborate chandeliers and ruffled curtains. A doorway at the side of the room opened into a huge dining area, with rows and rows of long tables. Wait staff were putting the finishing touches to the crisp white tablecloths and sparkling crystalware. Charlie had included these rooms in the building to hire out to charity groups for fundraisers. The ballroom was packed with men in suits and bow ties and women in evening dresses outshone only by their jewellery. An eight-piece jazz band was playing *Mack the Knife*, and waiters orbited the crowd with trays of drinks and hors d'oeuvres.

Eva felt warm with pride; it was worth all the phone calls and negotiations, dealing with infighting amongst committee members and last minute crises when it all came together so smoothly on the night. In her previous life she had insisted on the ball going ahead despite Charlie's death and the newspapers had done their usual gush. 'Despite her recent bereavement, Eva Dennehy looked magnificent in an off the shoulder ruby pink gown, and the MC of the evening, Deputy Mayor Collins, paid tribute to her courage in going ahead with the ball in the generous and civic minded tradition of her husband.'

She was wearing the pink gown tonight; it had been especially designed for the occasion. She shivered. Deja vu again. So many little details of her previous life she hadn't remembered, so it was like living a new life, but other times the deja vu was so strong she broke out in goosebumps.

She focussed on the steady stream of Council officials and other dignitaries flowing towards them, eager to pump Charlie's hand and offer their congratulations. Spotting Helga with Frances and Diana, who were also on the organising committee, Eva excused herself.

'Another success, darling!' Helga trumpeted, enveloping her in a hug.

'Did you read Bernard Brecht's column in this morning's Herald?' Diana asked. Bernard Brecht was a controversial commentator on modern culture. Eva shook her head.

'He called this building a triumphal blending of modern and conservative, old time grandeur perfectly balanced with cutting edge comfort and style. You know you've really made it when old Bernie praises you.'

'Saving the world one high rise at a time,' Frances said. 'What's his next project?'

Eva smiled. 'You know how it is. He's got a dozen things on the go.'

They all nodded; they knew exactly what she meant.

'I just wish Harry would let go of the reins long enough to take a holiday,' Diana said. 'I want to do a Rhine river cruise and I've threatened to go on one without him.'

'Just go,' Frances said, 'You can't put your own life on hold for him. Make sure you spend up big, then he'll be sure to go with you next time.'

'It's good for couples to have separate holidays,' Helga said. 'You appreciate each other so much more when you come back.'

As Eva surveyed the crowd, she spotted a face. Hair pulled back, smudged eyes, the sort of lips that instantly give men fantasies. Eva caught her breath. *Fucking cheek, what the hell is she doing here?* In her previous life, Veronika hadn't attended the ball—presumably she had no reason to, with Charlie dead. Had Charlie invited her? This was a public event—anyone could attend if they were prepared to cough up the two hundred dollars for a ticket. But you could lay money on her and Charlie planning her appearance.

A hard ball of anger lodged in Eva's chest. She moved a little so she could see Veronika more clearly. Plain strapless gown that showed off the creamy curve of her shoulders, a single strand necklace and tiny, diamond drop earrings; yet she exuded more elegance than all the other women in their sequins and ruffles and jangling layers of jewellery put together. She was talking to two portly, grey-haired gentlemen, who were listening with the rapt attention men often give to beautiful women, overcompensating for the fact that all they're thinking of is her naked body wrapped around theirs.

'That's Veronika Ettore,' Frances said at her shoulder. 'She's a model, of course, what else would she be with those looks?'

'I believe she has a master's degree in business,' Helga said. 'And she runs a PR Agency as well.'

'Brains and beauty, a dangerous combination,' Frances said.

'Lucky we're a rare species,' quipped Diana.

Eva's eyes searched the room for Charlie—he was on the other side of the room in a close knot of people including Sol and Andrew Thomason, a well-known criminal barrister. What was that scandal Thomason was involved in a couple of years ago? She racked her brains as they all moved into the dining room at the request of the MC.

Eva was seated opposite Charlie and she did her best to converse politely with the chatty councillor's wife beside her, while surreptitiously watching Charlie for any sign of secret glances in Veronika's direction. Veronika was sitting two tables behind them, right in the line of Charlie's gaze, but Charlie seemed engrossed in conversation with the convivial man beside him and hardly glanced away at all.

Then she remembered about Andrew Thomason. His ex-wife had publicly accused him of being involved in criminal activities with some of his own clients and hiding money in an offshore account to avoid paying his rightful property settlement to her. The forensic accountants' investigations supposedly found nothing untoward and the publicity faded away.

But Helga, as usual, had the real dirt. 'No-one, especially Andrew, could be so stupid as to get involved with their own clients, the ex was way off the mark there. But I happen to know that there was some hurried shifting of money and favours traded.'

Eva couldn't remember Charlie mentioning at the time that he knew Andrew. Maybe he'd just met him tonight.

A plate of smoked salmon and braised asparagus had appeared in front of her. She picked up her knife and fork.

'Anyway, the upshot was that he got caught out,' the councillor's wife, whose name Eva had forgotten, was saying.

'I beg your pardon, who got caught out?' Eva asked.

The woman looked at her reproachfully. 'Councillor Hughes. He resigned due to ill-health—that was the official story, but he was having an affair with his children's nanny. Very unoriginal, not to mention foolhardy—how was he not going to be found out? His wife hired a private detective, got photos, very racy so I've been told, so she sacked the nanny, kicked him out and threatened to go to the newspapers if he didn't hand over the house and most of their savings. Quite frankly I don't think the newspapers would have been interested. It's not as if he was anyone important and men cheat on their wives every day of the week, don't they?'

'They do,' Eva agreed.

After the main course and the usual platitude-driven speeches lauding Charlie's vision and Eva's hard work, the band started up again with *I'll Take Romance*, a waltz. Charlie led Eva on to the dance floor. He held her with the familiar closeness of a husband to a wife, not the urgent intimacy of a man to his lover. Her skin prickled and she knew that wherever Veronika was, she was watching the two of them.

Why did she come anyway? Were they planning to find a broom cupboard and steal a kiss and a grope? Or maybe they couldn't bear to be apart from one another on this important occasion, even if they had to keep up this pretence. If she wasn't so angry she'd laugh at the absurdity of it. She tightened her hold on Charlie and pressed her body into his. She smiled up at him as she felt his corresponding hardness and kissed him long and tenderly on the lips. *Cop that, you scheming bitch.*

As she and Charlie returned to their table for dessert, she caught a glimpse of Veronika in conversation with another woman a few feet away. She longed to say, 'Do you know that dark-haired woman over there?' Just to see his reaction. Of course he'd want to know why she'd asked and she'd brush it off with, 'Someone told me she runs a PR agency so I thought you might know her.'

But she stopped herself. She'd already taken him to La Bella—one coincidence was plausible, but any further references to Veronika and Charlie would twig that she knew. And it was important that he didn't know that she knew.

CHAPTER EIGHT

EVA was returning from her early morning walk with Dodie as Charlie walked out the front door to go to the office. The Mercedes was in the driveway, engine idling, Robert at the wheel. Charlie had recently changed tailors and his new slim line three-piece suit took years off him. Eva felt a warm rush of pleasure as she looked at him.

'When will you be home?' she asked.

Every morning she asked him the same question; it made her sound so wifey-dependent, but she couldn't help herself.

'I don't know. I'm going early to boxing, I'll do my usual shower and change there, and afterwards Sol and I are having dinner tonight with a couple of potential investors. It could be a late one, so don't wait up for me.'

He gave her a peck on the cheek and she watched as he got into the car and Robert whisked him away. Investors? Or a rendez-vous with Veronika? Though he had mentioned Sol, so maybe it was above board. As Charlie's legal advisor, Sol played a big role in his business affairs and often attended meetings with him. Not that she was inclined to give Charlie the benefit of the doubt.

She knew the boxing was genuine, because she'd spied on him once. A couple of years after they were married, Charlie had come home one night and told Eva he'd joined a boxing gym. At his recent medical check-up, his doctor had told him he'd be heart attack material if he didn't start exercising to offset the stress of his business life.

'Why a boxing gym?' Eva asked. It conjured up images of a sweaty, claustrophobic basement where bare-chested men in shorts and boxing gloves pummelled punching bags or each other while the trainer kept up a constant barrage of yelling. It didn't seem like Charlie's sort of place at all.

'It's short and intense,' Charlie said. 'I need something I can fit into my schedule. I can be in and out in less than an hour and the gym is two blocks from the office.'

He attended the gym religiously at six o'clock three evenings a week, showering and dressing there before coming home, as he didn't want to sit in his beloved Mercedes in sweaty clothes. It soon occurred to Eva that the gym might be a cover for his sexual liaisons. After all, he arrived home fresh from his shower and in a clean change of clothes—how did she know he'd even been boxing at all? Showering at the gym could be a good excuse for washing the odour of sex and perfume from him.

So one evening she drove to North Sydney, parked in a parking station half a dozen blocks away from Charlie's office and walked back, against the tide of weary-faced commuters hurrying to the railway station. It was the middle of summer, the day still bright and the heat still stifling at six-fifteen. She almost missed the gym, even though it was just as she'd imagined—a concrete basement in a commercial high-rise, underneath a Chinese restaurant. A tiny, shabby sign on the front announced it was *Jim's Boxing. Beginners Welcome*. The front door was closed, but as she drew closer she could hear yelling from inside.

She peered around the side of the building. Along the wall was a series of small, rectangular barred windows. Eva glanced around. A young couple strolling into the Chinese restaurant were too engrossed in themselves to notice her. A steady stream of pedestrians strode past; no-one was watching her.

She slipped around to the side wall below the first window. Standing on her tiptoes she slowly raised her head to look in, ready to duck and run if anyone saw her.

The room was as basic inside as it was outside—bare concrete walls and floor, a row of punching bags along one wall, a boxing ring in the middle of the room. In one corner a set of lockers, in the other a drinking fountain. A doorway beside the lockers presumably led to the showers.

There were about twenty men in total, of varying ages and build, but they all had one thing in common—their bodies glistened with sweat. And fortunately they were too absorbed in their individual torture to look up at the window. Some were giving the punching bags a good workout, another group was skipping, another was doing push-ups. A short, nuggetty man, presumably a trainer, watched them from the sidelines.

In the boxing ring, two men, one swarthy and the other fairer-skinned, were walloping each other while a burly man with a battered face yelled at them from outside the ropes. As the windows were the sort that didn't open, Eva couldn't hear him, but she could see his lips moving. She deduced he was Jim; he looked more authoritative than the other trainer.

Which one was Charlie? She studied the men more closely, realising with a shock that he was the fairer-skinned man in the boxing ring. Initially he'd had his back to her and she hadn't recognised him in his headgear and mouthguard.

She watched him now, her heart in her mouth, as his opponent drove him into the corner of the ring. But just as it looked as if he were beaten, he found a surge of energy and came out from the corner, raining blows on his opponent, forcing him back into the middle of the ring.

Pride welled up inside her as she watched Charlie holding his own as he ducked and weaved and pummelled, the solid bank of muscle in his back and shoulders contracting and gleaming under the lights. She hadn't noticed until now how much fitter he'd become.

Jim blew the whistle hanging around his neck. The two of them stopped mid-blow as he stepped over the ropes into the ring, talking and gesticulating. Eva ducked her head down again; she didn't want to push her luck in not being spotted. Anyway, she'd seen enough. More than she'd anticipated. Even with his protective gear on, the expression on Charlie's face as he attacked his rival was clear. Anger, because he needed anger to fuel him. But also a pure, primitive joy, a total absorption in his physicality, a delight in his ability to inflict damage.

Was it just a release from the stress of business, where emotion often had to be stifled in the name of diplomacy and competitiveness? Boxing was still the province of the working class, and in that gym, a wealthy entrepreneur would be in the minority, probably the only member of that minority. But in the boxing ring there was no class distinction; everyone was equal until punched into submission.

Perhaps it was a subconscious desire to connect with his past, though Charlie would have denied it vehemently if she'd suggested it. Or maybe a way of diffusing the anger he harboured towards his parents and two brothers for being what he termed 'failures at life.'

Maybe, Eva mused, on her way back to the car, it was all three. Whatever the reasons, she was relieved she'd proved to herself that the boxing was not a cover for Charlie's sexual liaisons. Not to say, though, he wouldn't use it in the future.

On the present occasion, going to dinner with investors straight afterwards, it was likely to be genuine, unless it was a hurried assignation. Eva pushed the thought from her mind as she went inside, unclipped Dodie's lead and let her outside. She stripped off and as she stood under the shower, an embryo of a plan was beginning to grow in her mind.

It was still formless, made up of fragments of information, most based on rumour, speculation and intuition. Charlie knowing Andrew Thomason. Even if Andrew was innocent of laundering money, he had criminal associations. The allegations of bribery by Councillor O'Brien and of underhand deals done at the Waterfront Club. Charlie was known as a tough, uncompromising operator—he had to be to get where he was—but until now Eva had heard no whispers of illicit activity. So maybe he was right and the allegations were false. Or not. But there was a way to find out.

•••

The Waterfront Club was known colloquially as a gentleman's club, with all the connotations that brought to mind, and rumour had it that many high profile men, including politicians and judges, frequented it. The criteria for membership were secret; you were either accepted or not, no explanations given. The no women rule, apart from those who worked there, was strictly enforced. Eva knew that Charlie had been there (only occasionally, he asserted) in the name of entertaining out of town clients. More than once she'd asked him what went on there, and he'd replied, 'It's a private club, where men have a couple of drinks and do business. That's all it is. The strippers are just eye candy. And none of them can hold a candle to you, my darling.'

She was about to find out the truth of that.

She took the dress out of its wrapping and laid it on the bed. Black with red trimmings, plunging neckline, mid-calf length with slits up the side to mid-thigh. It had been a shopping mission with a difference—to find a dress befitting a high-class stripper. She presumed that the strippers at the Waterfront Club, catering as they were to affluent clients who demanded quality, were a cut above the usual night club regulars with their kitschy costumes, blank faces and drug-dead eyes. If not (and after all, rich men were like all others, in that all they wanted to see were tits and pussy), perhaps she could set a new standard.

Not that she was going to strip, of course. But convincing them at the Waterfront that she was there for a job was the only chance she had of getting in. And the only way to find out what went on there, and if or how Charlie was involved.

On the bed beside the dress was another shopping bag. She slid out a G-string and suspender belt in purple and red lace, sheer black stockings and a shoebox containing a pair of diamante stiletto heels. Of course, no-one would see her G-string or suspender belt, but she had to wear them to psyche herself into the part.

Her stomach clenched with apprehension. Could she do this? Could she front up to the Waterfront and pretend to be a stripper?

Of course she could. She'd been dressing up and pretending all her life. Right back from kindergarten days, when she put on her cardboard and glitter tiara, her mother's shawl and high heels and transformed herself into a princess, because princesses' daddies didn't yell at their daughters for every little misdemeanour, real or imagined, and whip their legs with a belt until they bled.

By the time her father left, it had become an ingrained part of her life—raiding her own and her mother's limited wardrobes and becoming a movie star, pouting to an adoring audience, or a ballerina, gracefully leaping and twirling, or an explorer, circumnavigating the back yard in her wide-brimmed hat with her compass and backpack. It helped to relieve the loneliness of being an only child, whose mother was zonked out on sedatives when she wasn't working.

Later as a teenager, putting on a different persona—Jane Fonda, Janis Joplin, John Lennon's secret girlfriend—alleviated the stultifying boredom of life in a country town, where every day was Groundhog Day and it seemed as if she were trapped there forever, like an insect in amber.

Eva picked up the stockings, so sheer and silky to the touch. Her mind took her back to a fancy dress party she'd attended in her final year at school. She'd saved up her money from her part-time job and hired a stripper's outfit—a strapless, sequinned mini-dress with fishnet stockings and thigh-high boots, complete with suspender belt and garters.

Once dressed, sporting lashings of eye make-up, poppy-red lipstick and a wig of long, blonde curls, it was easy to immerse herself in the role. To become the stripper. When she strutted into that party, they all thought, for the first few moments, that she was the real thing—that the host had organised a stripper for the night's entertainment.

The just-lingering-long-enough eye contact, alluring smile and swagger of her hips were all part of the act. The males at the party, most of whom were still school students, gathered around her, trying to attract her attention and plying her with drinks.

It was a heady feeling, the awareness of her sexuality and the power it gave her, the desire she sparked and the instincts she aroused. She'd experienced that growing awareness since adolescence, but it was amplified now by this new person, her alter ego, Eva the stripper.

In the end, she'd performed a strip-tease, hasty and clumsy though it was, in the back seat of Neil Hanlon's father's Volvo, though they were both so drunk and high she couldn't remember the details. Just another high school party, another attempt to blot out the tedium of small town existence.

If she could do it then, she could do it now, with the added bonus that she wouldn't be ending the evening having a one night stand with the school heart-throb. She went into the ensuite and started with her face, smoothing concealer on it to hide her fine lines, then foundation and blusher. She suspected that most of the strippers at the Waterfront Club would be nowhere near her age, but with the help of make-up and dim lighting, she could shave a few years off her age.

Then false eyelashes and eyeliner, but with more restraint than she’d used at seventeen, and glossy red lipstick. She slipped on her underwear and stockings, then her dress and stiletto heels. With the blonde pageboy wig she'd worn while shopping for the aconite plant, her transformation was complete. She sashayed up and down in front of the full length mirror, thrusting out her breasts.

'Why, kind sir,' she said, fluttering her eyelashes at herself, 'I'd just love to do a show for you. And if the money's right, I'll fuck you as well. Sign a non-disclosure agreement? Of course, that'll be an extra two hundred.'

She picked up her handbag and went to call a taxi.

CHAPTER NINE

THE taxi driver pulled up in front of a three storey sandstone building perched on a hill overlooking the harbour at Milson's Point. It could be easily mistaken for an office block, as there was no sign. Eva paid the driver and disembarked. A beefy, running-to-fat security guard standing at the entrance had his mouth to his walkie-talkie.

His eyes flickered over her as she approached. *Act cool and calm. The worst thing he can do to you is refuse to let you in.*

'I don't know where the fuck Andy is,' the guard said into the walkie-talkie. 'It's not my fault he didn't turn up.'

'We need another body up here,' a nasal voice replied.

'I can't help you, I'm on my own here. Over and out.'

He clipped the walkie-talkie back on to his belt and looked her up and down properly. Spurred on by champagne bravado, she put on her most winning smile.

'I'm Angelique, I'm doing a strip show tonight.'

'I need to see your ID.'

She made a pretence of rifling through her handbag, then groaned. 'Oh, no! My driver's licence is in my other handbag at home! I was in a rush and I forgot to do my usual last minute check. I'm so sorry.'

'I can't let you in without ID.'

'Really?' She sighed, then looked up at him from under her eyelashes. 'This is my first job here, I was so looking forward to it. I'm going to lose a whole night's work if I can't get in; I've got two kids to feed and the landlord's on my back for the rent.'

The guard looked at her impassively. 'Who hired you?'

'I got a phone call, I forget the man's name.' It was sounding lame. She put on a look of anxious concern. 'I've been hired to do a private show. The gentleman concerned will be so disappointed if I don't turn up.'

'Which gentleman is that?'

'Charles Dennehy.'

'Mr Dennehy isn't here.'

'I was told he wouldn't be here until ten o'clock. I wanted to come early so I had plenty of time to get ready. I'm just so excited, this is a real step up in my career.'

She smiled at him as if he were her best friend and she was expecting him to be as excited as she was. 'You can phone Mr Dennehy yourself if you like and confirm it.'

If he did, she'd have to hotfoot it out of there.

The walkie talkie crackled into life again. ‘Base to Adam.’

‘For fuck’s sake.’ The guard snatched the walkie talkie from his belt. ‘Go ahead.’

‘We need you up here, pronto. Get Brent from the bar to relieve.’

'He’s as useless as tits on a bull. Roger, over and out.’

He poked his head in the doorway. ‘Ron! Can you tell Brent to come out here immediately?’

A tall, scrawny man in black trousers and white shirt loped out. ‘Mind the door,’ Adam told him. ‘I’m needed upstairs.’

He turned to Eva, who smiled demurely at him. He narrowed his eyes and inclined his head towards the club. ‘Go on. But I’m warning you—if you make one ounce of trouble you’ll be out of here on your pretty little arse.’

He dashed inside, and as she entered the foyer, she caught a glimpse of him disappearing up a flight of stairs beside the lift. She breathed a sigh of relief—her instincts to play ingénue rather than hardboiled had paid off.

Straight ahead of her was a set of double oak doors, leading to what looked to be a large lounge bar. She peered in. It was like looking into last century—rich red carpet, shiny brown leather armchairs grouped around small tables, paintings of dignitaries jostling for prominence on the dark panelled walls, huge gilt-edged mirrors, a crackling fireplace at the far wall.

A bar ran along the side wall, and chandeliers and candelabras gave the room a muted, intimate atmosphere. Men in business suits stood or sat in clusters, drinks in hand, in serious discussion. It reeked of establishment, power, and secret deals done behind closed doors.

A doorman in a suit and bow tie materialised. 'Can I help you, Madame?'

She flashed a smile. 'No, thank-you.'

She walked over to the lift, pressed the button and the doors opened immediately. On the first floor was another foyer, with another security guard stationed outside the doors. He could have been Adam's twin.

'I'm Angelique, I'm booked to do a strip show. Adam downstairs okayed me.'

The guard looked her over, then waved her through. The room was twice the size of the downstairs lounge bar, with the same sumptuous decor and furnishings. The difference here was the table service—bare-breasted waitresses in mini-skirts, fishnet stockings and high heels bustled around with trays of drinks. Filling up the far end of the room were half a dozen gambling tables, with men grouped around them, sometimes two or three deep. Cigarette smoke curled and wafted in the air. The croupiers were all female and also topless, sporting small bow ties at their necks which matched their black mini-skirts. A large bar ran along the side wall and on a small stage at the back of the room, a brassy blonde spilling out of a tight sequined dress belted out *Me and Bobby McGee* to the accompaniment of a three-piece band. Apart from the female staff, the room was a sea of men, all in formal or business attire.

Eva went over to the bar and addressed the nearest bartender. 'Excuse me, I'm doing my first strip job here. Where do I go?"

'Over there.' The barman nodded in the direction of a door in the corner.

She made her way over to the door and upon opening it, found herself in a dark room with a movie showing on a large screen. It was typical commercial pornography—a woman on her hands and knees being penetrated by a man with an impossibly large penis, accompanied by the obligatory sighs and moans. Men sat in armchairs watching the movie either alone or with a topless hostess on their knee.

The room, being only small, was dense with cigarette smoke, stifling when you weren't used to it. 'How did we non-smokers ever put up with this?' Eva wondered, trying not to breathe it in. As she watched, one of the men tweaked his hostess's nipple. She gave his hand a firm slap. 'You know the rules, Arthur, if you want hands on.'

Feeling like Alice in Wonderland, Eva opened another door into a large, dimly lit room. Clusters of men sat on couches drinking and staring transfixed at the spotlit stage on which two strippers in tiny, glittering bikinis gyrated to a disco beat. They whipped off their tops, threw them into the audience to loud cheers and pranced around the stage like show ponies, their round, hard breasts as still as rocks.

'Can I help you?' a husky voice asked.

A tall, topless woman in heels, jaunty hat and a lacy, see-through apron over a g-string was beside her, holding an empty tray.

'I'm Angelique,' Eva said. 'I'm here to do a private strip.'

'Which agency are you with, honey?'

Her voice was throaty. Eva gave her another look. Plastic boobs—they all had those—but in this one's case, a protruding Adam's apple. And large, raw-boned hands. All tastes catered for.

'I'm not with an agency, I work for myself.'

'Good for you. Nice work if you can get it.'

'This is my first night. Do all the girls come from agencies?'

'They do, but not just any agency. The club has strict criteria—the girls have to be clean, vetted regularly, and able to keep their mouths shut. You're the first one I've met who isn't agency. How did you get the job?'

'I have contacts,' Eva said.

'The woman raised her eyebrows. 'Lucky you. I'm Tabitha, by the way. Would you like a drink?'

Eva hesitated. She had to keep her wits about her, digging for information without giving away her motives.

'It's on the house,' Tabitha said.

What the hell, she'd stand out if she wasn't drinking. 'Thanks, I'll have a Scotch on the rocks.'

Eva stood at the back watching the show. After some kissing and fondling of each other's breasts, the strippers slipped off their G-strings, did the splits and disappeared side stage to a wave of applause and whistling.

Tabitha reappeared with Eva's drink.

'Thanks. They look after you here, then?'

'What do you mean?'

'Drinks on the house. That's generous.'

'You're allowed two free drinks before your show. Didn't the manager ask you to sign an agreement with a list of rules?'

Eva thought quickly. 'I didn't have time to sign it. I have to come in tomorrow and do it.'

'Well, I guess I'd better tell you. Your two free drinks before the show are to loosen you up if you need it. No blow or speed till after your show—supposedly, but no-one takes any notice of that. The management turn a blind eye; some of the girls need it to perform. No weed at all, it dulls you too much. None of that is in the contract, of course. No sexual contact during private shows, that's for the Fantasy Rooms only.'

Eva nodded as if she'd heard it all before.

'And of course, the usual non-disclosure stuff. Who's your client?'

'Charles Dennehy.'

Tabitha gave her an appraising look. 'Your contacts must be good, he's very particular. He usually only wants Candy or Dana.'

'Maybe he's decided he wants a change.'

'Could be.' She put her hand on Eva's arm. 'I hope he likes you, he's a very generous tipper.'

I bet he is. She watched the sway of Tabitha's tight, low-slung buttocks as she headed to the bar in the corner. That would be one woman safe from Charlie's advances. The disco music started up again and another two strippers strutted on to the stage in sequined, feathery regalia. Non-stop titillation.

Eva considered her options. It was apparent from Tabitha's comments that Charlie was more than just an occasional visitor and that he'd lied about the girls just being eye candy. No surprises there. But it would soon become obvious when Charlie didn't turn up for his private show that her story was fake. She didn't want to hang around for too much longer in case, by some horrible coincidence, he did happen to turn up after his meeting. Time and subtlety were of the essence.

She spotted a sign for the Ladies Restrooms, headed over and went in. There was a small room to the side of the entrance. Two young women in barely-there spangly bikinis and stiletto heels were bent over a long marble bench. Eva had come across women doing cocaine in rest rooms before at social functions, and the sight of them sucking it up through a straw into their nostrils repulsed her. Apart from the marble bench, there was nothing else in the room. Could it be there for the sole purpose of using cocaine?

She went in, peed and washed her hands. As she was leaving, she almost collided with one of the women coming out of the cocaine room at the same time, wiping her nose. She smiled at Eva, her eyes shiny. She had to be at least eighteen, but didn't look a day over fifteen.

'Hi! I'm Bonnie. Are you new?'

'Yes, I'm Angelique.'

'Do you want the dressing room? It's over here.'

Eva followed her slender, boyish figure to a room behind the stage. A table and a mirror ran the length of the room, the table covered with messy piles of make-up and associated detritus. Sweat and perfume mingled under the hot make-up lights. Two topless women in G-strings were chatting feverishly while primping and preening in front of the mirror.

'This is Angelique,' Bonnie said, taking a cowgirl costume from a hook.

'Hi,' they both said, pausing for a nanosecond in their conversation without taking their eyes off the mirror.

Eva pulled up a stool, took some lipstick out of her evening bag and began to reapply it. As soon as there was a lull in the conversation, she fanned herself, saying, 'It's hot in here isn't it? My make-up is melting already.'

The woman closest to her eyed her in the mirror. Her jet black wig, fake fingernails and fake tan gleamed under the lights. 'It looks fine.'

'They're not looking at your face anyway,' the other one said. She was identically fake except for a blonde wig.

'Are you on stage tonight?' Eva asked.

'Yep,' the black-haired girl answered. 'We're the titillating twosome, aren't we, Dana?'

They burst into giggles. Was this Charlie's Dana? They both exuded the sort of manic energy gained from artificial stimulation.

'What's your act?' Dana asked.

'I'm doing a private show for Charles Dennehy.'

Dana narrowed her eyes. 'Really? Is he here?'

'He's arriving later.'

'He must be getting sick of you,' the other girl said, nudging Dana. 'He wants some fresh pussy.'

'Shut up, Tash,' Dana said.

'So you know him pretty well?' Eva applied some more eyeliner.

'What's it to you?'

Eva shrugged. 'Just curious. I've heard a lot about him. Like he's a generous tipper.'

'You'll get a few hundred if you let him do what he wants.'

'I thought there was no sexual contact allowed in the private shows?'

'Who told you that?' Tash asked.

'Tabitha.'

Dana curled her generous lip. 'Tabitha wouldn't know a dick from a dildo. No-one sticks to the rules—you do anything if they pay you enough.'

Bonnie, dressed in a fringed midriff top, tiny fringed skirt and cowboy boots, was brandishing a whip. She looked like a kid playing dress-ups.

'See you guys later,' she said. At the doorway, she turned and said to Eva,' There's a party on later, round the corner. Highview Apartments, just ask for Benny.'

'Benny has the best mull,' Tash said. 'And you'd never know it to look at him. He looks like my grandfather.'

'So I guess there are a lot of fat cats who hang around here,' Eva said.

'You've got to be rolling in it to be a member,' Dana said. 'The only thing that makes this job bearable is the tips.'

'Absolutely,' Tash said. 'The richer they are, the kinkier they are.'

'I hear that a lot of illegal business goes on here too.'

Dana looked at Eva as if she'd personally accused her of it. 'Are you a cop?'

Eva glared back at her. 'Do I look like a cop?'

'I reckon you would if you were in uniform.'

'I'm not, I'd spit on a cop as soon as look at one. There was something in the news the other day about people doing shady business deals here, in fact, I think it was Dennehy they were talking about and I thought, I bet that happens all the time. I mean, it's away from the public eye and no-one's supposed to talk about what goes on here.'

'That's another rule that gets broken,' Tash said. 'But yeah, all sorts of stuff goes on here; I've seen Charlie-boy hanging out with a couple of guys I know for a fact do crooked shit. But it's the same for a lot of them here. Everyone has their price.'

'Okay, Miss Philosophy 101, let's beat it.' Dana said. They both donned a frilly, see-through negligee, placed an Alice-band sporting a huge pink bow on their heads, and clutching a teddy bear each, tottered out.

So Charlie had been seen consorting with crooks. Vague, but a starting point. Charlie never socialised for the fun of it; there was always a purpose to it, something that was in it for him.

Eva left the dressing room and stood for a while watching Dana and Tash on stage raising laughs doing some very un-childlike things with the teddies. She looked around and saw Tabitha at the bar chatting to the bar attendant. She'd just have time to pump her for more information before leaving; she'd booked a return cab for ten pm; she wanted to arrive home before Charlie to save awkward explanations.

'Your man not arrived yet?' Tabitha asked.

'Not yet. Gives me time for another drink.' Eva ordered a scotch on the rocks from the bar attendant. "Do you know Charles Dennehy well?'

'Not in the biblical sense,' Tabitha grinned. There was a smear of red lipstick on her front tooth. 'He's not into trannies, which is a shame, because I'd do him, he's a charmer.'

'So I've heard. I've also heard that he hangs around with some shady types here.'

'Depends what you mean by shady types. Why do you ask?'

'I did some illegal stuff myself a few years ago but I'm straight now and I don't want to get into any more trouble.'

'You don't have to worry about that. All he'll want to do is fuck you. And don't worry about the drugs either, just make sure you stay on the premises. As far as I know, this place has never been raided. It'd bring down the whole fucking government.'

'I hope he doesn't do drugs himself. I hate fucking men when they're high, they're so unpredictable.'

Charlie's views on drugs were well known. He had funded a number of well publicised 'say no to drugs' campaigns, as well as the construction of a drug rehabilitation centre, Hope Valley, on the outskirts of Sydney. In private he despised those who became addicted to drugs or alcohol, especially when they made fools of themselves in public. It arose from having two brothers who became drug addicts as teenagers, though Charlie never talked about them. In a place like this, principles could easily be compromised, but even so, Eva doubted that he'd be foolish enough to use drugs in public. But she had to make certain.

'You might not get a lot of work here if that's the case. But I've never seen Charlie use drugs. He even hates his girls using them. One night, Dana turned up absolutely off her face, and he told her to fuck off and hired someone else.'

She picked up her loaded drinks tray from the bar. 'Gotta go, good luck. I'm sure he'll love you.'

Eva finished her drink, then headed out of the room, hoping that none of the security guards would question why she was leaving so early. As she reached the door, she came face to face with a group of men coming in. Walking straight towards her was Charlie, accompanied by Sol and two other men.

She felt the blood drain from her face. Could she make a run for it? Too late, he'd seen her. And he was looking at her intently, frowning. Recognition dawned and his expression turned from disbelief to anger in a few heartbeats. There was only one way she could play it.

'Mr Dennehy, lovely to see you again,' she purred. She turned a dazzling smile on to the others. 'I'm Angelique, your hostess. Please follow me.' She turned and walked back into the room towards an empty table in the far corner.

She felt the presence of someone behind her and a hand on her shoulder. 'Eva, what the fuck are you doing?' Charlie hissed in her ear.

'I might ask you the same question,' she replied without turning around. At the table, she indicated to the men to take a seat. 'Tabitha will be with you shortly to take your drink orders.'

Sol was staring at her with a mixture of disbelief and derision. The other two men, who were Chinese, looking sleek and prosperous in their shiny suits, nodded and smiled. Ignoring the waves of anger radiating from Charlie, Eva perched on his knee and curled her arm around his neck, crossing her legs so that the side of her dress fell away to reveal the tops of her stockings and a glimpse of her suspender belt. The Chinese men stared at her exposed thigh as if they'd never seen one before.

'I've got a little treat organised for you and your guests,' she said, loudly enough so the others could hear. 'Your own private strip show.'

Charlie was rigid. 'Thank-you for the offer, but no thanks.'

She ran her fingers through the tufts of grey hair on the side of his head. 'Come on, baby, don't be a spoilsport, I've been looking forward to it. She turned to the others. 'What do you think, boys? Wouldn't you like your own striptease show?"

Sol said nothing, leaning back in his chair, as if to distance himself from the scene. The businessmen smiled politely and looked at Charlie. They obviously sensed that he disapproved of Eva for some reason unknown to them and they didn't want to offend him.

Charlie unwound Eva's arm from around his neck, lifted her from his lap and stood up. 'I'm not here for a strip show and I'd appreciate it if you'd go.'

She gave an exaggerated pout. 'I'm sure you'd change your mind if I was Candy or Dana.'

She watched his face as the reason she was there dawned on him. Snooping, catching him out. Proving the truth of what he'd denied for so many years.

'I'm afraid I'll have to call security if you don't leave us alone.'

Eva put her fingers to her mouth, kissed them and placed them on Charlie's mouth, leaving a smear of red lipstick on it. 'I don't think you'll be doing that, sweetheart. It only takes one phone call and your little outing tonight will be headlines in the Sunday rag.'

Charlie's expression could have frozen water. Eva smiled sweetly at him. Oh, the joys of revenge! The stage show had just finished, with Dana and Candy naked except for their heels and their teddy bears, to rounds of cheering and whistling.

Tabitha appeared at the table with two bowls of nuts which she placed on the table.

'Would you believe Mr Dennehy has changed his mind about a private show?' Eva said. 'There's just no pleasing some people.'

Tabitha arched her eyebrows at Charlie. 'If he cancels without notice, he has to pay you half the fee.'

'I'll waive it this time,' Eva said. 'But don't try it again, buster.' She gave Charlie a playful slap on the shoulder, then turned a brilliant smile on them all and said, 'Good-night, gentlemen.'

Tabitha placed her hand on Charlie's arm and looked deep into his eyes. 'Mr Dennehy, may I take your drink order?'

Eva sashayed out, swinging her hips like a hula dancer.

•••

She sat on the deck, still in her stripper's attire, sipping on a nightcap of Bailey's Irish Cream. She'd taken off her wig, as it had made her head hot and itchy. She heard the front door open and then Charlie was standing before her.

'What the hell do you think you're playing at?'

Dodie, sitting at her feet, gave a soft growl.

'You're the one who needs to explain.' Her voice was low, matching his. 'Dana and Candy and fuck knows who else. You can't deny it—I got it from the horse's mouth. Or should I say, the whore's mouth.'

'You're a fine one to talk about whores. Look at you.' Eva's dress had fallen away to reveal the tops of her stockings and suspender belt.

Charlie made a movement and instinctively she flinched. Her insides froze. For a moment she thought he was going to hit her. He'd never done it before, had vowed he would never be like his father. But she'd never seen him as angry as he was now.

He turned away and paced up and down in the living room, then he was in front of her again.

'What if someone had recognised you? How humiliating would that have been? For you and me.'

'Well, they didn't. Don't worry, I wouldn't ruin your reputation by letting anyone think that Charles Dennehy's wife was a woman of low morals. That's reserved for all the sluts he has on the side.'

'You've been drinking. It doesn't become you at all.'

'Would you rather me high on coke, like your little girlfriends?' She stood up and eyeballed him. 'I've known all along that you've been fucking other women and now that I've proved it, you can't even admit that I'm right and you've lied to me all these years.'

Charlie was still, the calculated stillness of a wild animal before it pounces on its prey. That inner chill gripped her again. Dodie growled again. Eva pushed past him into the kitchen and fixed herself another drink.

She half wished she'd taken up Bonnie's invitation to the party at Highview Apartments. But what would she have in common with a bunch of hookers and strippers?

CHAPTER TEN

THE phone rang just as Eva was about to head out the front door. She almost let it go to the answering machine, then at the last minute picked it up.

'What the hell were you doing at the Waterfront Club on Friday night masquerading as a stripper?'

Helga. Sol had obviously told her; she always maintained they had no secrets between them. Except who they'd fucked.

'It was just a bit of fun. I thought Charlie would play along, pretend not to know me and join in the role play, but he wasn't in the mood.'

'That's an understatement. Sol said Charlie was furious that you embarrassed him in front of their investors and he was annoyed as well.'

Fuck you Sol. 'I don't see why. The investors didn't know who I was.'

'Why didn't you just buy a pair of fluffy handcuffs if you wanted to spice up your sex life?'

'Sorry, Helga, I can't chat. I'm on my way to an appointment.'

●●●

Eva had imagined Odyssey Investigations to be like the classic private detective agencies from a novel or movie—a dingy office hidden in an alleyway with a faded sign and a bell on the door. So she was pleasantly surprised to find it in an upmarket office block right in the heart of the Surry Hills shopping precinct, surrounded by trendy cafes and boutiques. She took the lift to the second floor and found the office. She checked her reflection in the glass door, getting a momentary shock to see herself in a blonde wig and wrap-around sunglasses, and entered a modern, airy office simply furnished with inviting armchairs and glossy pot plants.

'Elizabeth Deakin, I have a ten-thirty appointment,' she said to the middle-aged, pleasant-faced woman at reception.

'Please take a seat, Mr Homer will be with you shortly.'

Eva sat in one of the armchairs and picked up a magazine, flicking through the pages. Her confidence in Pete Homer had soared and she hadn't even met him yet. If he could afford an office in such a prime location his business must be flourishing, which meant lots of satisfied customers. Then it struck her—Pete Homer. Odyssey Investigations. He had a sense of humour too. Even better.

A rotund man in a suit strode into the waiting room and held out his hand.

'Ms Deakin, I'm Pete Homer. Pleased to meet you.'

Eva stood up and shook his hand. It was plumply warm. She followed him into an office furnished like a gentleman's study, with a bookcase and a settee in the corner, and even a drinks cabinet. Cosy and intimate, designed to put anxious clients at ease. She sat in the plush chair across the desk from him.

'What can I do for you, Ms Deakin?'

Pete Homer leaned back in his chair, his hands clasped over his giant blancmange of a stomach, and regarded Eva with bright eyes, birdlike in their inquisitiveness. It was hard to gauge his age as his bulk, florid complexion and triple chins undoubtedly made him look older than he was, but Eva estimated he'd be forty at the most. She was glad he was nothing like the stereotype private eye—rumpled and cynical, bottle of Scotch in his top drawer. In Pete Homer's case, it was more likely to be a box of doughnuts.

Eva shifted in her chair and crossed her legs. 'First of all, Mr Homer, I'd better tell you that Elizabeth Deakin is not my real name.'

His eyes twinkled and she realised that he must hear that confession every day.

'Please call me Pete. And you can rest assured that nothing you tell me will be disclosed to anyone else, unless you give me permission to do so. That includes Barbara as well, whom you met at reception. Discretion is the fuel that our business runs on, and we do our utmost to ensure that.'

Eva's shoulders softened. There was something comforting and trustworthy about this man.

'My real name is Eva Dennehy. I'm Charles Dennehy's wife.'

He gave no sign of recognition. 'What can I do for you, Mrs Dennehy?'

'My husband is not a man to whom fidelity is important, I know he's been unfaithful to me countless times over the sixteen years we've been married, but he's always denied it and up until recently I've had no proof. As far as I'm aware they've all been purely sexual playmates. But things have changed. I've discovered that he's having an affair with a woman called Veronika Ettore, and he's planning to leave me for her.'

'How did you find that out?'

'I overheard a phone conversation between them.'

'So why do you need me?'

'Because I need proof.' Something more than a phone conversation. Hard proof, so that when the time came for her to confront him, he couldn't deny it. 'I want photos of them. In the act.'

'What are you going to do with them?'

'What business is it of yours?'

'None whatsoever. You're free to do whatever you like with them. Just a word of advice—don't act too hastily, take some time to consider your options. I've had more than one client confront her husband with proof of his infidelity, then found herself up to her ears in lawyers, all taking their chunk, not to mention the humiliation and publicity.'

'I'm well aware of the consequences,' Eva said coolly.

Pete opened a drawer, pulled out some papers, rifled through them and slid them over to her. 'This is our contract. One thousand dollars deposit, hourly rate of one hundred per hour, plus expenses.'

Eva read through the contract, all standard stuff. The fees were high; she hoped he was worth it.

'I have twenty years' experience in the business, particularly in your field of enquiry,' he said.

So he made a living out of spying on wealthy women's husbands.

'Just out of interest, how did you find me? Did someone recommend me?'

'I found you in the phone book. Hiring a private detective had never occurred to me—I thought it was the sort of sleazy thing people only did in books—until a woman at a social event told me about someone she knew who'd hired a private detective to investigate her husband, so I thought, 'why not?''

She signed the forms and handed them back. Peter picked up a notepad and pen. 'Okay, give me the facts.'

Eva told him everything he wanted to know about Charlie and what little she knew of Veronika. 'The only place I know the two of them have been together is La Bella Restaurant.'

She watched him write La Bella in his neat handwriting with his gold-plated pen.

'So what happens now?' Eva asked. 'Do you follow him until you catch him out?'

She couldn't imagine someone Pete's size following anyone, on foot anyway, without being noticed.

As if reading her thoughts, he said, 'You'd be surprised how well we large people can blend into the background. No-one looks at us, they're either disgusted or they don't want to be caught staring. I'm very discreet. Your husband will never know.'

Eva cleared her throat. He studied her. 'Is there anything else I need to know?'

'There's another matter I'd like you to investigate.'

He waited for her to continue.

'You may have heard in the local news that Councillor Tim O'Brien accused Charlie of bribery to speed up the approval for his new building Dennehy Towers.'

Pete nodded.

'At the gala ball for the opening of the building, a reporter mentioned allegations of Charlie doing underhand business deals at the Waterfront club. And on the same night, I saw Charlie and Andrew Thomason having a tete-a-tete. If you remember, Andrew Thomason was the barrister accused of hiding money off shore from his ex-wife during their property settlement. Charlie has never mentioned knowing him.'

'And?' Pete prompted.

'I want you to find out if Charlie is involved in any illegal activities.'

'And you're basing your request on what you've just told me?'

Eva nodded.

'It's a pretty flimsy basis for suspicion. Vague allegations of bribery and doing underhand business deals which haven't been substantiated, and your husband talking to a barrister who was cleared of allegations of impropriety. Do you think they're all linked in some way?'

'Probably not, but I'm working on the theory that where there's smoke there's fire. And there's something else.'

She told him about her visit to the Waterfront Club, and both Tabitha and Tash's assertion that they'd seen Charlie consorting with known criminals. 'And I can tell you that illegal activities go on there—drug use is rife, I saw a couple of girls doing coke in the Ladies. They have a room especially for it.'

Pete raised his eyebrows. 'That was a risky thing to do. What would you have done if someone had recognised you?'

'As far as I know, no-one did. Except Charlie and Sol, of course. And Charlie is still not talking to me.'

Pete made some doodles on his notepad. 'Still not a lot to go on. I'm not saying it's not possible he's crooked, but it will be difficult to get evidence. I assume you want evidence?'

'Yes.'

'What are you going to do with it?'

'Again, I don't think it's any of your business.'

She wasn't about to tell him she intended to use it to blackmail Charlie. If you leave me, I'll go to the police with this information.

'I'd hate to see a beautiful, intelligent woman like you come to any harm.'

It was a compliment she'd been given countless times; coming from Pete it sounded genuine.

'I can take care of myself.'

Pete sighed and picked up his pen again. 'Ok, fire away. Tell me what you know about your husband's business.'

Eva told him the names of the companies and projects that she could remember. 'I'm sorry, I can't tell you much, Charlie made it clear right from the start that the business was his domain, and I was happy to go along with that. We have a very traditional marriage—he makes the money and I spend it. If he is corrupt, my lack of knowledge is certainly convenient for him.'

'So I take it you have no access to any of his business documents or correspondence?'

'Definitely not. His secretary Ainsley guards him and the office with her life. She's been with Charlie longer than we've been married and she's like a mother—no girl is good enough for her Charlie and she's amazed our marriage has lasted as long as it has. Obviously she's underestimated my charms.'

'It would be an unwise person who would do that,' Pete said. 'Does Charlie have a home office?'

'Yes, but he doesn't do much there, it's mainly for show. And there's nothing important there, I've already looked. He gets all his bank statements and anything financial delivered to the business.'

Pete stared down at his notes and tapped his pen on his notepad.

'I've just remembered,' Eva said. 'He was audited by the Tax Office a couple of years ago. I don't know why; he was very tight-lipped about it. Maybe someone tipped them off, but the upshot of it was that they didn't find anything untoward.'

'If the Tax Office couldn't find anything, then I don't like my chances. We'll have to come at it from a different angle.'

'I agree. I think it would be easier to pursue the path of his supposed criminal connections. Surely you have contacts in that area?'

Pete regarded her with amusement. 'This isn't like the movies, where I meet my informant on a park bench and he passes me all the information wrapped inside a newspaper. You're right that I do have some contacts on the wrong side of the law, but there's no guarantee they'd be able or willing to pursue that line of enquiry without compromising their safety or my own.'

'I certainly don't want you to put yourself in danger. But I would appreciate it if you could do what you can.'

'I'll put out some feelers and see what I come up with. What's the best way to contact you?'

'You can phone me at home during the day or send mail to this address.' She handed him a card with the address of a post office box in Rose Bay she'd paid for that morning.

Pete hauled himself to his feet and held out his hand. 'It was a pleasure to meet you, Mrs Dennehy. I'll keep you regularly apprised of my progress. You can pay your deposit to Barbara on the way out.'

'Thank-you. Please call me Eva.'

She was nearly out the door when she heard, 'Eva!'

She turned around. 'No more visits to the Waterfront Club,' Pete said. 'You could be compromising your own safety as well.'

CHAPTER ELEVEN

ON the drive home from Odyssey Investigations Eva mulled over her discussion with Pete. She knew her reasons for suspecting Charlie of illegal business were weak, but she couldn't ignore her hunch. And she had a good feeling about Pete—if there was anything to find, he'd dig it up.

Something was niggling her though, and after she'd arrived home and fixed herself some lunch, it came to her. She jumped up and went into Charlie's office. It was true, as she'd told Pete, that she'd already searched it—she did so regularly, searching for evidence of his infidelity—credit card statements, letters, phone numbers, anything. Of course she never found anything—Charlie would never be so careless as to leave any evidence there.

But now she would come at it from a different perspective, that he might be hiding evidence of crime. What sort of evidence she had no idea—drugs, money, guns? That sort of thing only happened on TV crime shows. She started by searching the drawers of his antique rosewood desk, looking and feeling closely underneath them for something that might indicate a false bottom. Unlikely, but sometimes antique desks were constructed with secret compartments. There was nothing in the drawers except the usual office stationery, and two boxes of Charlie's business cards.

She then examined the entire wall, running her fingers over it, looking for a hidden safe, including behind the paintings. Original David Hockneys. Charlie would freak out if he knew she was touching them. Although he claimed to have an appreciation of art, Eva suspected that he'd acquired the paintings for their bragging rights, rather than their aesthetic value.

By the time she'd inspected the coffee table, and the bookcase crammed with books on business, property and investment, she was exhausted. She sank into the three-seater leather couch and as she leaned back the footrest popped up. She hadn't realised the seat was a recliner–she was never invited into the office and she'd never sat on the couch.

On impulse, she clambered out of the seat, leaving the footrest up, and examined the base of the chair, feeling underneath it. Nothing. The middle seat didn't recline, so she sat on the other end seat and leaned back until the footrest was up.

She jumped off and examined the base, sliding her fingers under it. She felt something hard, a lever, and pulled it. A compartment slid into view in the space above the base, about two feet square. There was no lock, just a hinged lid. Eva opened it. Inside, nestled in a piece of foam rubber was a revolver. Black, shiny, menacing.

Eva's heart stood still. She'd never seen a gun up close. Gingerly she took it out. It was lighter than she expected. Even though it gave her the shivers, she was fascinated. She ran her fingers over the smooth cylinder, found the latch and opened it. Six chambers, all empty. She closed the cylinder again and only then did she notice the small box in the compartment, half hidden by the foam rubber. She took it out and opened it. Bullets. Six of them.

She turned the revolver over, getting used to the feel and positioning of it in her hand. She swivelled around and pointed it at the bookcase. What would it be like to shoot someone? She couldn't do it–when it came to the crunch, she wouldn't have the guts to pull the trigger, to commit that final, irrevocable act. Which was strange, considering she was already a killer. But poisoning was different.

More to the point, what was Charlie doing with a gun? This was Australia—the average man in the street didn't own a gun, wasn't permitted to own one, unless he was a recreational shooter or a farmer. Charlie was neither; he had no reason to own a gun. No legal reason.

•••

The post office car park was bathed in pale wintry sunshine, but Eva didn't feel any of the warmth as she sat in her car, reading the two page report sent to her post office box by Pete Homer. Her head was hangover-heavy and she had to read it a couple of times for it to sink in. It outlined days and times over the past two weeks that he'd tailed Charlie, along with a tally of expenses.

The upshot was that Charlie and Veronika had been spotted on a couple of occasions having intimate lunches in restaurants on the other side of the city from his office, and also drinks at cocktail bars after work.

'There has been physical contact,' Pete wrote. 'Some handholding and kissing, but at this stage I have been unable to find any evidence of them sleeping together. After their meetings they both go their separate ways, Mr Dennehy to his office or home and Ms Ettore to Secrets International Models or Milestone Marketing, a PR agency of which she is part owner, or her home at Darling Point.

'From my observations, although Ms Ettore is obviously very attracted to Mr Dennehy, she is keeping her distance, for reasons I can only speculate on. I have enclosed photos and will continue to undertake surveillance.'

Eva slid out a half dozen colour photos from the envelope. Veronika and Charlie gazing into each other's eyes in a dimly lit bar. Veronika was facing the camera and Eva fancied she could make out a hint of triumph in her expression. The two of them holding hands across the table in a restaurant. In one photo Veronika was reaching across the table with her finger on Charlie's mouth, in a gesture as if to say, 'Hush.' Tender and erotic. A photo of them in a clinch in the shadows, bodies and lips pressed together like a book cover for a romance novel.

The photos slipped out of her hand on to her lap. Her head sank on to the steering wheel and she gave in to the spasm of sobbing that had bubbled up. When it seemed as if there were nothing left inside her, she checked her face in the side mirror and dabbed at it with a tissue. *Self-pity doesn't become you, Eva.*

She dug around in her handbag for her mobile phone before remembering she didn't have one. Mobile phones were still at the brick stage and only those who wanted to show how hip they were owned one. How had society ever functioned before instant access to a phone?

She phoned Pete after arriving home. 'I got your report. What did you mean by Veronika keeping her distance for reasons you can only speculate on?'

'I haven't been able to get close enough yet to hear conversation of any worth, so I'm going by body language only, which is something that we investigators get to be very good at. Veronika is a clever woman–she's obviously head over heels in love with your husband but she's keeping her cards close to her chest. She lets him think he's doing the chasing, but she's slowly reeling him in, and I'm guessing that she wants some sort of commitment, a declaration of love at the very least, before she consents to sex. It's old-fashioned, but it works a treat for men like your husband, who are used to women taking their clothes off for them at the click of a finger.'

'That bitch,' Eva said.

'She's certainly a woman who has no compunction about using her feminine wiles.'

So—something she and Veronika had in common. Eva would prove that she could out-wile her any day.

'How are you going with the other investigation?'

'I've done some probing about the allegations of bribery and Charlie's association with Andrew Thomason, but I've drawn a blank. I haven't been able to find any moles within the Council, they're all admirably tight-lipped, and as for the other, Charlie and Andrew have attended a few of the same social functions, but there seems to be nothing to suggest they're anything more than acquaintances.'

'I expected as much. You're wasting your time—'

'However,' Pete interrupted, 'I have discovered something which could be significant. I have a contact who is well-informed about the local criminal scene, and he informs me that Charlie's name has been linked to the owners of Downtown, a jazz bar in the city, who are rumoured to be involved in drug importation and money laundering.'

'Drug importation? Charlie? He's always been so anti-drugs.'

'It's only hearsay at the moment, though my contact's information is usually spot-on.'

'I have some information too,' Eva said. She told Pete about her search of Charlie's office and the discovery of his gun.

'You're becoming quite the private eye,' Pete said. 'Perhaps I should take you on as a partner. But that does lend some weight to the hearsay—what reason would a law abiding citizen have to hide a gun in a secret compartment?'

'I asked myself that question as well.'

'I'll let you know as soon as anything more comes to hand. Be careful, and remember, this is strictly confidential.'

Eva thanked him and hung up. Downtown. She'd never been there, not being an aficionado of jazz, and she couldn't remember Charlie mentioning it. Not that he would. Her head was woolly—she'd drunk a whole bottle of champagne last night after Charlie, barely speaking to her over dinner, had gone out again, God knows where.

She needed some exercise and fresh air. She took down Dodie's lead from its hook on the kitchen wall. Dodie came scampering in, her claws skidding on the marble tiled floor. She could be at the other end of the house, but somehow she always knew the minute Eva had her lead.

'Hullo, my darling,' she crooned, burying her face in Dodie's fur. 'Your daddy's been a very bad boy. He's breaking my heart. He thinks he's so damn smart but I'll get so much dirt on him, he'll have to get permission from me to blink.'

CHAPTER TWELVE

DOWNTOWN reminded Eva of a jazz bar from an old movie. A tiny entrance in a small alleyway between two shops in the outer part of the business district. Down a flight of steps into dim lighting and the odour of stale beer, greasy food and cigarette smoke. A band was playing on a small stage, surrounded by intimate alcoves of tables and armchairs. A banner proclaimed them as *All That Jazz*.

Eva paid her five dollar cover charge, and as there were no spare tables, she perched on a corner barstool and ordered a Scotch on the rocks. The clientele were mainly middle-aged, their dress code casual bordering on scruffy, faces etched with weariness, the sort of place where people came on a Friday night to wind down from the week and forget the boss, the mortgage and the family. Anyone who came to pose or be seen would stand out like a plumber's bum crack.

Eva was glad she'd decided to wear trousers and a jacket, though her blonde wig and heavy make-up, worn as a disguise, made her more conspicuous. She was aware of being sized up by both sexes. At a nearby table a dumpy, hard-faced woman in a garish flannelette shirt over floral leggings eyed her off, as if calculating what sort of competition for male attention Eva was likely to offer.

She grimaced inwardly. The nineties had a lot to answer for when it came to fashion—few women could carry off the floral leggings look, unless they were a supermodel like Claudia Schiffer. Who, come to think of it, Eva had never seen wearing them. She focused her attention on the band playing *Hello Dolly*. The lead singer, a heavy set man with a shaved head, was doing a passable imitation of Louis Armstrong.

The only reason Charlie would come to a place like this would be to do business. When he'd phoned that afternoon to say he had a meeting and wouldn't be home till late, she immediately thought of Veronika. But for once she was glad—it would give her the opportunity to do some investigation of her own. She'd left a note for him, suitably vague. 'Out for dinner with the girls, see you later tonight.'

Pete wouldn't approve of what she was doing, but he needn't know. It wasn't that she didn't have faith in him, but a woman using her feminine wiles, as he called them, could find out things a man could never hope to discover. If the rumours about Charlie were true, he was leading a whole other life of which she'd had no inkling. And for what reason? Money? Surely not. He had more than both of them could spend in a lifetime. She was curious and restless and still half-disbelieving, and something within her was driving her to investigate this other life herself, to find out what it was that attracted Charlie to it.

The band finished *Hello Dolly* with a flourish of saxophone to whistles and applause. 'Thanks, ladies and gents,' the lead singer said. 'We'll take a break and be back shortly. Don't go away!'

The members came down to the bar and ordered drinks. The lead singer stood next to Eva and ordered a beer. His face was shiny with perspiration.

'Are you enjoying the show?' he asked.

'Yes, your band is excellent. Do you play here often?'

'Most Friday nights. Every now and then they have a guest band.' He held out his hand. 'I'm Ray. I haven't seen you round here before.'

I'm—Sarah.'

They shook hands.

'This is my first time here,' Eva said. 'I heard it was a good night out so I thought I'd come and see for myself.'

'You like trad jazz? Jelly Roll Morton and Bobby Hacket and the like?'

'I adore them,' she replied, though in reality there was only so much jazz she could take before it all started to sound like a jumble of notes. 'Do you know the owners here?"

'I know Tommy and Sniper real well.'

'Sniper?'

'He was a sniper in the Vietnam War, one of the best, they reckon, and he was only eighteen when he was conscripted. It's affected his mind though, he's a bit crazy. You wouldn't want to get on the wrong side of him.'

'What's Tommy like?'

'Nice guy. Straight down the line, honest as the day is long.'

He gave her a more thorough look. 'Why do you want to know? You wanna buy the joint?'

'Just interested. It must be a tough job running one of these places.'

'They've both owned bars in Asia so they can handle anything. Are you going to be here for long?'

Eva smiled and fluttered her eyelashes. 'Depends how good the music is.'

'The best is yet to come. If you'd like to, you can join us for a few drinks after the show.'

'Thanks, I'll let you know.' Of course she'd go. Ray might have some useful information, knowing the owners.

He downed the rest of his beer. 'See you soon.'

Eva ordered another Scotch on the rocks to fortify her through the ordeal of another couple of hours of jazz. When a couple got up and left, she slipped off her bar stool and took their table. It was in a shadowy corner, a perfect vantage point to hide and observe people. When the band started up again, a few couples got up and shuffled around on the dance floor.

Relaxing in the mellow glow of her Scotches, Eva was surprised at how quickly the time went. She rebuffed a couple of offers to buy her a drink, to looks of disbelief. What was a woman doing here on her own if not to pick up a man?

At eleven thirty, Ray thanked the audience and the band packed up their gear. Frank Sinatra boomed out from the jukebox with *The Lady is a Tramp* and an older couple twirled around on the stage to whistles from the audience. Other couples joined them on the dance floor. The party wasn't over yet.

Ray scanned the room till he found Eva and made a beeline for her. 'Glad you're still here. Wanna come out the back and join in the party?'

Eva made a pretence of hesitation. 'I'll stay for a while.' Charlie was probably at home now, wondering where she was. Let him wonder.

She waited for Ray to take his gear out to his car, then followed him through a door behind the stage. It led out into a dark alley and the suffocating odour of putrid rubbish, and in through another door a few metres away. They were in what appeared to be a small bedsit—a living room with a double bed against the far wall, a couch and a couple of beanbags, leading into a tiny kitchen, with a bathroom to the left. Perhaps the owners stayed here sometimes instead of going home. Made sense if you were going to be partying.

A couple of stand-up lamps glowed in the living room, highlighting the shabby decor. A man and woman were cosied up on the couch. The other four band members, all men in their forties or fifties with the pale, unhealthy pallor of professional musicians, stood in a circle holding stubbies of beer. The room reeked of marijuana.

'This is Sarah,' Ray said. He did the introductions. The couple on the couch were Tommy and his wife Carol. Tommy stood up and shook her hand. He was a short, powerfully built man in his fifties; his round, rosy-cheeked face gave him the demeanour of a benevolent grandfather, belied by the look of shrewd appraisal he gave her. Carol was a tall, slender woman with a long, horsy face. She nodded coolly to Eva.

Ray went into the kitchen to get Eva a Scotch. There was another man in there and Eva heard Ray murmuring to him. Then he stood in the doorway with her Scotch and beckoned her in.

'Sarah, this is Sniper.'

Sniper was tall and rangy, bald on top, with a stringy pony tail. His face was pockmarked with the scars of severe acne.

'Hi.' Eva held out her hand, but Sniper ignored it.

'I've seen you somewhere before,' he said.

Heart racing, Eva put on a look of surprise. 'Really? I can't think where. This is my first time here.'

Sniper looked her over. His eyes darted constantly like small brown fish. He nodded at the wall. 'Stand over there.'

'Come on, Sniper,' Ray said. 'No need to frisk her. She's not a cop.'

'You know my motto. Trust no-one.'

'You'd frisk your own grandmother.'

Eva's indignation at the prospect of being frisked overrode her apprehension. 'I can assure you I'm not a police officer, but if you want me frisked, Carol can do it. I'm not ready for you and me to become that well acquainted.'

Sniper looked at her as if he wanted to kill her, then his face creased in a broad smile.

'You've got a feisty one there, Ray.' He poked his head into the living room. 'Hey, Carol!'

Carol appeared and Sniper nodded at Eva. 'Frisk her. Check she's not wired.'

Carol appraised Eva. 'Take your jacket off.'

Eva did so, Carol felt it all over, then frisked her with the professionalism of a seasoned security officer. 'She's clear.'

He grunted. 'Doesn't mean she's not a cop.'

Ray handed Eva her drink and she followed him back out into the living room.

'I see what you mean by him being a bit crazy,' Eva said. 'Why would he think I'm a cop?'

Ray shrugged. 'Paranoia's all part of the Vietnam stuff, I guess. You're lucky he's in a good mood, I've seen him beat people up for standing up to him.'

He dropped into one of the bean bags and Eva settled herself into the one beside it. 'I know this is a corny line, but what's a beautiful woman like you doing in a place like this? Don't you have a man waiting at home for you?'

Eva shook her head. 'I'm single and fancy free.'

'Me, too.' Ray told her about his divorce five years ago and his two teenage boys who stayed with him every second week-end. He too was the victim of a serial cheater, and in the end he'd had to leave his wife for the sake of his pride and sanity.

'I still love her. She's the same person I fell in love with and married. But I can't live with her because I know she'll never stop doing it. It's the saddest thing in the world, to love someone and not be able to live with them.'

'I understand,' Eva said. 'I had a husband like that.'

He looked at her with new respect and the joy of someone who'd found a confidante.

'Do you know,' he leaned closer to her and Eva was aware of his strong masculine odour. 'One night I was so mad at her, because she was denying she'd been out with lover boy and I knew she had, that I wanted to kill her. I put my hands around her throat and squeezed, just a little, to see how it felt, and she looked at me with such fear in her eyes, I realised what I was doing and I let go.'

'I can believe that.'

He took her hand. 'You're a very understanding woman.'

'You're getting a bit cosy over there, Ray!' Steve, one of the band members, called out. He and the others were now lounging on the floor near the couch, sharing a bong with each other, and with Tommy and Carol. Sniper had come in from the kitchen and was sitting on the bed, leaning forward with his legs apart, swigging straight out of a bottle of bourbon.

'Mind your own beeswax,' Ray said. He and Tommy exchanged glances and Tommy nodded almost imperceptibly in the direction of the kitchen. Ray put his mouth to Eva's ear. 'Wanna do some charlie?' His breath was hot in her ear.

It took her a few seconds to remember that charlie was slang for cocaine. She hesitated. She'd had plenty of opportunities to do coke in her previous life; many in her social circle used it recreationally. Helga swore that sex after cocaine was 'off this planet,' but Eva had always abstained because Charlie disapproved of drug use. As did her inner good Catholic girl.

As a teenager she'd experimented with marijuana and party drugs, as a form of rebellion against her upbringing, but after seeing the consequences of heavy use in many of her peers—addiction, unemployment and crime, she stopped as soon as she left school.

She thought of Charlie again—what would he think if he could see her now? It suddenly struck her as funny—Charlie disapproved of charlie. She giggled. What the hell, if she was going to have any credibility with this group, she had to go with the flow.

'Sure,' she whispered back. Ray grinned at her, took her hand and helped her out of the beanbag.

They followed Tommy into the small, drab bathroom in seventies mustard yellow. On the bench was a large hand mirror. Tommy pulled a ziplock bag of white powder and a handful of cut down straws out of his pocket, emptied a pile of the powder on to the mirror, and cut it into lines with a business card. He bent over, held one nostril shut with his finger and stuck the straw in the other nostril. Eva watched the line of powder disappear up the straw. Tommy removed the straw and stood up. Ray gestured for Eva to go next.

'You go,' she said to him. She needed more time to prepare herself. She watched Ray stick the straw in his nostril and suck up the powder. He stood back and nodded at her.

'Take your time,' he said. 'You don't need to suck too hard.'

So it was obvious this was her first time. Her chest was tight with apprehension, but she couldn't back out now. She'd do it this once and that was it.

She stepped up to the mirror. Hands shaking, she closed one nostril and pushed the straw up the other. She was aware of their eyes on her. She bent over and slowly inhaled the line of powder, feeling a cold tingling in her nostrils. As she stood up, she met Tommy's gaze.

'What's your story, Sarah?' he said. 'You came here tonight to pick up a man and try some coke?'

Eva mustered a frosty look. 'I don't know what your problem with me is. I'm recently divorced and just moved to Sydney, so rather than sit at home alone I decided to go out and enjoy myself. All I wanted to do was have a couple of drinks and listen to some good music, and this is how the night worked out.'

'I like a woman who goes with the flow,' Ray said. 'Leave her alone. You're getting as bad as Sniper.'

Tommy shook his head. 'She's too classy for you.'

'That's for her to decide.' Ray put a protective arm around Eva's shoulders and gave her a squeeze. 'Wanna come for a drive?'

'Where to?' Though she had a fair idea.

'My place. Not far away, about twenty minutes' drive.'

She'd sensed Ray's attraction to her when they met at the bar, and suddenly the thought of sex with this unprepossessing, virtual stranger was incredibly exciting. Besides, she could pump him for more information, which was the whole purpose of this encounter. Pump him, all right. She laughed out loud.

Ray drew her into him and kissed her, a long and hungry kiss. Her nose and the back of her throat were numb, but the rest of her body was zinging as if she'd just got an electric shock. A very pleasurable electric shock. Her knickers were already damp.

Ray led her out through the back door of the kitchen to a small, dirt carpark. He unlocked the passenger door of a battered panel van; it creaked as he opened it. Eva stepped in. It smelt of beer, cigarettes and stale body odour.

As she fastened her seat belt, piles of take-away rubbish at her feet, she had a flashback to her high school days and going out with Eddie Farraday in his van, the back crammed with surf boards, wetsuits, and dank towels. Amongst all the junk he'd wedged a grimy mattress, on which she'd lost her virginity—fumbling, suffocating sex, too quick to be pleasurable, but satisfying in the sense that she'd achieved a goal. That was a lifetime ago, but she had the weird sensation that she was about to go right back there.

'Sorry about the mess,' Ray said, as he heaved himself into the driver's seat. 'The kids treat this van like a rubbish tip.'

The van shuddered and growled as he pulled out into the traffic. It had been raining, and the roads gleamed in the streetlights. The world was fresh and vivid—the traffic that whooshed past, the shops huddled together as if they were sharing a secret, large brooding blocks of houses and apartments, the sliver of moon like a jewel pasted on to a black canvas.

Eva put her hand on Ray's knee and stroked the fabric of his jeans. She fancied she could feel his muscles and the heat of his skin through it. He grinned and placed his hand over hers. Sweaty. But she didn't mind. Sweaty was exciting.

'Nearly there,' he said. 'I'm afraid my humble abode is as messy as my car, but I can only partly blame the kids for that. If I'd known I was going to get lucky tonight, I would have had a spring clean.'

Eva squeezed his knee. 'I'm sure I'll be too preoccupied to notice my surroundings.'

Ray's humble abode turned out to be a two bedroom duplex apartment that screamed 'bachelor slob'. She followed him into the living room. He gathered up a blanket and a pile of clothes and newspapers from the brown velveteen couch and dumped them onto another chair. He indicated to her to take a seat. 'Would you like a glass of wine? I only have chateau cardboard.'

'No thanks.' Eva approached him, kissed him on the lips and slowly unbuttoned his shirt, exposing his pale, doughy belly. She ran her hands over it and rubbed his nipples. He groaned and lunged forward to reciprocate, but she put her hand up. 'You'll get your turn!'

She peeled off her jacket and began to undo her blouse, one slow button at a time. She gyrated and twirled and pouted as she divested herself of her clothes. She imagined herself as Dana or Candy from the Waterfront Club, performing to an adoring audience, men desiring her, longing to touch her, fucking her with their eyes. She was their goddess, their fantasy, the woman they thought of when they were fucking their dumpy, uninspiring wives. She caressed her nipples; they were so erect they hurt. Ray had unzipped his pants and was stroking his erect cock, his eyes fixed unwaveringly on her body. She slid off her g-string and threw it to him and he put it to his nose.

Eva lay on the threadbare carpet and did some soft porn poses, teasing him with glimpses of her pussy and then hiding it with the demureness of a nineteenth century painting.

'Show me,' Ray groaned.

'All in good time, lover boy. And quit the hand job, you'll be finished before I've even started.'

He obediently stopped caressing his cock and she eventually showed him, parting her legs and rubbing and stroking herself. She plunged her finger inside her pussy.

'I'm wet, baby,' she breathed. 'Wet and hot for you.'

She began to stroke her slippery nub and before she could stop herself she was climaxing, and it seemed to go on forever.

Then Ray was on top of her, slipping his cock inside her and he came instantly as well, shuddering and moaning before collapsing on top of her.

'Oh, wow!' he breathed in her ear. 'That was hot!' He raised himself up on his elbows and grinned down at her. 'You're a one woman show! You didn't need me.'

'Of course I needed you! You came in at the just right time to finish me off.' Eva ran her fingers through his chest hair. 'If you want to do it again, I can make sure you have a bigger part next time.' She giggled. 'So to speak.'

'Are you always this insatiable? Or is it the coke?'

'Insatiable is my second name, baby.'

He laughed. 'Okay, Sarah Insatiable. I'll need a bit of time to recover. Do you want that drink now?'

'That would be nice.' The buzz from the cocaine was already starting to fizz out and she'd need something else if she was going to fuck Ray again.

Ray came back with two chipped glasses of wine and they lay naked together on the couch under a rug and sipped the wine. Eva stifled a grimace, but it was the effect she wanted, not the taste, so she gulped it down.

'So, the others in your band are not into coke?' she asked.

'You kidding? On our wages? The only reason Tommy shares his with me is because we've been mates for ages—we went to high school together.'

'You must know him pretty well, then.'

'Yeah. We got into plenty of trouble at school together, but we lost contact after that. He got an engineering degree and went to Africa to build bridges, and I got married young and was working three jobs to support my family. We met up again years later and stayed in touch. When the boys and I put the band together, he'd just taken over the club and I asked him if he'd give us a go. And the rest, as they say, is history.'

'So what does he do apart from run the club?'

Ray shrugged. 'I dunno. Play golf. He's got heaps of dough. The club's just a sideline.' He traced his fingers around her nipple. 'Why are you so interested in him? He's married, you know. He and Carol are very close.'

'I'm not interested in him in that sense. I just thought he seemed like an interesting person.'

'You talked to him for all of three minutes.'

'I can read people, I don't have to talk to them. Like you, for example,' Eva slid her hand under the blanket and stroked the tops of his thighs, sensing his cock stirring, 'I knew as soon as I met you that underneath that kind and decent exterior was an exciting, sexy man.'

'The way you say that, I can almost believe you.' Ray threw the blanket off, flicked his tongue over her nipples and nipped them with his teeth. She stopped herself from flinching and moved her hand down to caress his balls.

'I'm curious as to how Tommy avoids getting arrested for the cocaine. I always thought the police kept a pretty close eye on bars and clubs. I mean, you and I were both taking a risk tonight as well,' she added, to move the emphasis away from Tommy.

'Life's a risk, baby. You were taking a risk coming home with me tonight—I could have been a serial killer and chopped you up into little bits and stuffed you into my freezer.'

'That's true. Note to self—in future, check the freezer on the way in.'

Ray looked up from licking circles around her navel. 'So do you do this a lot?'

'Do what?'

'Pick up men in clubs and go home with them.'

'Of course not. I'm very picky when it comes to men. If I hadn't met you I would have gone home by myself.'

'Well, you don't have to sit at home alone any longer. Big Daddy Ray is here.'

Eva moved her hand up and started stroking his cock. Ray groaned and she shifted herself further down and ran her tongue all around it as if she were licking an ice-cream cone. His breathing became ragged and she stopped.

'Keep going,' he gasped.

'You haven't answered my question.'

'What question?'

She took his cock into her mouth and gave a couple of sucks.

'About Tommy. I want to know, how come he doesn't get caught?'

'I dunno, he mentioned once about having friends in high places.'

'What did he mean by that?'

She sucked him long and hard, then stopped. Ray groaned. 'You're torturing me, you devil-woman.'

'Answer my question.'

'He didn't tell me their names, but I assume he meant police.' He laughed. 'It's more like friends in low places.'

Eva stopped sucking again. 'Police who are criminals?'

He gasped. 'I suppose so. Don't stop now.'

If he knew anything more he wasn't going to let on. She closed her mouth around Ray's cock again and finished him off.

CHAPTER THIRTEEN

IN the cab on the way home, Eva took off her wig and false eyelashes and stuffed them into her handbag. She took out her small hand mirror and some tissues and wiped off most of the make-up, so she looked as much like her normal self as was possible.

When she walked in the front door, Charlie was in the living room in his silk bathrobe talking on the cordless phone. 'Talk to you later,' he said, and threw the phone on the couch.

'Where the hell have you been?'

'Out with the girls, as I said in the note.'

'You said you were having dinner. It's one thirty!'

'We decided to make a night of it and went to a couple of bars afterwards.'

'What bars?'

'Micky's and The Skyline.' They were a couple of upmarket bars in the city she'd been to before. They were always overflowing on Friday nights and it would be impossible for him to verify if she'd been there or not. If he wanted to go that far.

'I don't know what's got into you, lately, Eva.' The look he gave her was pure disgust. She felt her insides curl up into a tight ball, and she wanted to run into his arms, promising she'd never do it again, so he'd forgive her and everything could be like it was before.

But she looked him in the eye and said, 'So it's fine for you to go out until all hours of the night, tomcatting around, but not me?'

'Firstly, I don't go out tomcatting, as you put it, I'm out earning money so you can spend your days having facials, going out to lunch and buying clothes. And secondly, by saying that, you're implying that you yourself were out tomcatting.'

'Don't be ridiculous,' Eva said. 'I'm going to bed.'

She started off down the hallway and then Charlie was in front of her, blocking her way. He put his hands on her shoulders. 'Eva, what's going on?'

She took a deep breath to quell the anger rising inside her. Her hands itched to slap that hypocritical concern off his face. It was on the tip of her tongue to confront him about Veronika, but she stopped herself. *Wait till you've got the evidence.*

'Take your hands off me before I call the police.'

Charlie stared at her in bewilderment, then dropped his hands down to his side. 'The police? For what?'

Eva said nothing. She swept past him to the bedroom.

•••

'It hurts every time I laugh,' Frances groaned. 'That woman is a sadist.'

'We'll promise not to tell you any jokes,' Helga said. Eva wondered not for the first time how Helga managed to finish a Pilates class looking as immaculate in her designer gym gear as she had at the start. She herself felt drained and on edge after coming down from her cocaine high last night and had been tempted to miss her class. But in the end she decided it would take her mind off her suffering.

'I can certainly notice the difference,' Diana said, patting her stomach.

'Honey, if your stomach was any flatter, it would be sucked right into your backbone,' Helga said.

The waitress brought them their skinny cappuccinos. The cafe, near the Pilates studio, was humming with Pilates disciples in lurid leotards and tights breakfasting on low fat muesli and health shakes. Diana, a compulsive trend follower, had persuaded them to try this latest fitness craze by attending Saturday morning classes with her.

'It's not all about having a flat stomach,' she said. 'It's about strengthening your core muscles.'

'Sex will do that for you and you don't need a fit ball,' Helga said. 'Contract your pelvic floor muscles while you're having sex and you not only strengthen your core but you have explosive orgasms. As does your partner.'

'Trust you to bring everything down to a base element,' Frances said. 'I'll have to try it,' she added to peals of laughter from the others.

'The class must have worn you out, Eva,' Helga said.

Eva forced a smile. 'I had a late night. Watching TV,' she added, to pre-empt awkward questions. She was analysing the information she'd got from last night. Nothing concrete, apart from Tommy having criminal contacts in the police force, if she believed Ray's account. She hadn't been able to link Charlie to Tommy and Sniper—yet. The only thing she'd proved was that Helga was right—sex under the influence of cocaine was out of this world.

'Eva, are you okay for the meeting next Tuesday night?' Frances asked.

'What meeting?'

'We've only been talking about it for the last ten minutes—to organise the fundraiser for Mercy Ships.'

Eva had other plans for Tuesday night.

'Sure thing.' She'd plead illness on the day. There were plenty of others on the organising committee to cover her absence. She often got fed up with the cattiness and power plays that seemed to be an inevitable part of being on a committee.

'Watching TV?' Helga said as they were walking to their cars. 'You need to get a life, honey. Has Charlie been working too hard to take you out?'

'He hasn't been at home much lately,' Eva said. 'He's got a couple of big projects on at the moment.'

'You haven't been tempted into any more moonlighting as a stripper?'

Eva glanced at her. It sounded like an innocent question.

'No.'

She hesitated as she unlocked her car door. She wanted to confide in Helga, to tell her about Veronika, although she probably already knew. It was probable that everyone knew; the old adage that the wife was always the last to know was amusing until you were the wife. In her previous life, Eva hadn't let on to anyone that she knew about the affair, so as not to be seen to have a motive to kill Charlie.

Now she couldn't confide in Helga because she couldn't be certain that she wouldn't tell Sol, who would then tell Charlie that Eva knew about Veronika.

And she didn't want to play her hand just yet. If she confronted Charlie about the affair, he might take that as a sign that it was time to leave her, before she'd had time to gather the dirt.

'As I've said before, find yourself a playmate,' Helga said. 'What's good for the goose is good for the gander. Early twenties is ideal—old enough to have some experience but young enough to learn new tricks.' She winked. 'I'm off to play right now, with Felippe. A massage with extras.'

CHAPTER FOURTEEN

TUESDAY nights at Downtown, if this was typical, were a more subdued affair than Fridays. The club was almost full, but the clientele sat staring into their drinks or chatting desultorily. It was hard to let your hair down when you knew you had to front up to work the next day. Even the band was more restrained—just a three piece band playing a crossover of jazz and blues.

Eva ordered a Scotch and sat on a couch at the opposite end from a man in jeans and bomber jacket cuddling a woman in denim overalls. She'd dressed down this time in blue jeans, pullover and boots, though she still wore her wig and make-up. She looked around, wondering if Tommy or Sniper would make an appearance or if she'd have to seek them out; she'd decided to approach them on the pretext of buying some cocaine, in the hope of gleaning some further information about their activities and their link to Charlie.

It was a dangerous road she was going down, but the compulsion that gripped her overrode her fear. A compulsion that made her reckless—after all, that's why she was back in this life again. To change things.

The couple beside her were into the music, tapping their feet and jerking their heads to the beat. The band were rough around the edges; they didn't have the professional slickness of Ray's band. That Ray wouldn't be here was one of the reasons she'd turned up tonight—she didn't want to encounter him again. There was no point, as she couldn't pump him for more information about Tommy and Sniper without arousing his suspicions. He'd asked her for her phone number and she'd given him a false one—easier than telling him she didn't want to see him again.

The other reason was that Charlie had flown out that morning for three days in Melbourne, supposedly on business. Was he taking Veronika, or meeting her there? He had to be doing one or the other; even if the business was genuine, it would be too good an opportunity to miss. Eva had informed Pete so he could organise surveillance.

She checked her watch. Eight thirty. They'd probably be out at dinner, somewhere intimate, sparks of desire crackling between them like lightning. A searing pain ripped through her chest and for a few moments she thought she was having a heart attack. She gulped down the rest of her Scotch and went to the bar to order another.

She picked up her drink, turned around and found herself face to face with Sniper. His mouth was smiling but the rest of his face wasn't.

'Back again? Can't keep you away, can we, Sarah?' He leaned closer to her. His breath reeked of sour cigarette smoke. 'Or should I say, Mrs Dennehy?'

Eva swallowed. 'How did you know?'

Sniper put his arm around her shoulder. She shuddered inside as he led her away from the bar.

'A lot of people think I'm mad, and maybe I am. My shrink certainly thinks so.' He laughed, a strange, high-pitched cackle. 'But I picked you for a phony straight away. I had you followed after you left here, back to lover boy's place and then to your little love-nest on the harbour. Does your husband know about your little party?'

'I fail to see what business it is of yours, but yes, he does. We have an open marriage.' *We may as well have.*

'Lucky you. You get to fuck whoever you want and keep the money. What's it like to be a rich man's whore?'

Eva slapped his face. *Shit, why did you do that? He was goading you.*

Sniper looked stunned, dropping his arm from her shoulder, then burst out laughing. 'Hey, a woman with spirit! I like it.'

'I'm surprised you've got any customers left, if that's the way you treat them.'

He leered at her. 'No, darling, only the ones I like. Now tell me, what brings you here tonight? Besides good music and good looking men.'

'What makes you think there's any other reason?'

'Women like you always have ulterior motives. This is not exactly the Ritz, is it?'

'I don't know so much. I bet you could buy cocaine at the Ritz if you knew the right people.'

Sniper stood still, eyes flickering non-stop, then he nodded for her to follow him. They went out the back door behind the stage, and in the side door to the small bedsit. As soon as they were inside, Sniper slammed the door shut and pulled her towards him, his arm around her neck. She couldn't see the knife but felt its cold steel against her throat.

'Who sent you?'

The room was whirling. She felt the warm gush of urine soaking her knickers.

'No-one,' she croaked.

He tightened his arm and pressed it against her throat. 'Tell the truth, bitch. Did Charlie send you?'

'No, I swear! He doesn't know I'm here.'

Sniper took his arm away and watched her as she caught her breath, coughing and spluttering. 'You're lying. You said he knew you were here on Friday night.'

'He did, he doesn't know I'm here now.'

He lunged at her and she felt the knife against her throat again.

'Okay!' Eva gasped. 'I lied, I'm sorry. He doesn't know I've been here at all.'

Sniper released his hold, but dangled the knife in front of him. It was just a kitchen knife, frightening in its ordinariness. Tears sprang to Eva's eyes and she quickly wiped them away. They were tears of shock and relief, but Sniper wasn't the type to be moved by tears.

'He wouldn't care anyhow,' she said. 'He's got a girlfriend, so he doesn't care what I do.'

'Is that so? So if I were to call him and tell him you were here buying cocaine he wouldn't give a rat's arse?'

Eva averted her eyes from Sniper's gaze. It would be impossible to come up with a convincing story to tell Charlie and the game would be up once he knew. 'What's it worth for you not to tell him?'

Sniper moved closer. 'Now we're talking. I like a woman who sees reason.' He pierced a hole at the top of her pullover with his knife and cut a neat line right down the centre as if he were slicing a ham on a butcher's hook. He pulled aside the two halves of her pullover to reveal her bra.

'Let's negotiate a method of payment you're familiar with.' He reached behind her, the knife still in his hand and deftly unhooked the bra. He sliced through the straps with the knife and the bra fell to the floor.

'Nice tits.' He pressed the cold blade of the knife against each nipple. They betrayed her by immediately becoming erect.

'I take that as a yes.' Sniper grinned. 'Seeing as you're so co-operative, I'll strike a deal with you. I'll sell you some blow, and in return for me keeping your little secret, I get to ravage your beautiful body. Deal?'

Eva gritted her teeth. 'Deal.' The only way she could get through having sex with Sniper was to be high, she didn't have to think twice about it this time. 'Can I have the blow now?'

•••

'So you've got photos?'

Pete picked up an A4 envelope from his desk and handed it to her. 'They were taken at the Royal Carlton in Melbourne.'

She opened it and slipped out a dozen colour photos, standard five by seven. She flipped through them. They were all of a man and woman naked, having sex in a hotel room. In some of the photos the faces were blurred, but it was clearly Charlie and Veronika. In one photo they were lying on their sides on the bed, facing each other. Charlie was facing the camera, and had his hand on Veronika's breast. In another, Veronika was sitting on the edge of a chair, head tipped back, and legs wide apart. Charlie's head was in between them, his bald head gleaming in the light. From the angle the photo was taken, Veronika's thick tangle of dark pubic hair was easily visible and Eva felt a burning rush of jealousy. Charlie liked her neat and well-trimmed and she had regular bikini waxes to keep herself that way.

She shoved the photos back in the envelope. 'How did you get them?'

'It's probably best that you don't know, my methods are not always within the law.'

Eva stared him down until he shrugged and said, 'Hotel room attendants are paid peanuts, so for the right price it's not too difficult to persuade one of them to let my tech guy into the room to install a couple of hidden cameras.'

Peter took a large bite of one of the cream doughnuts Barbara had brought in with the coffee. 'Do you want me to keep up the surveillance on them?'

'No, this is all the proof I need. How are you going with the other enquiries?'

'I've got a couple of leads. You realise that even if I can get photos of Charlie consorting with criminals, it's not enough for him to be charged with anything. Maybe not even enough to interest the police.'

'If he's crooked, there's got to be some way of getting proof. He's clever, but he's not invincible. All criminals make mistakes sooner or later, don't they?'

He stuffed the last bit of doughnut into his mouth. 'Depends on how long you're prepared to wait.'

'Can you tell me about the leads you have so far?'

He studied her with pursed lips and clasped his pudgy hands on the desk. 'If I tell you, you have to promise not to breathe a word to anyone. You could be endangering your life if you do.'

'You have my word.'

'It's rumoured that the owners of the Downtown club, two fellows called Tommy Cranstoun and Richard Farthing, known as Sniper, have been linked with Melbourne gangland figures, specifically the McCarthy family. The McCarthys have their fingers in a lot of pies, especially in the amphetamines trade. It's big business at the moment.'

'I know about the McCarthys.'

Peter raised his eyebrows. 'You do?'

Whoops. There hadn't been much publicity about the McCarthy family in 1995. It was only in subsequent years that they had become infamous for playing a major part in the Melbourne gangland wars.

'I read something the other day in a newspaper.' To change the subject, she said, 'So if Charlie's linked with the owners of the Downtown club, must he by association be linked with the McCarthys?'

'It's certainly a strong possibility. And you can guarantee that if he's involved with the McCarthys, he's in the drug trade. Everything they do is tied in with it.'

'What else do they do?'

'Prostitution, gambling, money laundering, protection rackets. You name it, they're into it. Multi-skilling, it's called.'

'So Charlie's anti-drugs stance is just a convenient front?'

'Either that, or he's prepared to compromise his principles for the sake of a few million dollars.'

Eva thought back to the opening of the Hope Valley rehabilitation centre and all the publicity and homages paid to his generosity. *Fucking hypocrite.*

She stood up, clutching the envelope of photos. 'Thank-you for what you've done so far.'

Pete stood up and shook her hand. 'You might not be thanking me by the time I've finished. The truth can be painful, as you're already aware.'

•••

For once, the view of the harbour from the deck failed to lift her mood. The cloud banks scudding across the dull winter sky amplified the heaviness that hung around her like a shroud. Dodie licked her hand, jumped on to her lap and snuffled into her armpit. The images of Charlie and Veronika replayed in her mind like clips from a movie. She could no longer pretend it wasn't happening or turn a blind eye. Was it any better this way than it had been in her previous life? At least she hadn't been subjected to the images of them having sex.

And the indications that Charlie was mixed up in criminal activity were mounting. Apart from Pete's findings, Sniper's comments had confirmed it. It was apparent from the way he spoke that he knew Charlie well enough to phone him, knowing he'd be furious that Eva was buying cocaine. Admittedly, Charlie's so-called aversion to drugs was public knowledge and Sniper could have been bluffing, but instinct told her she was right.

From that point of view, her night at Downtown had been a success. She'd established a link between Tommy and Sniper and Charlie, though not in the way she'd anticipated. But her cover was blown, so how much more information she could obtain was uncertain. And the other downside was being forced to have sex with Sniper.

The image loomed in her mind. She'd kept her eyes closed throughout, imagining it was Charlie's hands roving over her body and that it was his body on top of hers, even though Sniper was nothing like Charlie. His body, though thin, was rock hard with muscle, his touch impatient and rough. But she found the experience surprisingly erotic and despite herself, had climaxed easily.

Watching Sniper afterwards, his snores like bugle calls, and the craters on his face still discernible under several days of beard growth, she deduced it was the effect of the cocaine; it was not an experience she intended to repeat.

Purging that memory from her mind, she went into her bedroom and paused at the entrance to her walk-in wardrobe. At the back hung her fake fur overcoat and in its pocket was the cocaine she'd bought from Sniper. It was tempting her, and her inner good girl was telling her to resist it, to throw it out and forget about it. *But I need to distract myself from thinking about Charlie and Veronika and Sniper and Tommy, and it's not as if I'm addicted.*

She entered the wardrobe, dug deep into the overcoat pocket and hauled out the clipseal plastic bag. She went into the ensuite and snorted a line of cocaine through a cut-down straw from the packet she'd bought at the supermarket. Within a couple of minutes she felt the rush of euphoria and suddenly it was boring to be at home by herself with her thoughts. She fetched Dodie's lead and Dodie immediately scampered in.

She crouched down and Dodie jumped up and licked her face. 'Oh darling, I've been neglecting you, haven't I? I'm so sorry, being depressed is no excuse. Let's go for a nice, long walk.'

Dodie ran around in circles with delight, her claws doing a tap dance on the floor.

'No, even better, let's go to the dog park. Then you can run around to your heart's content.'

With Dodie in the back seat of the car, her face pressed eagerly against the window, Eva drove along South Head Road towards Potts Point, where there was a large off-leash dog park. She'd taken Dodie there many times and watching her bound through the trees, nose along the trails and make friends with other dogs never failed to delight her.

Though the sun was still trying in vain to burst through the clouds, the greyness had lifted from the day. A sensation of well-being filled Eva's body; she was as light as a souffle. She wanted to jump out of the car and embrace the world, the trees, the road, the bent-over old man hauling his shopping cart, the mob of teenage boys sloping along in back to front baseball caps and baggy jeans.

She turned up the car radio. Bryan Adams was singing his latest hit, *Have You Ever Really Loved a Woman?* She sang along at the top of her lungs, the haunting melody and poignant words spearing her insides with an exquisite pain.

She saw the red light too late. The car in front of her loomed large. She planted her foot on the brakes. There was a resounding bang, the airbag burst out of the steering wheel and her face slammed into it.

CHAPTER FIFTEEN

A YOUNG, neatly bearded man in a white coat with stethoscope accessory appeared at Eva's bedside in the emergency outpatients ward of Parklands Private Hospital.

'Hullo, Mrs Dennehy, I'm Anthony McVeigh, one of the physicians here. How are you feeling?'

'I'm fine.' She rubbed her face. 'Apart from feeling like I've been hit in the face with a soccer ball.' And a pounding head and a dry mouth and wanting to get the hell out of here. 'Do you have any news on Dodie?'

'Your dog's fine, one of the paramedics contacted your husband and a bystander looked after her until he arrived.'

Relief flowed through her. She'd heard a yelp as Dodie was flung off the seat on to the car floor, but fortunately she wasn't hurt.

The doctor pulled the curtain around the bed, picked up her chart and studied it. 'Your obs are good. Can you tell me about the accident?'

'I already told the nurse.'

'I'd like to hear as well.'

She gave an impatient sigh. 'I was on my way to the dog park at Potts Point and was a couple of blocks away when I didn't see the red light, and ploughed into the car in front of me. It was a young guy in a beat-up old Holden and he was very upset, to put it mildly. I got Dodie out of the car and was examining her to make sure she was all right, and he was yelling, 'Who cares about your fucking dog? What about my fucking car?'

'So I yelled back. Who the hell did he think he was? You should see my car! The police arrived and took our details, and then I called the towing agency, and after I made the police promise to take care of Dodie, the ambulance brought me here. And as my obs are normal, as you said yourself, I'd very much like to go home.'

'Not just yet. The police have instructed me to take a blood sample to be tested for drugs, specifically cocaine.'

She was aware of him watching her.

'Why would they think I've taken cocaine?'

'Dilated pupils, constantly blowing your nose, and you were agitated and aggressive at the scene of the accident. Textbook symptoms.'

Fuck. The doctor sat on the edge of the bed, the chart on his lap.

'So when did you take the cocaine?'

Just answer his questions so you can go home. 'About ten o'clock this morning.'

'How much did you have?'

'I don't know, just enough for a snort.'

He was scribbling on her chart.

'This is confidential, isn't it? I don't want my husband to know.'

The doctor looked up. 'Of course. But he'll know anyway, if the blood test comes back as positive. You'll be charged with driving under the influence of a dangerous drug.'

Double fuck. But she didn't want to think about the implications of that right now.

'How often do you use cocaine?'

'Not often. That was only my second time.'

Third, actually.

He stopped scribbling, placed her chart back on the end of the bed and poked his head out of the curtain. 'Jodie! Can we do this now?'

A chubby blonde nurse hurried in with a trolley and prepped Eva's arm. The doctor took the sample of blood, sealed it and labelled it, then Jodie took off with it. He put a Band-Aid on her arm and stood looking down at her.

'I'll give you some advice; you can take it or leave it. Stop taking cocaine as from right now. Apart from the embarrassment of being charged with this offence, you're setting yourself up for destruction of your nose tissues, heart attack or stroke, liver, kidney and brain damage and a host of mental health issues such as depression, chronic anxiety and psychosis. And don't think it can't happen if you're just a social user, it doesn't take much to become addicted.'

'Thanks for the lecture,' Eva said. 'Can I go now?'

The doctor gave her a forbearing look, as if he were used to his advice being ignored. 'There's some paperwork to sign, then you're free to go. Make sure you rest and drink plenty of water.'

He left and returned a few seconds later holding a pamphlet, which he handed to her. 'Here's the phone number of a drug counselling service. Keep it handy, you might need it one day.'

●●●

'Morning!' Helga trilled, bowling in past Eva as she opened the front door. She was carrying a cardboard tray with two coffees and a newspaper under her arm. Eva was still in her bathrobe, drained after a restless night's sleep.

'Thought you might need one,' Helga said, handing her a coffee. She scrutinized Eva's face. 'So you've seen today's Telegraph?'

'No. Why?'

She took in a deep breath. 'Oh, shit. You'd better sit down.'

They sat on the living room couch and Helga passed her the newspaper. On the front page screamed the headlines 'Socialite in public slanging match, full story, page three.'

Below it was a photo of Eva on the sidewalk, face puckered in ugly anger at the driver whose car she'd rear-ended, who had his back to the camera. Off to the side, the crumpled bumper bar and rear of the Holden were clearly visible.

Eva groaned. 'Oh, fuck.' The newspaper photographer and reporter had materialised from nowhere as she was waiting for the police to arrive. In her distress about the accident she hadn't noticed them until the camera flashed in front of her, then she rounded on them both and abused them as well. How did they get there so quickly? Did a bystander recognise her and call the newspaper?

Eva opened the newspaper to page three. 'Eva Dennehy, the glamorous wife of mining magnate Charles Dennehy, was involved in a car accident yesterday in Park Road at Potts Point. Her car collided with a Holden sedan belonging to twenty-five-year-old Martin Langley, with both cars being extensively damaged. While waiting for the police to arrive, Mrs

Dennehy and Mr Langley became involved in an argument, with plenty of expletives exchanged by both parties.

When asked to comment on the accident, Mrs Dennehy turned on the reporter and photographer and swore profusely at them, calling the media "a pack of vultures always hunting for a victim to attack and demolish."'

Eva closed the newspaper, folded it in half and threw it on the coffee table.

'You weren't hurt?' Helga said.

Eva shook her head. 'Only my pride.'

'Is it true? The report?'

'If you call the occasional 'fuck' swearing profusely, then yes. And of course, typical of the tabloids, it's fine to swear if you're a twenty-five-year-old man, but if you're a woman, you're nothing better than a tart.'

'It sounds like you really lost it. It's most unlike you, I've never heard you swear in public in all the years I've known you.'

Eva shrugged. 'I was having a bad day.'

Helga raised her eyebrows. 'I take it Charlie hasn't seen it?'

Eva sighed. 'I guess not. I would have heard about it if he had.'

She'd given Charlie only the bare details of the accident, and nothing about the argument or the blood test. After getting over his annoyance at the damage Eva had done to her car, he'd organised a hire Mercedes for her to drive while hers was being repaired.

Helga stood up. 'I'd better go. I'm on my way to Bridget Kerry's house—you know, the wife of the politician, to quote for redecorating her guest wing. She tells me she's going to have some Very Important Visitors. Top secret.' She put her finger to her lips. 'I'll keep you posted.'

'Thanks for the coffee.'

Helga gave her a hug. 'Don't worry about the newspaper report. It'll be forgotten tomorrow, they'll find some other scandal. Make sure you remind Charlie of that.'

At the door Helga said, 'You know if you need to talk, I'm here for you. Any time.'

•••

Eva had been expecting a visit from the police, crossing her fingers they wouldn't turn up when Charlie was home. But they phoned instead.

'Mrs Dennehy, this is Senior Sergeant Berrigan from Woolloomooloo Police Station. We've received the results of your blood test conducted last week and it was positive for cocaine. We're saving you the embarrassment of us coming to your home, but you will need to come to the police station as soon as possible. You're going to be charged with driving under the influence of a dangerous drug.'

'Thank-you, officer, I'll be there shortly.'

At the police station Senior Sergeant Berrigan and another officer, Constable Maloney, took her into an interview room. Berrigan handed her a notice of her rights. 'You are advised that you do not have to take part in an interview to answer questions about this offence and anything you say will be used in evidence against you.'

She sensed their curiosity, some sympathy from Berrigan, the older of the two, and disdain from Maloney, who barely looked old enough to have left school. She refused to take part in a record of interview or to contact a lawyer. She just wanted to get the hell out of there as quickly as possible. After half an hour she was able to leave, with her summons to appear in Sydney Central Local Court in three weeks' time in her handbag.

CHAPTER SIXTEEN

'AND now would you please give a warm welcome to the patron of ReadWrite, Mrs Eva Dennehy.'

Eva rose from her seat at the front table and walked up to the stage in the function room of Dennehy Towers. She looked down at the sea of faces. A couple of newspaper photographers stood at the side of the room, their cameras clicking and flashing.

Eva had been clammy with anxiety during the first few speeches she made as Mrs Charles Dennehy, but after years of experience, she was now able to project an air of poise and self-confidence. At a function such as this, a fundraising lunch and fashion parade, she was only expected to make a token speech about the charity and the good work it did.

'Ladies and gentlemen,' she said. 'And I can see a few brave gentlemen here today.' The smile faded from her face as she spotted a familiar figure. At a table at the back, by himself, sat Sniper, leaning back in his chair, his gaze fixed upon her. A cold spasm shot through her. What the hell was he doing here? It wasn't to look at fashion, that was for sure; he looked as much at home as a gangster at a garden party.

'We have to be here,' yelled a man from the back. 'We've got the credit cards!'

The ripple of laughter gave Eva time to pull herself together. 'The ReadWrite organisation,' she said, annoyed to hear a slight tremor in her voice, 'began five years ago, the brainchild of Lesley Hunt, a primary school teacher who could see that children from disadvantaged and dysfunctional families were falling through the cracks when it came to numeracy and literacy—'

She managed to get through the rest of the speech and the audience applauded as she stepped down from the stage and resumed her seat.

'Good work, darling, as usual,' Helga said. 'Although I detected a few nerves at the beginning.'

'Must be out of practice,' Eva said.

'At least you'll be in the papers for the right reason this time,' Frances said.

'And you didn't swear once,' Diana added.

Eva gave a token smile. Frances and Diana made light of the newspaper report, but there was a certain wariness in their attitude towards her now, as if they were holding their breath wondering what embarrassing thing she'd do next. She wondered if Helga had told them about her appearance at the Waterfront.

She watched the models strutting their stuff in their Carla Zampatti and Collette Dinnigan outfits, Sniper's presence an ominous niggle in the back of her mind. Around her women were oohing and aahing and noting which outfits they were going to buy. Half the takings from the clothes, if bought at participating stores in the next two days, would go to ReadWrite.

'The men can't complain about us wearing out the credit cards,' Frances said. 'It's all for a good cause.'

The end of the fashion parade signalled the official end of the function, although many stayed behind for more drinks. Helga beckoned the waitress over and ordered another bottle of champagne. Eva glanced behind her and to her horror, saw Sniper making his way to her table.

'Excuse me.' She got up and strode towards him, meeting him half way.

He affected an expression of surprise. 'Just thought I'd drop by to catch up with the latest fashion and who do I run into?'

He was wearing his usual faded jeans, his only concession to the occasion being a collared T-shirt. He cast an appreciative eye over her. 'I must say, you're much sexier when you're not in disguise. Blonde makes you look trashy.'

'Just tell me what you're doing here and get the hell out.'

He grinned. 'Don't want those stuck-up bitches to see me with you and ruin your reputation? It'll be ruined anyway when you go to court.'

'Keep your voice down. How did you find out?'

'I have friends everywhere. That's why you should be nice to me.' He ran his hand over the smooth curve of her hip. 'Very nice to me.'

Eva swallowed hard. 'I don't want to talk here. Let's go outside.'

'Haven't got time to chat, much as I'd love to. Meet me tonight at Kings Motel in Kings Cross. Room five, eight-thirty.'

'I have a prior engagement. And what makes you think I would possibly want to meet you in a motel room?'

'Oh I think you'll change your mind very quickly. Unless you want me to tell your husband what a naughty girl you've been.'

'He'll find out soon enough, anyway.'

'I'm not talking about your arrest, darling. I mean everything. How you like slumming it in bars, picking up strange men, snorting blow up your pretty nose.' He grinned at the expression on her face. 'You didn't think our little tryst the other night was going to be the only one, did you? When you're on a good thing, stick to it, that's my motto.'

He came up close to her. Her spine prickled; he radiated menace. ‘Don’t even think about not coming,’ he said in a low voice. ’Because I can snuff you out. Just like that.’ He clicked his fingers. ‘As long as you do what I tell you, we’ll get along fine, and Charlie boy will be none the wiser.’

He grinned as if they’d just shared a risqué joke. ‘See you tonight. Wear something sexy.’ He winked and ambled out.

'Who was that?' Helga asked when Eva returned to the table.

'Just someone who thought he knew me. Turns out he was mistaken.'

'You look shaken,' Frances said. 'Was he harassing you?'

'Not at all.' Eva picked up her handbag. 'I've got a headache. I think I'll go home.'

'You're coming tonight, aren't you?' Helga asked.

Helga was holding a party for Sol's sixtieth birthday. She'd been organising it for months and had narrowed the list down to two hundred of their closest friends.

'Of course,' Eva said. 'If I go home and rest now, I'll be rid of this headache by tonight.'

•••

'This is a screamer.' Eva was propped up in bed with a heat pack pressed to her forehead. 'I've been popping pills all afternoon but it hasn't made any difference.'

'Sol will be very disappointed if you don't come.'

We both know that's a fucking lie. She bit her tongue to stop herself saying it. Charlie was fresh out of the shower, a towel wrapped around his waist. Eva longed to tear it away from him and run her tongue over his body, from his toes up to the delicious, vulnerable flesh of his inner thighs, circling them with her tongue, inching closer and closer to his erect cock. Did Veronika do that? There she was again, the bitch, popping up and ruining her fantasy.

'There are a lot of important people coming who'll be disappointed as well.'

It was all part of her unwritten job description as Charlie's wife, to be at his side in public, like the Prime Minister's wife, meeting and greeting, charming the men and forging friendships with the women. She'd happily accepted the role; indeed, had craved it. She relished the pride in Charlie's face when he introduced her to his associates and watched as they fell under her spell.

But that was before Veronika. It struck her like a blow to the stomach how dispensable she was. When Charlie ditched her, Veronika would be ready take her place. Eva had seen it happen countless times. In a well-orchestrated strategy, the new wife or partner slipped into her role without any fuss, attending a function here and there, supportive of her man and quietly self-confident but never assuming too much, gradually increasing her visibility until she was part of the social circle and people were hard put even remembering the previous wife's name.

But that wasn't going to happen this time.

Eva lay back against her pillow and grimaced. 'If I came I wouldn't be very good company, for you or anyone else. I'm sorry, honey, you'll have to go without me.'

She watched him dress in his formal suit and adjust his bow tie. He looked as if he were born to wear a suit, yet he was twenty-five before he could afford to buy one. Had he shared that with Veronika? Had he told her about his childhood in a decrepit apartment block in Cabramatta, his father a drunk who beat his wife and children, his mother, in and out of psychiatric hospitals, his two older brothers already seasoned drug users by the time they were adults? His years of working in dead end jobs, denying himself every pleasure to save money, educating himself by reading, attending seminars, cultivating the right contacts, and scrabbling out of bankruptcy before he found success?

Veronika would never understand Charlie the way she, Eva, understood him. His demons, sly whispers that burrowed into his brain like parasites, never allowing him to be content, constantly urging him to prove himself, that he was worthy of wealth and status. They fed on the fears that made him toss and turn in the middle of the night, fears that if he stopped, he'd backslide and be back in Cabramatta before he knew it. Eva understood those demons because she had them herself; she'd married Charlie to escape them.

Charlie came over and stood by the bed, looking down at her. He bent over, stroked a strand of hair away from her forehead and kissed her on the lips. A lump rose in her throat. 'All right, I'll pass on your apologies. You rest and get well.'

The room was empty now, sucked dry of energy. Her loneliness was an ache deep in her bones, and she realised it had always been there, right from the beginning of their marriage. Because Charlie had never been hers, not the way she wanted. But she'd covered up her loneliness with clothes and champagne and cocktail parties and spa days and committee meetings, subduing it with more shopping sprees or champagne whenever it popped its head up. And now *she* was on the scene, determined to make her claim on Charlie, to possess him in the way that she, Eva, had not been able to do.

She longed to dig again into her coke stash, despite the fact that it had already landed her in a heap of trouble. She longed for the lightness, as if she were floating in the air on a magic carpet, as every cell in her body filled with bliss. But if she were going to carry out the plan she'd thought of while in bed with her fake headache, she'd need her wits about her. Though God knows how she was going to fuck Sniper without the aid of any mind enhancing substance. She got up, had a shower and dressed in her plainest underwear, jeans and jacket. Contrary to his request, she wasn't going to make herself look sexy for him.

She wasn't hungry, but forced herself to eat a toasted sandwich. Not being in the mood to drive, she called a cab, stopped at a bottle shop on the way and bought a bottle of Bourbon. She arrived at the Kings Motel at precisely eight twenty-five. An icy wind whipped around her as she got out of the cab.

The motel was a grimy brick box, huddling into itself as if to keep out the cold. As Eva walked down the concrete path to room five, a woman in a tracksuit hanging off her scrawny frame came out of room three, banged the door behind her and scuttled through the car park, not before Eva noticed the festering sores on her face. Undoubtedly typical of the clientele, people shooting up drugs and buying sex at hourly rates. She knocked on the door of room five.

Sniper opened the door. He was wearing just his underpants and he already had a glass of what looked like Bourbon in his hand. Good, it would make her task of getting him drunk easier.

'Right on time, top marks for punctuality. And a present as well.' He grabbed the bottle from her as she stepped inside and placed it and his glass on the sideboard. Yelling and shooting blasted out from the TV. Sniper shut the door, grabbed her by the shoulders and slammed her against the wall.

'You stupid bitch, getting the cops involved. Did you tell them where you got it?' His face was right up against hers, his breath coming at her in acrid waves, his fingers digging into her shoulders.

'No. Let go, you're hurting me!'

His hand shot out and slapped her hard on the face, her head banging against the wall with the impact. She let out a yell. 'That's the idea, you stupid bitch. Swear to me you didn't squeal to the cops.'

'I swear I didn't. I refused to be interviewed.'

He released his grip on her. 'At least you got something right. If the cops get wind of a connection between you and me, I'm screwed. Thanks to you, we can't hang out at my place anymore.'

Eva put her fingers to her face. It was stinging like hell.

Sniper nodded towards a bar fridge in the corner, 'There's ice in there.' He downed his drink and handed her the glass. 'And while you're there you can fix me one of your bourbons.'

He sprawled out on the bed, his eyes fixed on the TV. Burning with humiliation and anger, Eva wrapped some ice cubes from the freezer in a greasy, stained tea towel and pressed it against her face. The sooner she and Pete got something on Charlie the better. Then it wouldn't matter if Sniper told Charlie of their association and she could tell him to fuck off.

The ice was soothing and relieved the pain a little. More shouting—'Freeze! Police!' and gunshots from the TV. It sounded like the police drama *Law and Order*—which would have struck her as amusing any other time.

After a few minutes, she took the tea towel off her face and refilled Sniper's glass with a generous shot of bourbon on the rocks, using the ice wrapped in the tea towel. She got another glass from the cupboard, rinsed the dust off it and made one for herself. She couldn't do this without alcohol; she'd take it slowly.

Part of her wished she could go through with her original plan to spike Sniper's drink with a sedative, just for the satisfaction of revenge. But she'd decided it was too risky. Firstly there was the issue of judging the right amount to knock him out without killing him and secondly, if he realised afterwards what she'd done, his retaliation would be swift and painful. As she'd already experienced.

She carried the two drinks over to the bed. Sniper was on his back, naked, his cock erect. Eva took a gulp of her drink, placed it on the bedside table, and slowly took off her clothes.

'Come for a ride, baby,' Sniper said, stroking his cock.

'Not so fast, cowboy.' Eva stretched out on the bed beside him. The mattress was as unyielding as a plank of wood. 'I need to get in the mood.' *And you need to get drunker*. 'Let's have a drink first.'

•••

Eva watched Sniper in the subdued glow of the bedside lamp. She'd turned the TV off and his snores punctured the silence. On the previous occasion they'd had sex, he'd fallen asleep quickly afterwards and he'd done the same tonight, as she'd hoped.

'You've slowed down,' Sniper had observed at one point, as she bobbed up and down on top of him. Alcohol appeared to have no adverse effects on his erectile function.

She increased her tempo, breasts jiggling in time. Sniper guffawed and tweaked her nipples. 'I meant your drinking.'

'Just being careful—I don't want to get so drunk that I pass out.'

'It wouldn't be the first time I've fucked an unconscious woman.'

She'd swallowed her disgust and had to look away. Was that what war did to people? Or was it in his genes? Looking at him now, mouth open, oblivious and vulnerable, it occurred to her that if she killed him, he could no longer blackmail her. She allowed herself to fantasize about it for a few seconds before her rational mind took over. Besides not having a weapon, she'd never get away with it.

He let out a groan. She held her breath, but he resumed his snoring. He wouldn't stay asleep for much longer, though. Eva eased herself slowly out of the bed. He didn't stir.

She padded over to the chair in the corner of the room where he'd thrown his clothes when he undressed. She picked up his jeans and felt in the back pocket for his wallet. Brown leather, battered around the edges, but good quality. She glanced at Sniper again. Still asleep. She tiptoed over to the fridge, opened the door and squatted down so she see in the light. She opened the wallet and flipped through the contents.

Credit cards, an RSL membership card, driver's licence with a photo taken some years ago when his face was fuller and his eyes softer—he almost looked normal. A dog-eared faded photo of a young blonde woman with a radiant smile holding a small girl of about four, also blonde with a cheeky grin, on her lap. His wife and daughter? Where were they now? She couldn't imagine that Sniper had ever been a normal guy living an ordinary life.

In one of the pockets were several folded scraps of paper. She slid them out and unfolded them. Most were receipts—car tyres, a TV from Harvey Norman, chemist shops, groceries. The last was a torn scrap of white paper with numbers written on it in pen. 2506 7834. A phone number? Bank account number? What she wouldn't give for a smartphone to take a snapshot. She quickly memorised the numbers and stuffed all the papers back in the wallet. She was suddenly aware of the silence in the room; the snoring had stopped. Her skin prickled.

'What are you doing?' Sniper said.

Eva shoved the wallet in the fridge, opened the freezer door and grabbed the ice cube tray. 'Just getting myself a drink of water. Do you want one?'

'No.'

He watched her as she filled her glass with ice cubes and water and returned to the bed. Sniper got up, went into the tiny bathroom and stood in front of the toilet. He had his back to her as he peed and luckily his stream was loud and long enough to give her cover. She crept over to the fridge, retrieved the wallet, stuffed it back into his jeans pocket, draped the jeans over the chair exactly as they were before, and was back in bed by the time Sniper came out of the bathroom.

He sat on the bed beside her and placed his hand on her pussy. He parted her lips and plunged his fingers inside.

'Still nice and juicy. Good for another round.'

'It's getting late. I have to go.'

Charlie always stayed the distance at parties, particularly if there were plenty of opportunities to schmooze, but it would be just her luck for him to come home early for once and find her not there.

Sniper pulled her towards him. 'I'm sure you've got time for a quick one.'

CHAPTER SEVENTEEN

'IF you're here to check on my progress there's nothing concrete so far,' Pete said. 'My informant has a contact who's had some dealings with the McCarthys, so I'm relying on him for information. I'm sure you appreciate that I have to tread carefully; the last thing I want is for the McCarthys to find out I've been asking questions.'

'I understand,' Eva said. *But can you tread carefully a bit faster?*

'If you don't mind me asking, how did you get that bruise on your face?'

She'd covered it as well as she could with make-up, but it was impossible to completely hide the blue-purple blotch on her cheek.

'Did your husband do it?'

'No.'

She knew what he was thinking. She was lying about her husband or she had a lover who was beating her up.

'I tripped over in my bedroom and my face hit the edge of the doorway,' she said. That was the story she'd told Charlie. It was a lame variation of the hackneyed 'I walked into a door,' story, but she couldn't come up with anything else.

She'd pretended to be asleep when he arrived home from the party at two am and again when he got up four hours later, and showered and dressed to go to the office. Saturdays were just another work day for him. But she couldn't hide it from him when he arrived home later in the day.

Charlie's mouth tightened. 'Do you really expect me to believe that?'

'You can believe it or not. It's true.'

'It's plain as day that someone's hit you. Where were you last night when you were supposed to be in bed with a headache?'

'I was at home. I'm sorry if you don't believe me but it's the truth.'

'How about I book an appointment with the doctor and get his opinion?'

'I don't need a doctor. Nothing's broken, it will heal in a few days.'

He looked at her with disgust. 'You know, when you started all this bizarre behaviour I thought you'd changed, you weren't the woman I married, but now I know this is exactly who you are. You've deceived me all these years; you're nothing but a two-timing whore.'

He turned to go. 'And cancel all social engagements until that bruise is gone. Apart from the fact that it will cast aspersions on my character, you look hideous.'

'You can't get rid of me that easily, you fucking hypocrite!' she'd shouted after him as he strode out and slammed the front door. That was four days ago and he hadn't spoken to her since.

It was obvious Pete didn't believe her story either, so she quickly changed the subject. 'I've come by some information that could be useful.'

She handed him a piece of paper on which she'd written the numbers from Sniper's wallet she'd memorised. After puzzling over it for a couple of days, she decided to hand it over to Pete; he had more sophisticated resources at his disposal than she had.

Pete looked at the paper. 'Could be anything. Where did you get it?'

She had to tell him; it was all going to come out now anyway. 'From Sniper's wallet.'

He blew out a sigh. 'I think you need to fill me in on a few things.'

There was a rap on the door. Barbara entered with a tray of coffee and blueberry muffins, placed them on the desk with a sideways glance at Eva and left. Today Eva was wearing a wig of jet black hair that fell in a shiny sweep down her back. If anyone recognised her going into the building she could ostensibly be visiting any of the businesses there, but she felt safer in disguise. The gossip rags would have a field day if they knew that Mrs Charles Dennehy had visited a private detective.

Pete handed Eva her coffee and held out the plate of muffins. She shook her head.

He picked up a muffin and took a bite. A blueberry fell on to his desk blotter and he scooped it up. ‘I have a feeling this is going to be a multiple muffin situation. Fire away.'

Eva recounted the events from the night she met Sniper and Tommy to her most recent rendezvous with Sniper, leaving out the part about him hitting her.

He wiped his mouth with a napkin and threw it on the desk. 'Do you have any idea what you're getting yourself into? These people are dangerous and if they find out what you're doing, you're gone. You won't even hear the gunshot.'

Eva crossed her legs and drew herself up in her chair, her skirt riding up her thigh and her breasts straining against her tight sweater.

'I'm giving you the benefit of my assistance. I need to get this evidence as quickly as possible before that bitch gets her manicured claws any further into him.'

'What makes you think it's not just another fling, and it will all be over in a couple of months?'

'Take it from me, it won't. Besides, as soon as I have enough dirt on Charlie, I can tell Sniper to go find some other fuckbuddy. The only way he can get a woman is to blackmail them.'

'You always pay a price in this game. Favours, sex, money—and bruises.'

Eva gave a resigned shrug. 'Okay, it was Sniper.'

'Why?'

It would be all over the news next week. 'I've been charged with driving under the influence of a drug and he thought I'd ratted on him to the police.' She told him the full story.

'For God’s sake, Eva! This is like a red flag to a bull for the McCarthys now. They'll be watching you like a hawk. If they find out you've been buying your cocaine from Sniper, that will be curtains for both of you. They won't want any publicity that might shine a light on their activities. For all you know, the police might have you under surveillance as well.'

'All of which proves we need to get this information as quickly as possible. Give your informant double pay if you have to.'

'I'll do my best. What did your husband say about the cocaine charge?'

'I haven't told him.'

Pete pursed his lips. 'However Sniper got that information, Charlie may well have the same contacts.'

'I'm pretty sure he doesn't know. He'd confront me about it, there's no way he could hide his anger.'

Pete checked his watch. 'I've got another client to see in a couple of minutes.' He saw her to the front door. 'Eva, promise me you'll stay out of this, this is what you're paying me to do. None of this will matter if you're dead.'

The prospect of her death loomed before her for the first time since her travel back in time. Was it possible for her to die in this life? Was that part of the deal? Father O'Halloran hadn't said anything about it, but as she was living her life over again as if the first one hadn't existed, she had to assume that if she died in this life, that was it. Lights out. Irrevocable.

A creeping chill pervaded her body. She looked Pete in the eye. 'I promise.'

'And stay away from coke, it will get you into more trouble.'

She gave a grim smile. 'I know.'

She'd flush the rest of her stash down the toilet as soon as she got home.

●●●

Helga's Lotus roared up and stopped at the kerb just as Eva was heading out the front gate with Dodie on her lead. Damn—she wasn't in the mood for company. Helga got out of the car and trotted over in her heels and tailored pantsuit, silk scarf flapping in the breeze.

'Good morning! It's a glorious day, isn't it? Hullo, you little bundle of cuteness!'

She bent over to fondle Dodie, who jumped up and snuffled her as if she were a long lost friend.

'I'm just off for a walk,' Eva said.

'I'll come with you. I could do with some exercise.'

'In your heels?'

'I do everything in my heels, honey. I was born wearing Manolo Blahniks. No wonder my mother had such a hard time of it in labour.'

Helga fell into step beside Eva as she walked down the side track that led down to the harbour foreshore path. It was the first week of spring and Nature had put on a show, right on time, as if to affirm it. The sky was clear, the sun soft, and warm and the breeze gentle. The harbour sparkled and the path was alive with cyclists and walkers, basking in the day. Dodie was beside herself with excitement, straining at her lead as if she'd never been on a walk before.

'So what's up?' Helga asked.

'What do you mean?'

'I haven't seen you for over two weeks. You didn't make the art gallery opening and you missed Fran's do at the Golf Club. I know you said you had other commitments but I don't believe it for a minute.'

It was just over two weeks since Sniper's assault on her, and the bruise was barely visible; with make-up, it wasn't discernible at all. She'd refused social invitations not because Charlie had ordered her to, but to avoid awkward questions. Charlie continued to give her the silent treatment—he ate out every night, came home late and turned his back on her in bed, with no acknowledgment of her presence beside him. The space between them in bed was as vast and desolate as the Sahara Desert.

'Are you and Charlie having problems?'

It was pointless denying –it—Helga knew her better than anyone.

Of course I can trust her. She's my best friend. If the boot were on the other foot, I'd keep her secret, even under torture.

'Helga, if I tell you something, will you promise not to tell a soul—not even Sol?' *Especially not Sol.*

'Promise, cross my heart.'

'Charlie's got it into his head that I'm running around town screwing every guy I meet.'

'Where did he get that idea?"

'I haven't a clue.'

'Are you having an affair?'

'No.'

Something told her not to mention her assignations with Sniper; in any case, she'd hardly call them an affair.

'He's in love with Veronika Ettore.' She glanced at Helga. 'You knew, didn't you?'

'I've heard whisperings.'

'And you didn't think to tell me? '

'Honey, if I told you every rumour I heard about Charlie's love life, we'd talk about nothing else. I didn't know if it was true, and knowing how you feel about his dalliances I didn't want to upset you unnecessarily.'

'Anyway,' she added, 'how do you know he's in love with her? Did he tell you?'

'No, he doesn't know I know. I overheard a phone conversation between them a while ago, he's planning to leave me and she's going to have his baby.'

'He hasn't done it yet, has he?'

'He told her he's waiting for the right time, whenever that is.'

'That proves it's just another affair. He's stringing her along with promises, he has no intention of leaving you.' Helga patted her arm. 'Don't lose hope, honey. Charlie loves you, I know he does.'

It's not enough, not Charlie's type of love. He has no concept of what it means to love someone the way I love him.

And for once Helga was wrong about Charlie stringing Veronika along; she didn't hear the phone conversation, she hadn't seen them together. Whatever the reason was that Charlie hadn't left her yet, she was in no doubt that he would.

They arrived at a park, a pocket of lush grass with a couple of seats, a swing and slippery slide. A small boy and girl on the slide jumped off and ran over to them. Dodie strained at her lead to jump up at them.

'Dodie, down!' Eva ordered.

The children's mother was sitting on one of the seats, breast-feeding a baby. 'Children, ask first if you can pat the dog!' she called.

'Can we pat the doggie?' the girl asked. She looked about five, a dainty blonde angel in pigtails, and the boy, snowy haired, looked about three, still carrying some residual toddler chubbiness.

'Of course you can,' Eva said. 'Dodie, sit!'

Dodie sat and luxuriated in the attention as the children patted and stroked her with tentative little hands.

'Todd, gently!' the girl said, with big sister bossiness as Todd pulled one of Dodie's ears.

Eva smiled and exchanged an 'aren't they gorgeous?' glance with their mother. Her body ached with wanting—she longed to scoop up both the children and take them home with her. In her blackest moments of despair, she'd toyed with the idea of going off the pill without telling Charlie and getting pregnant, just to spite him and fulfil her own yearning. If she couldn't have him, at least she'd have his child. But she knew it would just make him despise her more for deceiving him. She told herself it wouldn't be fair on the child—but how could he fail to love a child that she, Eva, bore him when he was willing to have a child with Veronika?

In any case, she'd left it too late—at forty, her chances of conceiving were low. Non-existent now that she and Charlie weren't having sex. That's where he went every night—to be with *her*, perhaps already making a baby.

'That's enough, kids!' the mother called. 'Say thank-you to the lady and come and have some juice.'

'Thank-you!' the children chorused, gave Dodie a last hug and dashed over to their mother.

'Well behaved kids,' Helga observed, as they continued on. 'Makes a nice change.' She was childless by choice, declaring that whatever maternal hormones she possessed had been quashed by Sol's two grandchildren, courtesy of his son from a previous marriage. She referred to them as the brats from hell, and needed at least two days of shopping and massages to recover after they visited.

They had to walk single file now, due to the oncoming pedestrian traffic. Helga took the lead. Even in her heels she set a cracking pace. Her self-assurance was almost a visible force—it had won her as many enemies as friends, but if she ever had any doubts or had to wrestle any inner demons, she'd never admitted to it. Perhaps she was born with chutzpah, along with her heels.

They veered off the path to a grassy knoll amongst the trees and sat on a bench seat overlooking the harbour. Dodie lay at Eva's feet, snapping at butterflies. Yachts and fishing boats skimmed along the water, scarcely making a ripple on the smooth surface, and three canoes glided past close to the shore, the occupants shouting and laughing to each other.

'If you had the chance to relive your life, would you do anything differently?' Eva said.

'That's just a roundabout way of asking if I have any regrets. And the answer is no. Why do you ask?'

'Just interested.'

'Bullshit, you're asking me because you've got regrets yourself.'

'Maybe.'

'Come on, spit it out.'

What would Helga say if she told her the truth? That she'd murdered Charlie in her previous life and had regretted it for twenty years? She'd laugh outright at the unbelievable notion that Eva had travelled through time and was now living her life a second time. But after Eva had killed Charlie, she had the feeling that Helga suspected the truth. It was nothing she said, it was more what she didn't say—the way she looked at Eva sometimes, as if they shared a secret. It was one of the reasons Eva moved to Melbourne six months after Charlie's death—much as she missed Helga's friendship, her presence made her uneasy.

'The only thing I regret is allowing Charlie to fall in love with Veronika,' Eva said, 'and that's something I have no control over anyway.'

'That's true, so don't beat yourself up about it. It's not your fault. I guarantee it will blow over just like all the others. Once he discovers her faults—and even someone as gorgeous as Veronika has faults—he'll ditch her and realise how lucky he is to have you.'

Eva gazed at the horizon, where the iridescent blue of the harbour met the softer blue of the sky, where the white sails looked like toy yachts in a bath. If she closed her eyes and wished really hard, as she'd done as a child, could she make it come true? It had never worked then—every birthday and Christmas she'd wished for a pink bike with streamers on the handlebars and a basket, but every time she got a new schoolbag, shoes or pencil case. So she'd stopped wishing. Until she met Charlie.

'Let me give you one piece of advice,' Helga said. She took off her sunglasses and looked directly at Eva. 'Don't let your emotions get the better of you.'

•••

'Come in for a coffee,' Eva said as they arrived back at her house. She was glad after all that Helga had joined her—she always felt uplifted after being in her company.

'You relax,' Helga said. 'I'll get it.'

Helga had been to Eva's home often enough to know her way round the kitchen as well as Eva did herself. Eva let Dodie out into the back yard and perched on a stool at the kitchen bar, watching Helga's competent hands as they filled the kettle and switched it on and scooped out the coffee from the jar into the plunger. There was something soothing about watching someone else doing tasks in the kitchen.

The front door slammed, causing them both to jump and Charlie appeared in the doorway. His tie was askew and his top shirt button was undone. Anger was emanating from him in waves.

'I need to speak to you, Eva,' he said. His voice was terrifying in its calmness.

Helga picked up the bottle of milk she'd just got out of the fridge, opened the door and put it back. 'I'll go outside and talk to Dodie.'

'I'd prefer it if you went home.'

Helga said nothing, and looked at Eva. Eva dropped her gaze, embarrassed for her friend.

'Fine,' Helga said. She went out and picked up her handbag from the living room couch.

'I'll talk to you, later, Eva,' she said, pointedly ignoring Charlie. As soon as the front door closed behind her, Charlie turned on Eva.

'So when were you going to tell me about your cocaine charge? Or were you just going to let me read about it in the newspapers?'

'I didn't need to do either, you found out anyway.'

As she knew he would. She was surprised it had taken him this long; her court appearance was less than a week away.

'And here was I, feeling sorry for you for being in an accident and it was all your goddamned fault!'

His face was a dull red and the veins were bulging in his neck. Eva felt gratified that she'd been able to arouse such a reaction. This meant he loved her, didn't it? You only get really angry at the people you love.

He was so close to her now that she could see the hairs in his eyebrows, the way they knotted and tangled together and the deep pale gullies under his eyes that spoke of long hours and important decisions. How had she never noticed them before?

'Where did you get the cocaine from?'

'Just an acquaintance. No-one you'd know.'

He grabbed her shoulders; his grip was powerful and she flinched. 'Tell me!'

She had a flashback to the incident with Sniper and she saw Charlie smashing her face as if she were his opponent in the boxing ring. Her legs began to shake. 'Go on, hit me! That's what you're itching to do, isn't it? But you can't, because you always vowed you'd never be like your father and you've kept that promise to yourself and you can't break it now. Can you?'

She was shaking all over now, but she held his gaze until he dropped his hands from her shoulders.

'And while you're snorting that stuff, you don't give a fuck about the effect on me. After next Monday, everyone will know that the wife of Charles Dennehy, anti-drugs benefactor, has been convicted of driving under the influence of an illegal drug. The media will have a field day and I could very well lose investors!'

Eva was silent. There was nothing to say; apologies would only inflame him more.

'And to add insult to injury, you're buying an illegal drug with my money! I'm closing off your access to my bank accounts. In future, everything you spend will need to be approved by me.'

He turned and strode out. The front door slammed. Eva ran to the front window. Charlie's Mercedes was parked on the curb, Robert standing at the driver's door smoking a cigarette. As soon as he spied Charlie, he stubbed out his cigarette in a pocket ashtray he was holding, hurried around and opened the back door. Eva watched as Charlie got in, the engine started, and the car glided down the street.

'Don't go!' she cried out. 'Come back and I'll make it right again.' Her insides crumpled in on themselves and she sank to the floor on her knees. She was six again and her father was angry with her for spilling a jar of paint water on the kitchen table, all over a pile of important documents he had to take into his work as an insurance agent. She was doing a school project, spending hours on it, determined to get top marks so he would wrap his strong arms around her and say,' I'm proud of you, honey', just like other kids' fathers did.

But instead he took her out to the back shed where he kept the whip and lashed the back of her legs until she couldn't feel the pain any more, shouting at her all the while. 'Do you want me to get into trouble with my boss? Because that's what you've done, you've ruined those documents! You're a clumsy, thoughtless little girl and I'm ashamed to call you my daughter!'

She got the top mark in her class for her project, but her father had already packed his suitcases and left to try his luck with another woman, another casino, another town. He promised to visit, but never did and years later, her mother told her he'd died of cancer. And as she knelt on the floor sobbing, she didn't know if it was for her father, Charlie, or herself.

Robin Storey

CHAPTER EIGHTEEN

EVA'S barrister, Justin Fellowes, self-proclaimed 'best representation money can buy,' assured her he could get her off with a fine and no conviction recorded.

'We've got plenty of material to work with,' he said, with a toothy smile. 'Your previously unblemished record, all your community fundraising, character references from charities you've assisted, all these will go in your favour. It would be an exceptionally harsh magistrate who would fail to give you another chance, particularly as this incident of cocaine use was an aberration which you've assured me won't happen again.'

He looked at her intently. Eva nodded.

This was Eva's second visit. On her first, she'd told him, that she wanted the case dealt with on her first appearance. Adjournments would only drag it out and prolong the public exposure.

He shook his head. 'Impossible, I need more time to prepare—'

Eva interrupted him. 'I can always take my business elsewhere.'

He paused, no doubt weighing up the exposure he'd get for representing her against the lower fee for not being granted at least a couple of adjournments. He sighed and nodded, and since then had managed to prepare his submission in record time.

He twirled his gold pen in his pale, slender hands. 'The only thing I can't guarantee is that the media won't be buzzing around like a swarm of flies. The best we can hope for is that they get the main facts right. Come to my office at eight o'clock on Monday morning; we'll go in my car and I'll get you in the back entrance of the courthouse.'

On Monday morning at eight thirty Justin and Eva approached the back entrance of the Sydney Local Court. Justin was in suit and tie, carrying a fat, shiny leather briefcase. Accompanying them was his instructing solicitor Patrick, a tall, gangly man with a barely-there moustache that looked like a gravy smear. The difference in status was evidenced by his well-worn briefcase, with its scuff marks and tarnished buckles. Despite the cool morning, Eva was perspiring in her tailored skirt, blouse and jacket, and her hands were clammy. A throng of journalists advanced upon them.

'Let me do the talking,' Justin muttered out of the side of his mouth. 'You go ahead with Patrick. '

Patrick carved a path through the crowd, Eva following close behind, bowing her head as cameras flashed and microphones were thrust at her. 'Mrs Dennehy, is it true that you have an addiction to cocaine? What does your husband think about your charge? When are you going into Hope Valley Rehab? Will you get special treatment there?'

Behind her Justin was answering the questions with a calm and unwavering, 'No comment at the moment, I'll be making a statement after court. '

Patrick rapped on the back door of the courthouse and it immediately swung open. A security officer stood beside it. Patrick stepped back for Eva to enter, then hurried in after, followed by Justin.

'Thanks, Mick, ' Justin said to the security officer.

'Are you okay?' he asked Eva. She nodded. They went up in the lift to the courtrooms on the first floor. The foyer was busy; the seats were all occupied, and people huddled in crowds. Young punks in hip hop jeans and matching bravado, sharp-faced young girls in low slung jeans and baggy tops preening and giggling, young mothers, flush-faced and sour-mouthed from chasing after toddlers and soothing restless babies, a sprinkling of middle-aged people.

A well made-up woman in a tailored suit sat staring straight ahead of her, as if oblivious to the noise around her, an expression on her face that said, 'This is all a mistake, I shouldn't be here.' Eva felt an affinity with her as she walked quickly past, avoiding eye contact.

Justin led the way, stopping at the furthest courtroom. 'We're in this one. '

The door was locked; through the glass panel the only person visible in the courtroom was a young male depositions clerk shuffling papers. Justin rapped on the door and the clerk, young and bespectacled, looked up frowning. He came over, opened the door a crack and poked his head out

'Hi Matthew,' Justin said, 'I believe Eva Dennehy's matter is being heard in this court.'

'That's right. '

'Would you mind if she waited here? I know the court's not open, but the media—you know how it is.'

He spread his hands in a gesture of supplication. Matthew glanced at Eva, nodded and opened the door wider. 'Sure, come in.'

'We'll be back shortly,' Justin told her. He strode off with Patrick close behind.

Eva sat in the front row; she was more visible there but she wouldn't have to clamber over people to get out when her matter was called. Matthew went back to his work.

It was the first time she'd been in a court room. She looked around her to take her mind off her churning insides, at the glassed-in dock—thank God she didn't have to sit there—the bar table, the magistrate's bench, the small desk at the side which she presumed was for the court reporters, visualizing everyone in their rightful places so she'd be prepared when court convened. Justin had requested that her matter be heard as early as possible.

'Will your husband be at court?' he'd asked.

'No,' Eva said.

He raised his eyebrows, but said nothing. Charlie had paid for her representation, only because he also wanted the matter dealt with as soon as possible, but he drew the line at fronting up to court. Besides, that would mean he'd have to talk to her for appearances' sake, and he was still maintaining his stony silence.

In the end, her court appearance was not the traumatic experience Eva had feared. Hers was the second matter heard, and although the courtroom was packed, including at least half a dozen reporters, she had her back to them as she sat at the bar table next to Justin, with Patrick on the other side.

The magistrate's unassuming demeanour was belied by his flinty gaze and Eva was aware of his scrutiny as the police prosecutor read out the facts. Justin got up and did his spiel with much gesturing and dramatic turn of phrase in a bid to convince the magistrate and everyone in the court of Eva's impeccable character, her remorse for her offence and her determination to make amends for this out of character behaviour.

As soon as he sat down, Eva stood up.

'Mrs Dennehy,' the magistrate said, surveying her over his glasses. 'I've taken into account the facts as stated by the prosecutor, the letters of recommendation tendered to the court and Mr Fellowes' submission on your behalf. You're fined six hundred dollars, with three months to pay, and disqualified from driving for six months from today. I order that a conviction not be recorded. Please hand your licence to the police prosecutor.'

Eva fumbled in her handbag, took out her driver's licence from her purse and handed it to the police prosecutor. All eyes were upon her as she, Justin and Patrick left the courtroom, but she put her chin up and looked straight ahead.

'A great result,' Justin said as soon as they were outside the courtroom. 'We couldn't have hoped for better.'

Eva's knees were weak with relief. 'Thank-you. I'm so glad it's over.'

'Not quite,' Justin said. After they got out of the lift, he steered her towards the front entrance. 'It doesn't matter which entrance we use, they'll be waiting,' he said. 'Patrick, can you assist Mrs Dennehy please?'

Sure enough the press were there, flocking around them as they descended the steps. Patrick guided Eva, his hand in the small of her back. Eva shook her head at the microphones thrust in front of her, keeping her eyes averted. Justin answered their questions with a brief statement.

'It was a satisfactory result and I'd appreciate it if you would allow Mrs Dennehy some privacy so she can recover from this ordeal and get on with her life.'

•••

Even though she vowed not to, Eva found herself watching the six o'clock news. Unfortunately it had been a quiet news day, and she was the second headline after a fatal six car pile-up just outside Sydney.

'Eva Dennehy, wife of mining millionaire Charles Dennehy, appeared in Sydney Central Local Court today charged with driving under the influence of a dangerous drug. She was apprehended four weeks ago after she was involved in a car accident and tested positive to cocaine. Mrs Dennehy admitted to having taken cocaine, but her barrister Justin Fellowes claimed in his submission to the court that it was a one-off incident and Mrs Dennehy had vowed it would not happen again. Mrs Dennehy was fined six hundred dollars with a conviction not recorded, and was disqualified from driving for six months.'

The report finished with a brief film clip of Charlie's speech at the opening of Hope Valley Rehabilitation Centre, followed by Justin making his statement on the steps of the courthouse, Eva behind him wearing her big sunglasses. She could see now that he was enjoying the attention and had probably steered her down the front steps deliberately so he could have his few moments of fame.

Watching herself, she was reminded of news clips she'd seen of movie stars after they'd been to court for a drug offence, hiding behind the slick Hollywood front of their lawyer. That's how the average joe would see it—another high roller bites the dust. That's what you get for being rich and beautiful.

The shrill clamour of the phone made her jump. Let it ring, it would only be the media. Their home number was unlisted, but reporters had a way of finding these things out. The answering machine message kicked in and after the beep, she heard Helga's voice.

'Eva, I've just seen the news. Why didn't you tell me? Ring me back as soon as you can.'

She wasn't in the mood to talk about it, and certainly not to Helga, who'd castigate her for her stupidity—not in using coke, but driving afterwards. When Helga had asked her later what Charlie was so upset about when he came home unexpectedly and asked her to leave, Eva made up a story that Charlie had accused her again of running around with other men. Although she sensed that Helga didn't believe her, she was so insistent it was true she almost believed it herself.

Eva pressed the off button on the remote control. Dodie, snuggled up beside her on the couch and looked up at her with adoring eyes. She was only allowed on the couch when Charlie wasn't home; as soon as she heard the key in the front door, she'd spring on to the floor and lie at Eva's feet.

Eva stroked her ears. 'What would I do without you, girl? At least I know you'll always stand by me.'

She thought of the coke in her coat pocket that she'd meant to throw out, but hadn't. What if Charlie came home and found her high? She got up, went into the wine cellar, and returned with a bottle of Dom Perignon. It was a gift which she and Charlie had decided to keep for a special occasion.

Except there never seemed to be any these days. If she couldn't get high, she at least deserved the best champagne. She popped the cork and poured it into her glass, watching it froth over the sides on to the carpet.

CHAPTER NINETEEN

HER head was throbbing and the nausea was rising. She swallowed it and looked at the bedside clock. Seven-thirty. She turned over—Charlie was already up. Had he even come home? She tried to focus her memory—she'd drunk the whole bottle of champagne and fallen asleep on the couch. She woke up at two am, an old war movie on the TV, turned it off and made her way into the bedroom. Yes, Charlie had been there, she remembered now, huddled on the other side of the bed. If he was awake when she stumbled into bed, he gave no indication of it.

She got out of bed, threw on her robe and padded out to the kitchen. Charlie was dressed for work, standing at the kitchen counter making himself a coffee. He didn't look up as she came in. She walked up and stood right beside him, almost touching him.

'Stop this right now! I'm your wife. You can't keep pretending I don't exist!'

He reeled back. 'You reek of alcohol! So that's going to solve everything, drinking until you pass out!'

'At least it's legal.'

He poured himself a coffee and took it to the front deck. She followed him out. The sun, weak as it was, made her head hurt. Charlie stood at the railing and looked out over the water. She came up beside him. 'Do you remember we're having the cocktail party here next week?'

Stupid question. Of course he'd remember. They'd planned it two months ago to coincide with the launch of Dennehy Developments, another arm of the Dennehy Corporation. Not content with making a fortune in mining and construction, Charlie was now branching out into property development. Eva had already sent out invitations and received over a hundred acceptances, and was looking forward to catering for one of 'Eva's soirees.'

'I haven't forgotten,' Charlie said. He looked sideways at her. 'Are you up to it?' He was sizing her up, and she could see he was wondering if he could trust her to keep herself together and not embarrass him with any rash behaviour.

'Of course I'm up to it. Honey, I'm sorry about this whole business, I promise it won't happen again. Please give me another chance.' *Give me another chance to make you see that you love me more than her.*

Charlie looked at her for a few moments, and in his eyes was something she'd never seen there before. Pity. He gulped his coffee and went inside without saying a word.

●●●

'You know, you can phone and place an order and it will be delivered to your home,' Helga said, as they stood in the supermarket with a packed trolley of goods at the end of a long checkout queue.

She'd insisted on driving Eva to the supermarket to buy provisions for the cocktail party. On occasions like this when there was a large number of guests attending, Eva hired a catering company to help out with the food, but liked to prepare as much of it as she could herself.

Helga looked on with annoyance as a young mother ahead of them in the queue grappled with a screaming toddler.

'I know,' Eva said. 'But I like grocery shopping. Looking at all the varieties of food and choosing what to buy. It's all part of the preparation process.'

'What on earth are you cooking with all this stuff?'

Eva counted on her fingers. 'Oyster vol-au-vents, savoury scrolls, Mexican dip, spinach and feta cheese pasties, chocolate truffles, macaroons, lemon meringue tartlets—'

'You're a genius. Julia Child's got nothing on you.'

On the way home Helga asked, 'How are things with Charlie?"

Eva had returned her phone call the day after her court appearance and told her the story. She was glad she couldn't see Helga's expression, though surprisingly, all Helga said was, 'You dodged a bullet there. It could have been so much worse. You could have killed someone—or yourself.'

Up until then, Eva had avoided thinking about that scenario.

'He's speaking to me now. That's a start.'

'He'll come round, give him time. And the public memory is short, thank God. Did you see today's headlines? Marlene Michaels, a teacher at Roseville Grammar, has been accused of having an affair, with one of her female students—your story's already in the archives.'

She was right. The phone had rung constantly for the first couple of days after her court appearance, and Charlie had hired a security guard to stand at the front gate to chase away reporters. But in less than a week, the fuss had dwindled away.

'You're not getting in too deep, are you, honey?' Helga asked.

'What do you mean?'

'With the coke.'

'Of course not, it was just one incident.'

'I'd hate to see you being dragged down by it. To misquote Francis Bacon, drugs are a good servant but a bad master.'

'Thanks for the advice. I'm fine.'

As they hauled the bulging plastic bags of groceries from the garage to the house, Eva said, 'I wonder where Dodie is. She's usually tripping me up as soon as I walk in the door.'

They dumped the grocery bags on the kitchen counter, and while Helga went out to the car to fetch the rest, Eva wandered through the house calling out to Dodie. She checked the daybed on the sun porch and the mat in the laundry. She went out into the yard and looked in her kennel, and searched places where Dodie couldn't possibly be—the guest wing, the garden shed, both locked when not in use.

She ran back into the kitchen where Helga was unpacking the grocery bags. The hook where Dodie's lead usually hung was bare. She looked out the window into the yard and noticed for the first time that Dodie's food and water bowls were gone.

Helga looked up, a tin of condensed milk in each hand. 'What's the matter? Where's Dodie?'

'I don't know. I'm about to find out.'

●●●

'Dennehy Corporation, Ainsley speaking.

'This is Eva, may I speak to Charlie?'

'I'm sorry, Mr Dennehy is in a meeting at the moment. May I take a message?'

'You may not. I need to speak with my husband urgently.'

'Mr Dennehy's instructions were that he was not to be interrupted.'

I bet they were. He knew damn well I'd be calling him.

'If you don't put me through now I'll come to the office and create such a scene you won't be able to ignore me.'

A pause, as if Ainsley were picturing such a spectacle. 'Let me see what I can do,' she said coolly. It took a lot to rattle her.

After a couple of minutes of hold music—of course he'd keep her waiting—she heard a click, and then Charlie's voice. 'Eva, what do you want?'

'You know damn well what I want. What the hell did you do with Dodie?'

'I organised for her to go to another home. Don't worry, she's in good hands.'

'Why, for fuck's sake?'

'There's no need to swear. It's quite obvious that you're not capable of looking after her. Taking her in the car with you while you're high on cocaine is not the act of a responsible owner—she could have been seriously hurt or killed.'

'As if you'd care! And I've told you, it won't happen again, I've quit using cocaine.'

'Why do you keep a packet of it in your coat pocket if you don't intend to use it? Testing your willpower perhaps?'

'You bastard! You went through my things!'

'I only did what you do all the time. Don't think I don't know that you go through all my things trying to find evidence of God knows what.'

'Charlie, please, I'll promise you anything, I'll get rid of the coke right now, just get her back.'

She hated herself for begging, for sounding so pathetic.

'I have to go, Eva. And it's too late, I flushed the coke down the toilet.'

He hung up. Helga came out from the kitchen.

'I heard what you said. Is it true?'

Eva nodded. 'He gave Dodie away because he thinks I'm not fit to look after her. How dare he! If he walked in the door right now, I swear I'd kill him!'

She sank to the floor on her knees, rocking back and forth, her hands over her face, tears spilling out through her fingers.

●●●

Helga helped Eva off the floor and on to the couch and fixed her a brandy from the living room bar.

'That's better, you've got some colour in your face. If it were anyone else but Charlie, I'd say divorce him!'

'What do you mean, anyone else but Charlie?'

A shadow flitted across Helga's face. 'Just a throw-away comment.'

'You must have meant something by it.'

Helga hesitated.

'Tell me, please!'

'How much do you know about Charlie's financial affairs?'

'Not a lot. He made it clear from the start that the business was his domain, so I went along with that.' As long as he kept her in the manner to which she had quickly become accustomed. 'I suppose it was naive of me, but I didn't want to rock the boat and I trusted him.'

'What I'm about to tell you is what Sol has told me, in the strictest confidence, so you mustn't let on to Charlie that you know.'

Eva nodded.

'Charlie has most of his income and assets tied up in his business in such a way that if you were to divorce him you'd get very little.'

'I'm aware of that.'

Helga raised her eyebrows.

Whoops, another tactical error. In her previous life Sol had informed her after Charlie's death, in his capacity as Charlie's lawyer, that all she was entitled to was his life insurance. And it seemed to her that Sol had taken a quiet delight in breaking the news.

'Charlie told me, I think it was his way of warning me not to divorce him.' It was a lie, but it sounded plausible to her ears. 'What else has Sol told you?'

'About what?'

Did Helga know about Charlie's links to crime? And possibly Sol's? Eva couldn't ask her outright or even hint at it, as word would get back to Charlie through Sol that Eva was on his trail.

'Nothing. My brain's fuddled, I'm still in shock over Dodie.'

'Everything I know, I just told you. And you knew it anyway.'

Helga gave her a hug. 'I'm sorry to leave you when you're still upset, but I have a coffee date with Lady Gwendolyn Harvey to see if I can talk her into re-decorating before she sells. And then another massage with Felippe.'

'You've been seeing him for months now,' Eva said. 'Are you settling into a long term relationship?'

'Not likely. He's getting married on Saturday so we're having a farewell rendezvous. He's a good Catholic, he believes in fidelity in marriage. More's the pity.'

CHAPTER TWENTY

'YOU'VE excelled yourself again, Eva!' said Brian Appleby, editor of Sydney Business magazine, as he bit into a savoury tart, spilling a trail of pastry crumbs down his ample front.

'The vol-au-vents are to die for!' trilled his wife, Maria. 'Did you make them yourself?'

Eva smiled and nodded.

'You're a marvel! How do you do it all?' Maria waved her arm around to encompass the huge marquee on the back lawn humming with chatter and laughter, the lit fountains and the soft, lilting tones of the violin duo in the corner. A couple of press photographers prowled around, taking photos for the social pages.

To an outsider it would look like just another cocktail party; to those in the know, it was not up to the usual standard of Eva's soirees. A third of the people who'd previously accepted the invitation had pulled out at the last minute or failed to turn up, including some high profile invitees such as the Lord Mayor of Sydney and the local member of parliament.

'I have lots of help.' Eva gestured in the direction of the wait staff from the catering company, who were floating around making sure that no-one was without a drink and finger food.

'But you still have to organise it all!' Maria said. 'I'd be hopeless at something like this—Brian says I couldn't organise a party in a brothel.'

She gave a peal of laughter, her plump cheeks flushed.

'I think you've had enough to drink, darling,' Brian said, shooting Eva a look of apology. He took Maria's arm. 'Come on, let's get some more of those tarts.'

Eva gave an understanding smile and continued weaving her way through the crowd, acknowledging the comments on the way. 'You look gorgeous, Eva! Love the party!'

She headed to where Helga and Sol were standing, near the violin duo. She'd only had time for a brief greeting when they arrived. Sol's arm circled Helga's waist, drawing her close to him. They were part of a group, but were oblivious to those around them. Helga was saying something to Sol and he was gazing down at her, his face soft with affection. The only time Eva saw Sol show any warmth was when he was with Helga. They hadn't seen her, so she walked straight past them, tears stinging her eyes. Tears of jealousy. And grief. Once Charlie had looked at her like that, but it was part of his armoury of charm; she suspected he did it to all his women. She had no doubt that despite their open marriage, Helga was the centre of Sol's world.

'Eva!' Vivienne Crawford, a fund raising acquaintance, hailed her and came hurrying over. Eva hastily wiped her eyes. Vivienne was the last person she wanted to see her crying.

'How are you?' Vivienne's bulbous eyes, masacara'd and eyelined so they almost popped out of her face, scrutinised Eva. Her tone dripped with sympathy, but the meaning behind her words were clear. 'How are you coping with the world knowing about your cocaine charge and all the nasty gossip it's triggered?' Which Vivienne herself would contribute to, putting her own interpretation on whatever Eva said and reporting back to her poisonous friends.

'I'm very well, thank-you,' Eva said, mustering a radiant smile. 'In fact, I've never been better.'

'I'm so glad to hear it! By the way, is Yvette Porter here? I haven't seen her since her fabulous pottery exhibition and I was hoping to catch up with her tonight.'

Yvette and her husband Rupert, a well-known QC, had cancelled, pleading a clash of social engagements which they blamed on Rupert's secretary. And Eva was sure that Vivienne knew that, the bitch.

'I haven't seen her yet,' Eva replied. 'But why don't you go and look for her? She's bound to be somewhere near the bar.'

Yvette had a reputation for liking a drink or six. Eva smiled to herself as she turned and walked off, her first genuine smile of the night. She almost ploughed straight into Ainsley, looking barrel-like in an unflattering pleated voile skirt and blazer. Ainsley held her drink aloft and just managed to avoid spilling it over herself.

'Sorry, Ainsley,' Eva said. 'How are you?'

Ainsley gave her usual smile, the smile that said, 'let's not pretend we could ever be friends.' If she was holding a grudge about Eva's threats on the phone to come into the office and make a scene, she didn't show it. She never gave anyone the satisfaction of getting under her skin.

'I'm very well, thanks. And you?'

Was she imagining the emphasis on 'you?' Eva could imagine Ainsley's reaction to the news of her court appearance: *I knew she'd stuff up sooner or later*.

'I'm fine. Are you enjoying the night?'

'It's lovely. You've done a marvellous job, as usual.'

Eva had become adept at small talk over the years—it was the price she had to pay for this life. One of them. But sometimes it seemed as if that was all her life consisted of. Shallow trivialities. Her face ached from smiling and she felt as if she'd explode if she had to make one more vacuous comment.

'Thank-you. Excuse me, I've just seen someone I need to talk to. Nice to see you again, Ainsley.'

She scanned the crowd and saw that Charlie was working the room as befitting the star of the show. Champagne in hand, she made her way out of the marquee on to the lawn. It was a clear, star-studded night, with just an edge of spring coolness. But the beauty of the scene before her, the dark expanse of the harbour reflecting a rainbow of city lights, failed to move her. *Just like my life. Shiny and glittering on the surface, dark and murky underneath.*

The anger she'd felt towards Charlie for giving Dodie away had dissipated, leaving her in a fog of sadness and grief. For the second time. Another feeling of deja vu so strong it gave her the shivers. In her first life, she'd had Dodie put down after the bone cancer became so bad that she could hardly walk, and had never entertained the thought of getting another dog.

Because Dodie was irreplaceable. There could never be another dog who understood her moods so well; knowing when to play, when to relax, when to comfort. Eva was sure it was because she'd rescued her from an abusive owner. She and Dodie had both experienced childhood trauma, were both damaged. Another dog, no matter how endearing, would make her miss Dodie even more.

She felt exactly the same way now, even though Dodie wasn't dead. But she may as well be. Eva pictured her navigating her way around a new home, sleeping in an unfamiliar bed, being cuddled by complete strangers, and wondered if she was pining for her, Eva, and her old home. Then she pushed the image out of her mind; it was too painful.

'There you are.'

Eva jumped. Helga was beside her. 'Sorry, didn't mean to frighten you. What are you doing, hiding away at your own party?'

'Just admiring my own view.'

'You've done a fantastic job, as usual.'

'Even though over thirty of the guests didn't show? Just a coincidence they all cancelled after my court appearance.'

What had hurt most was that Frances and Diana were amongst those who'd cancelled, both pleading sudden family crises.

'And the others have just come out of curiosity to observe the damage, like passers-by at a car accident. Maybe they're hoping to catch me coming out of the bathroom with tell-tale bits of white powder on my nose.'

I should do it, just to see their reaction. She pictured herself circulating the crowd, her nose decorated with a light sprinkle of bicarbonate of soda, and she almost laughed.

'You're dead right, honey. People are fickle and cruel and ghoulish,' Helga said. 'And a lot of them are thinking, "Thank God it wasn't me," because you committed the one unforgivable sin above all others—you got caught.'

She squeezed Eva's shoulder. 'I think Sol's giving his speech shortly.'

She accompanied Helga back into the marquee and grabbed another champagne from a passing waiter. 'Well, look who's here,' Helga murmured.

At the opposite end of the marquee, being escorted in by the butler they'd hired for the night, was Veronika. Jessica-Rabbit-voluptuous in a silver cocktail dress, with the cool poise of a film star who is used to being gaped at. Beside her was a woman of about the same age, of squat build and homely appearance.

'That fucking bitch,' Eva said between clenched teeth. She craned her neck to find Charlie. He was holding court to a group of women, who were laughing at something he'd said. Like everyone else, he watched Veronika make her entrance, but his gaze didn't linger and he resumed his conversation as if she were just another guest.

The woman next to him, a young blonde whose breasts almost spilled out over her dress, placed her hand on his arm and leaned forward as she listened. The group burst out laughing again and another woman gave him a mock slap on the face.

Veronika was looking around, not even acknowledging Charlie's presence. Spying someone she knew, she swanned over to a group to be greeted with hugs and kisses, her friend following in her wake.

'She wasn't on the guest list,' Eva said. What was Charlie playing at? Was he trying to provoke her? But that presupposed he knew that Eva knew about Veronika. Which he didn't. Unless Helga had broken her confidence and told Sol.

Someone nearby tapped a glass loudly. 'Good evening, ladies and gentlemen!' Sol was standing on a makeshift stage near the entrance of the marquee holding a microphone.

He waited for the crowd to quieten. 'We don't want to take up too much of your time with speeches but as we're here tonight to celebrate yet another business venture for the Dennehy Corporation, I think it's fitting to acknowledge the achievements of Charles Dennehy.'

Sol bowed his head to acknowledge the applause. 'Charlie and I go a long way back. We went to different schools but we knew each other through football. Charlie was a very talented footballer. He could have gone pro if he'd wanted but he left school at fifteen to become a millionaire—those were his exact words.'

Eva tuned out. She'd heard this speech or variations of it countless times before. Sol had also made this speech numerous times, but his tone of admiration for Charlie's accomplishments never wavered. She hated to admit it, but it was kind of touching. Although Sol had been brought up in a private school, overseas skiing holidays, first car a Maserati kind of family, he'd also been taught to revere the work ethic, and had worked hard for success in his law firm and property investments. Eva knew that that was why he despised her, seeing her as a leech who'd married purely for money and did nothing to earn her keep. For Charlie's sake he was never less than unfailingly polite, but the contempt he reserved for fools was never far below the surface.

That's your mistake, Sol. Whatever I am, I'm not a fool. Eva couldn't picture him consorting with the likes of Tommy and Sniper. Perhaps he didn't; perhaps he and Charlie had minions who did all their dirty work. It stood to reason—the further removed they were away from the action, the less likely they were to be implicated. Unless the minions squealed of course, which was what Pete had hinted he was working on.

After Sol had finished his speech to a hearty round of applause, Charlie took the microphone and thanked Sol for his kind words.

'I'm proud of Dennehy Corporation and what we've achieved, building this business up out of the ashes, and now this new arm, Dennehy Developments. We aim to do not just residential but also commercial development, to be in the forefront of creating the infrastructure of the new suburbs and satellite towns that are mushrooming everywhere.'

He paused, looking around and making eye contact with the audience. Eva watched him lock eyes with Veronika, and move on. 'I've been asked many times why I continue to expand my company. After all, if I retired tomorrow, my wife and I could live in luxury for the rest of our lives without having to lift a finger. But at the risk of sounding like a cliche, it's not about the money. It's about challenge and learning new things—what's the fun of doing the same thing over and over again that you could do in your sleep? The day you stop challenging yourself is the day you die.'

Challenge. Was that really what it was all about? Was Veronika a challenge? Every woman he'd slept with? Perhaps Helga was wrong—it wasn't insecurity and the need for admiration driving him, it was the incessant need to test himself, to prove himself to the father who'd died years ago and would never know of his achievements. Was it also the reason for getting into crime—pushing the boundaries, new territories to conquer, the adrenaline of the high risk venture?

'But as the saying goes, behind every successful man is a good woman—'

'Hey, Charlie,' yelled a male voice. 'Bite the bullet and lose the cliches! '

Titters resounded around the room. Charlie smiled. 'And I've been lucky enough to have the love and support of my beautiful wife, Eva, who has kept the home fires burning and has, as usual, organised a spectacular night.' Charlie scanned the crowd until he found Eva and beckoned to her. 'Come on up, Eva.'

You bastard. After everything you've done, you want me to play happy families.

Eva weaved her way through the crowd up to the stage to stand beside Charlie. He put his arm around her waist and squeezed her and the guests applauded and whistled. She managed a smile as the cameras flashed. She couldn't help her gaze wandering to Veronika. She stood only a few feet away next to her friend, her eyes on Charlie. When she caught Eva looking at her, she looked away. But not before Eva had caught her expression. Triumph.

And then Eva saw it, clear as a summer sky. Charlie's plan. Charlie putting on the persona of the loyal, supportive husband, getting brownie points from the public for it. 'Isn't he lovely? His wife's gone and disgraced herself and made him a target for ridicule, but he's still standing by her.'

She could see it now in the faces staring up at her. Then one day, Charlie would quietly and with dignity make a public announcement that the marriage was over. 'We did our best but we just weren't able to save the marriage.'

He'd refuse to go into details, gentleman that he was, but the public would read between the lines. 'It was his wife, into cocaine, you know, when she went to court that was the beginning of the end.' The gossip mags would make up their own stories and he would do nothing to deny them.

He and Veronika would lie low for a while, then after a decent interval had passed, they would appear together in public as the next Golden Couple. She, Eva, had given Charlie a prime opportunity to exit the marriage and make it look as if it was all her fault.

•••

It was midnight, late for a cocktail party. Eva's feet were killing her and all she'd wanted to do for the past two hours was sink into bed, pull the sheet over her head and make the world go away.

She went over to the bar. Drinks were officially over and the bar staff were packing up, but she persuaded them to make her a double strength espresso before they turned the coffee machine off. There was a small knot of guests left, Charlie in the midst, the ones who always overstayed their welcome and whom you practically had to take by the arm and lead out the door.

Veronika and her friend had left about an hour ago after exchanging a few words with Charlie in the manner of guests thanking the host for a wonderful evening. Eva watched the body language between Charlie and Veronika—a slight leaning towards each other, glances exchanged that were a shade too long. Much as they were trying to be discreet, it was impossible to be around someone you were in love with without giving something away, no matter how minute.

Eva looked around to see if anyone else was watching them. Apparently not, but she'd bet her bottom dollar that more guests knew about the affair than didn't. Was that pity applause she'd received on the stage with Charlie? Pity that she was such a failure as a wife that he was forced to find comfort elsewhere?

Helga and Sol broke away from the remaining guests, and came towards her, arm in arm. Helga's champagne flush glowed in contrast to Sol's steadfast sobriety. Like Charlie, he drank very little; he liked to be in control.

'We're heading off,' Helga said. 'I'll just get my shawl.'

'I'll get it for you,' Sol said.

'It's only over there on the chair.' She hurried towards the back of the marquee.

Eva was about to break the uneasy silence by thanking him for coming when Sol said, 'You've got a natural talent for this, haven't you?'

His tone was not dismissive or mocking; it sounded like a genuine question to which he wanted the answer.

'I suppose so. I enjoy doing it, so that helps.' Seeing as he'd brought the subject up, she'd take advantage of it. 'I know you think there's not much brain power involved in organising something like this, but I challenge you to do it and make a success of it. As to the worth of it to society, the reason I charged twenty dollars a head for people to come tonight was because every single cent of that money will be donated to the Cancer Council for research.'

'Very admirable.' Sol leaned forward and said to her in a low voice, 'My advice to you is to stick to what you're good at. That way you'll keep yourself out of trouble.'

Helga was back with her shawl. 'See you soon, honey. Thanks for a lovely evening.'

She hugged Eva, Sol gave her a peck on the cheek and she watched them go, Helga matching Sol's loping stride. What the hell did Sol mean by sticking to what she was good at? Was he referring to her doing coke, or something else? Could that be a veiled warning to stop her investigations into Charlie's activities? If it was, how did he know?

•••

Sol's comment was still churning through her mind when Charlie came to bed. She watched him as he methodically undressed, hung up his suit and put his washing in the laundry hamper. He was a model husband in that way, she never had to pick up after him.

He cleaned his teeth, peed, turned out the light and got into bed. Before he had a chance to turn his back on her and go to sleep, she slid over to his side of the bed and draped her arm over his chest.

'It was a great night, baby, I was very proud of you.'

Charlie stroked her arm. 'And you too, sweet pea. Everyone said how much they'd enjoyed it.'

'I told you I could do it, didn't I? I promise you, no more coke and all that other crazy stuff. From now on, it's just you and me.'

She ran her hands through the hair on his chest and down to the softness of his belly. His body felt so good—when did they last have sex? Charlie had been so busy being disgusted with her and not talking to her, it had seemed like forever. And now she'd realised how much she'd missed it. Her hand moved down further. She ran her fingers through his pubic hair and felt his cock respond. She leaned down and took it into her mouth. Charlie groaned.

Fuck you, Veronika. You went home with your ugly friend and he's all mine tonight. She sucked Charlie's cock hard then slid on top of him, riding him as he tweaked her nipples. She got off and sucked him some more, tasting her juices on him, and alternated the riding and sucking, bringing him to the edge then stopping, until he begged her to let him come. And finally she did.

As she lay beside him in the aftermath of warm flesh, sweat and juices, she watched him as he slept, the rise and fall of his chest, his mouth slightly open, every now and then giving the occasional gentle snort. She hadn't climaxed but she didn't care; that wasn't her aim. She wanted to feel once more the power, the hold she had over him. It was erotic and exciting, and she craved more.

She drifted off to sleep and at dawn she woke Charlie by stroking his cock until it was hard, then climbed on top again. But this time she allowed herself the pleasure of climaxing, and her orgasm made Charlie come and she collapsed on top of him, her face nuzzled into his neck, her heart beating against his.

She wanted to stay in this moment forever. She was outside her body watching herself, taking note of every small detail, every sensation, so it would remain in her memory for the rest of her life.

CHAPTER TWENTY-ONE

THE hotel was in Darlinghurst, a run-down converted terrace house with a patchy frosting of mould over anaemic yellow paint. A small plaque on the front door announced it was the Apollo Budget Hotel.

The front door creaked as Eva opened it. An old Chinese man in a cardigan was sitting at a front desk watching a small colour TV. The blinds were drawn and the room was dim, reeking of stale oil and boiled cabbage. The man turned his head and looked at Eva, expressionless.

'Mr Henderson,' she said. That was Sniper's nom de plume. The man stared at her, unblinking and she wondered if he'd heard her.

'Twenty-four,' he finally said, and pointed up a flight of stairs.

Her assignations with Sniper were twice weekly, each one at a different venue—grimy, hourly-rate places, the managers indifferent and often surly. As long as you paid your money upfront, they didn't care who you were or what you did.

The stairs creaked as she went up them. Room twenty-four was at the end of a narrow hallway. The pervading odour was the same, no matter which hotel they went to—a mingling of musty carpet, sweat, sex, pleasure and desperation.

She knocked and opened the door, walking straight into a dingy bedroom. Budget hotel—what a euphemism. Sniper was sitting on the faded bed cover, naked with an erection. Beside him sat Ray, in his underpants and clearly not aroused. Sniper was grinning and Ray was looking apologetic and uncomfortable.

'What the hell is going on?'

'Thought you might like a little company,' Sniper said. 'I'd hate for you to get bored.'

He had that manic air about him—he was already high. Ray, on the other hand, looked stone cold straight.

'What's that supposed to mean? And what's Ray doing here?' She looked from one to the other. 'Are you two—?'

'No we aren't,' Ray said quickly. 'I told Sniper, no funny business between him and me.'

Sniper shrugged. 'Ray here hates queers. Me? I don't care one way or another, there were so many in Nam. I'm not one myself, though I don't think he believes me.' He looked at Ray. 'I'm not touchin' you mate, you're far too ugly for my liking. It's you and her and me and her.'

'Wait a minute,' Eva said. She looked at Ray. 'How did you get roped into this?'

'I was talking to Sniper the other night after we'd done our gig and I mentioned you and how you'd given me a false phone number—‘

He looked accusingly at her. 'And how I had no idea how to track you down and Sniper—' he swallowed, 'suggested I come along today so I could see you again.'

'So you thought, the more the merrier,’ Eva said.

'You got it,' Sniper said. He winked at Ray. 'She catches on quick, doesn't she?'

He stroked his erect cock. 'Just looking at you gives me a hard-on, baby.' *And a nose full of coke.* Ray locked eyes with Eva, his gaze saying, 'I'm sorry I got you into this.'

Eva gave Sniper an icy look. 'Contrary to your opinion, I'm not a whore. I don't have much choice in fucking you, but I refuse to do him as well.'

Sniper sprang up, slammed her against the wall and put his hands around her throat. 'Listen bitch, I think you're forgetting the reason you're here. You're here for my pleasure, to do whatever I want you to do and if I tell you to fuck a goat, you say, "Yessir, how many?" Got it?'

Eva was choking, gasping for breath. Her head was spinning. *For God's sake, don't pass out.* She nodded.

'You'll do it and enjoy it.'

She nodded again. Stars whirled before her eyes. Sniper released his grip. She bent over double gasping and coughing.

'For an intelligent woman, you're taking a long time to learn your lesson,' Sniper said.

When she'd regained her breath, she straightened up. Sniper was watching her, eyes as unfathomable as a dark well. 'Get your gear off.'

Eva took off her jacket and unbuttoned her blouse. She was in desperate need of some coke; Sniper always brought some and they did a line together before sex. But he'd already had his fix, and she was too frightened to ask him in case he lost it again. *I can do this. I can do it and pretend I'm enjoying it.*

As she stood naked before them, she fondled her breasts, pulling her nipples to make them erect, and rubbed her pussy. 'Okay, guys, who's first?'

•••

After Sniper had pulled on his jeans and left the room to go to the communal toilets, Ray stroked the matted hair away from Eva's face. 'I'm so sorry, Sniper wouldn't tell me anything about you. This was the only way I could get to see you again.'

Eva lay on her back on the bed, Ray on his side leaning over her. 'Don't apologise, it was fun.'

'Seriously? You enjoyed it?'

'I had no choice but to do it, so I decided I may as well enjoy it.'

It wasn't the truth, but it would do for Ray. She had put on a persona, like slipping on a costume, the hot and horny chick who could never get enough, as she fucked Ray and Sniper in turn, Sniper masturbating as he watched her and Ray, then taking his turn as soon as they'd finished. Sniper had then demanded that she and Ray do it again and it had taken some time to get Ray erect again, while Sniper had a second round of voyeuristic stimulation. She'd been too engrossed in her role-playing to get any pleasure herself and now she was drained of energy, empty of feeling. She was aware of only one thing—she badly needed some blow.

Ray would know where to get some. She looked into Ray's soulful eyes and laid her hand on his cheek. 'Well, I enjoyed it with you.'

'So what's with you and Sniper anyhow? Have you got something going with him?'

'No.'

'What then? What's the attraction?'

'There's no attraction, believe me. Not like there is with you.' She sat up and kissed him, letting her lips linger. 'He'll be back any minute. Can you meet me later today? Say, four o'clock at Ginger's, the bar near Circular Quay?' Somewhere well away from Downtown.

'Sure can, baby.'

The door opened and Sniper reappeared. 'Fun's over kiddies, we gotta split.'

He put on his shirt and as Eva stepped into her knickers, Ray moved out of the line of Sniper's vision, and gave her the thumbs up.

•••

'Pete, I have some bad news.'

Eva's hand was shaking as she held the phone receiver. She took a deep breath and steadied it. What a mess she was, she'd never craved coke as much as she did now. Ray had better come up with the goods this afternoon.

'What's up?'

'Charlie has cut off my access to his bank accounts, which means I can't afford to pay you any longer.'

She'd been paying Pete by withdrawing cash from Charlie's bank account in instalments, so as not to arouse his suspicions. He always assumed any cash withdrawals were for the usual purchases—clothes, lunches, beauty treatments—and never queried them.

'All I have is my personal credit cards, which are just about maxed out.'

Silence. Pete blew out a sigh. 'I'm in too deep to stop now, Eva. I'll put the rest of it on tick and you can pay me when your circumstances improve. I'm pretty sure we're on to something. My contact knows someone who's a computer genius, he can hack into anything and he's working on those numbers you gave me.'

Thank God for some good news. 'How much longer it will take?'

'I can't give you a time. But hang in there. We're doing everything we can.'

She wanted the whole sordid affair over and done with now. She'd had it with being blackmailed by Sniper. The morning's assignation with him and Ray had left her depleted—as if all her thoughts and emotions, her very identity had been sucked out of her, so that she no longer had any will of her own. And how did she know that Sniper was keeping his end of the bargain? For all she knew, he could be feeding Charlie all sorts of information. But she couldn't risk the chance that if she refused any further assignations, he would make good his threat to 'snuff her out.'

'Eva, are you okay?' Pete asked.

'Yes, I'm fine,' she whispered. She hung up the phone. She couldn't breathe. The room was closing in on her. She wanted to be Dorothy in *The Wizard of Oz*—stamp her feet and be back in her hometown, or in her case, her former life. Being a cynical old alcoholic carrying a swag of guilt around was not a great existence, but it was comfortable and predictable. And with no prospect of being killed, except maybe drinking herself to death.

CHAPTER TWENTY-TWO

AT four-thirty she was sitting alone in the cool dimness of Gingers, sipping a Cosmopolitan and wondering if Ray had stood her up. Had she been fooled by his apparent devotion to her? But then he came hurrying over to her table in a fluster of apologies.

'I'm so sorry, it was my turn to pick the kids up from school and I had to stay behind and talk to Joey's teacher—he's been acting up a bit in class.' He shook his head. 'Kids, you know how they are.'

'No, I don't.'

He was surprised. 'You don't have children?"

'No.'

'That's a shame. You're missing out on one of the best experiences of your life. '

The waitress was hovering. Ray ordered a beer for himself and another Cosmopolitan for Eva.

Eva put on her most demure look. 'Ray, I'm wondering if I can ask a favour of you.'

Ray took her hand and sandwiched it between both of his. 'You can ask me anything you want.'

'Do you know where I can get some blow?'

He stroked her hand lightly with his thumb. It put her teeth on edge, but she smiled.

'Sure I do. I can take you there. On one proviso.'

'What's that?' *Another fuck? Cheap at half the price.*

'Tell me who you really are and why you're hanging around with Sniper.'

Eva plucked the swizzlestick from her cocktail, removed the little parasol from the end and with slow deliberation sucked the cherry off the stick and into her mouth.

Ray's eyes never left her face. 'I know your name's not Sarah.'

'My real name's Eva. I think first names are fine between us—I only know you as Ray.'

Recognition dawned on Ray's face. 'Oh, Jesus, I know who you are. You're that mining guy's wife, the one who got busted for coke. I saw your photo in the papers. When you turned up at the hotel this morning, I thought your face was familiar. Apart from the night I met you, I mean.'

'I like your real hair better,' he added.

'Thank-you and please keep my identity to yourself.'

'Sure thing, baby. You're a hell of a woman; I can't believe I've made love to Eva Dennehy.'

Eva flinched inwardly at the 'made love.'

'So why are you hanging around with Sniper? He's not fit for you to wipe your feet on.'

'Didn't you know that some of us society ladies like to slum it every now and then? A bit of rough trade to add some spice to our lives?'

She looked away from the hurt look on Ray's face. He obviously assumed he was one of the rough trade. She slid a crescent of orange off her swizzlestick and sucked all the flesh from it, flicking her tongue around her lips after each bite.

'Anyway, you're worth ten of Sniper,' she said.

'What about your husband?'

'What about him?'

'You're obviously not happily married, otherwise you wouldn't be hanging around in bars picking up strange men.'

'Some would say that's a naive assumption, but in my case it's the truth. Charlie and I are going through a rocky patch at the moment.'

'That's not surprising, after your court case. I can see why you didn't want to give me your right name.' He stroked her forearm. 'If you need someone to talk to, I'm here.'

She put on a grateful smile and was just about to bring up the subject of the cocaine again, when Ray said, 'I know you're slumming it with me, but I know I can make you happy.'

'What are you saying? That you want to have an affair with me? Or you want me to leave my husband for you?'

'How about both?' Ray grinned. 'I'm greedy when it comes to you, Eva. I can't get enough of you. I fell in love with you the night I met you.'

'Ray, how can you be in love with me? We hardly know each other.'

'That's the fun of it, getting to know each other. True, I don't know your favourite foods or your hobbies or what your childhood was like, but I don't need to know those things to love you. I know what you're like inside, you're a good, kind, loyal person underneath that cynical front.'

'You think so?'

'See what I mean about the cynical front? And the best thing about me, Eva, is that I'm not after you for your money. If your husband cut you off with nothing it wouldn't worry me at all, I've never needed money to be happy. Of course I know you're used to a certain standard of living—'

This was like something out of a B-grade movie. No doubt he was hoping she'd say, 'As long as we can be together, that's all that matters.' At least acting was something she could do well.

'There's just one thing,' Ray said.

'What do you mean?'

'If we're going to be together, you'll have to stop seeing Sniper.'

Eva almost laughed out loud at the absurdity of it. She'd give anything to stop seeing Sniper, though not to be with Ray. How could he, with his dingy apartment, musician's wages and clumsy naivety, possibly think he could make her happy? But she couldn't afford to put him offside if he was going to get her some coke.

She blew out a sigh. 'You've certainly taken me by surprise. I'm going to need some time to think it over.'

'Of course, take all the time you need.' He grinned. 'But not too long. If you eat any more fruit out of your cocktail I'll have to jump you right here on the table.'

•••

'That's the place there.' Ray pointed to a block of modern apartments just off the main road in Paddington. The setting sun bathed their pristine white exteriors in a gentle glow and bounced off the angled glass. Ray continued down the street and parked around the corner in front of another, identical apartment block.

'It would be better if I went in alone,' he said. That suited Eva; she had no intention of accompanying him.

She dug into her handbag, pulled out a handful of fifties she'd got as a cash advance on her credit card and handed them to Ray. He counted them and stuffed them in his wallet. He'd rung his contacts from a public phone before they'd left Gingers to arrange the pickup.

'I'll be back in a few minutes.'

He shambled down the street and around the corner, his jeans bagging around his backside and shirt half untucked underneath his faded, stained denim jacket. Eva slunk down in the seat and rifled aimlessly through her handbag, anything to look busy and not attract the attention of passers-by. Ray's battered van would do that on its own, out of place amongst the late model cars parked on the street and in driveways.

This was a well-heeled part of town, as you'd expect of a cocaine dealer, full of yuppies and arty types, who would soon be arriving home from work with their briefcases, bottles of wine and take-away curries.

The driver's door opened and Ray got in. 'Mission accomplished.' He drew a plastic ziplock bag of white powder out of his jacket pocket and handed it to her. Eva slipped it into her handbag. She'd have to find a new hiding place for it at home, where Charlie was not likely to look.

Ray put his hand under her dress and stroked her thigh. 'Do you want to come back to my place? My ex will be picking the kids up in a few minutes and then we can get high and get dirty!'

His hand travelled up her thigh and stopped just short of her knickers. The offer was tempting, only from the point of view that it was more fun to be high with someone than alone, and even sex with someone as dull in bed as Ray was exciting when you were high. But it would only add more fuel to his hopes for a relationship and she had what she wanted now.

'I know my place is pretty crappy, compared to what you're used to,' Ray said, 'but I'm saving up to rent a better place. A nice little terrace house here in Paddington.'

Eva caught his hand before it went any further. 'I'd love to, but Charlie is expecting me home shortly and I don't want him to get suspicious.' She gave him a teasing smile. 'You're ready to go again after this morning? You're insatiable!'

'You make me that way, I get a hard-on just thinking about you. I've had the best sex with you I've ever had in my life.'

He cupped his hands around her face. 'When can I see you again? Can you give me your phone number—your real one?'

'I'm sorry, I can't risk it. I never know when Charlie's going to be home, he pops in and out at all sorts of hours.'

'You should get one of those mobile phones, then I could ring you whenever I wanted. A mate of mine's got one. Takes it everywhere in the car.'

Eva smiled. 'I'd need a bigger handbag, I think. If you give me your number, I'll ring you.'

Ray drew out his wallet, dug out a business card and handed it to her. 'Promise?'

Eva crossed her heart. 'Cross my heart and hope to die.'

He started up the engine and drew out into the street.

'Just drop me back at Ginger's,' Eva said. 'I'll go home from there.'

Ray stopped in a loading zone around the corner from Gingers. With the engine still running, he turned to her, kissed her hard on the lips, then put his hands on her shoulders and looked into her eyes. 'You make sure you phone me, or else—' he paused and added with exaggerated menace, 'I know where you live.'

She wriggled free from his hands. 'I already said I would.'

She opened the door and scrambled out. Ray pulled out into the traffic, waving and beeping his horn. She watched his van until it disappeared out of view. Surely he didn't know where she lived. It was said in jest, so perhaps she'd just imagined the undertone of irrationality, a thread of derangement borne of obsession. She hoped so, because she had no intention of phoning him.

CHAPTER TWENTY-THREE

'MESSAGE received four thirty today,' the answering machine intoned. Then Charlie's voice. 'Darling, just letting you know I've got meetings tonight and won't be home for dinner. See you later.'

'Meetings.' Probably the clandestine kind with Veronika. Eva pressed the delete messages button and sank onto the living room couch. She'd caught a cab home from Ginger's, darkness already closing in as she unlocked the front door.

The emptiness of the house echoed around her. Being alone felt so much worse in the evenings. Eva still expected to see Dodie racing out to greet her, weaving in and out of her legs. She still went to fetch her dinner bowl, or put her hand out to stroke her as she watched TV. Often she'd feel a tickle of fur on her leg, and whip around, but there was nothing there. Or she'd hear a 'walkies time' bark and search the house, even though she knew she'd find nothing. Once she looked outside at Dodie's kennel and saw her little moppet head peering out at her.

Was this how parents felt when they lost a child? She could hear Charlie's voice. 'Don't be ridiculous, Eva, she's an animal, you can't compare her to a child.'

She opened a can of baked beans. Her eating habits were atrocious these days; if Charlie wasn't home for dinner she wouldn't bother cooking. She scrabbled through her record collection and hauled out Rod Stewart's album *Blondes Have More Fun*. Charlie had somehow managed to find an album signed by the singer himself and had given it to her as a first wedding anniversary present. She placed it on the record player, which had pride of place beside the CD player, cranked up the volume and opened a bottle of champagne.

Rod's gravelly tones filled the hollow spaces in the house as she drank her champagne and ate the beans cold out of the tin with a spoon. 'Ain't love a bitch,' Rod rasped as she succumbed to her sadness and let the tears flow. When the record finished, she played it right through again. It felt good, this self-pity, turning the knife in the wound. Better than numbness. At least she could feel something and put a name to it.

But the wound was not painful enough. It needed to be burning, throbbing, filling her consciousness. She went into the library adjoining Charlie's office, unlocked the door of the antique rosewood cabinet and hauled out an armful of photo albums. She took them back into the living room, put the record on again and flicked through the albums.

Their wedding day, Charlie as debonair as James Bond in his suit and Eva in her ivory gown, as sweet and rosy as a doll on a wedding cake. Charlie teaching her to ski in Switzerland on their honeymoon, posing on the deck of the boat on their Rhine River Cruise, lounging on a picnic rug in a bushy glade, nuzzling Eva's ear as she was getting something out of the picnic basket. The two of them at a function she'd long forgotten, Charlie's arm around her waist, squeezing her into him as if to say, 'This is my woman.' Emerging from a dazzling aqua ocean, Charlie's head turned towards her and she smiling at him. A knowing, confident smile, a woman sure of her man.

She threw the last photo album on the floor, got up and swiped the needle off the record. She wrenched open the French doors and stepped out on to the deck. The moon was floating, pale yellow in the inky sky, suspended like a lost balloon. She threw her head back and shouted. 'Father, wherever you are, take me back. Give me back my old life!'

Her voice was shrill in the stillness, skipping over the water. She stared at the moon, as if he might be there.

'Please!'

She waited for a thunderclap, the roar of the wind, anything to signify that he'd heard her. But there was only the sky and the moon and the water and the brisk night wrapping itself around her.

●●●

She went into the walk-in pantry in the kitchen and took down a large jar of castor sugar from the back of the top shelf. She emptied out half the jar into a bowl, put her hand in and pulled out the bag of coke Ray had got for her. Even if Charlie suspected that she'd obtained more cocaine, he'd be unlikely to empty every jar in the pantry looking for it.

She took it into the ensuite and did a line on the marble bench top. Within minutes it had kicked in, that beautiful sweet release, the heaven after the hell. She put the bag back in the sugar jar, poured the sugar over it again making sure it wasn't visible, and put the jar back in the pantry.

After a quick shower, she dressed and made up her face. Wig, auburn pageboy. Her favourite; she had quite a collection now. Cleopatra eyes. Luscious, red, blow-you lips. Short black cocktail dress, hugging her body like cling wrap, suspender belt and black stockings, fuck-me heels. Just wearing a suspender belt made her feel sexy. Classy with slutty undertones. Forget the classy.

She called a cab, giving the address of the house three doors down, where it picked her up. The driver, an olive-skinned man in a turban looked her up and down out of the corner of his eye as she got in.

'Where to, lady?' he asked in a heavy accent.

'The city, please. Where's a good nightclub?'

The driver pulled out on to the road and studied her in the rear view mirror.

'There are many. Depends what you want to do. Drink? Dance?'

Pick up men? The unsaid sentence floated in the air.

'Both.'

'The Silver Spoon is good. So I have heard.'

'The Silver Spoon it is, then.'

She relaxed and watched the world roll past her like scenery on a stage—shadows of faces in passing cars, the garishly-lit windows of office blocks, neon lights glaring over shops. Darkness and light. The lights were so rich and vibrant, always changing, she could marvel at them all night. But something was pulling her towards the dark like bats to the night sky. An urge so strong it had no regard for consequences. Even if it meant self-destruction.

The Silver Spoon was in an alley between two office blocks, a narrow doorway with a neon silver spoon perched on top. As she paid the cover charge to the attendant, a large Goth girl who looked bored, or possibly drugged, out of her mind, the relentless bass of an unrecognisable song boomed from upstairs.

Was this club going to be full of young trendies in baggy jeans, jerking away to hip hop? She walked up the stairs and breathed a sigh of relief. A live band was playing a Bon Jovi song and the clientele, from what she could discern in the dim lighting, seemed to be at least over thirty. She had underestimated the cab driver's ability to assess her needs.

She joined the crowd at the bar. The effects of the coke always lasted longer if she was drinking as well, so she ordered a double bourbon and soda. The stronger the drink, the better. The place was packed, with the sort of hard-living crowd that liked to start coasting into the week-end on a Wednesday night. She found a square inch of space to stand, beside a group of young girls, on the default teenage setting of rapid, inane chatter, hair flicking and looking around to see who was noticing.

She watched the lead singer of the band in black singlet and crotch-tight jeans, leaping around the stage in imitation of Jon Bon Jovi, muscular shoulders gleaming in the spotlight. Eva imagined licking the sweat off them, her tongue moving down and across to the tufts of chest hair sprouting from the top of his singlet. She felt a spasm of tension in her pussy.

It was what she loved most about cocaine, every physical sensation was amplified as if someone had turned up the volume button. She stared at the singer, willing him to look at her, but he was too busy leering at the group of girls on the dance floor shaking their bums and tits at him.

'Can I buy you a drink?' someone shouted in her ear. She turned to see a woolly haired guy, probably in his thirties, in jeans and t-shirt grinning at her, revealing a mouthful of crooked teeth. It looked like her chances of attracting the Jon Bon Jovi pretender were slim; it never hurt to have a reserve.

'Thanks, a bourbon and soda, please.'

He disappeared into the crowd and came back after a few minutes with two bourbons. He handed her the drink. 'A woman who likes the hard stuff, eh?'

'You bet, baby,' she said, with arched brow and suggestive smile.

His eyes lit up and she could almost see the thought bubble above his head. 'I've struck it lucky tonight!'

'I'm Archie.'

'Caroline,' Eva replied.

'So what are you doing here all on your own, Caroline? Your friends deserted you?'

Eva smiled. 'Not at all. I just wanted to come out on my own, you meet more people.'

'You've met me, that's a start. Wanna dance?'

Eva looked at the dance floor, bodies jammed together in a bumping, jerking mass. She hadn't been nightclubbing since she was a teenager and the prospect of attempting to dance with a drink in one hand and her evening bag swinging over her shoulder, was not enticing.

She shook her head. 'No thanks, I'm not a dancer.'

'Me neither. Let's split.'

Eva hesitated. The singer was prancing up and down the stage to the strains of *You Give Love a Bad Name*, although he was more shouting than singing it. His jeans had slid down, revealing the top of his underpants. Not a good look, but he did have a nice arse. She imagined herself digging her fingernails into the firm, rounded flesh.

'You fancy him?' Archie asked. He leaned closer, mouth warm on her ear. 'He's a player. Got women everywhere, including a wife. I heard he's got one of those diseases, you know, like VD.'

His face was deadpan, but his eyes glinted with mischief, like a naughty schoolboy. 'A guy I know told me about a party that's on. Lots of piss and candy. Wanna come?'

What the hell. She wasn't going to hang around and try to compete for the attention of Mr Pretend Bon Jovi. Often the good looking ones turned out to be duds in bed. This one at least might turn out to be fun; if not, she'd make it fun.

'Okay,' she said.

'Hang on, I'll just go get the address.'

She watched him as he pushed his way through the crowd to a beefy man in denim, with a row of eyebrow rings on his right eyebrow. They exchanged a few words, then he returned and said, 'It's in Sydenham.'

They took a cab to the address. In another twenty years Sydenham, like many suburbs in the inner west, would become gentrified and the home of the upwardly mobile middle class, but now it was the province of the low income and welfare recipients, shabby and run-down.

The apartment was in a block of sad-faced apartments in a dead-end street full of similar apartments. As Eva got out of the taxi, she was assailed by an aroma of stale urine, burnt rubber and cooking oil. The party was in the front apartment. Raucous laughter and giggles wove through the head banging music and party-goers spilled out the front door and on to the footpath.

Archie paid the taxi driver, took her hand and led her across the road. They pushed their way through the crowd on the stairs and into the living room, thick with marijuana fumes and crammed with people shouting over the music.

'Wait here,' Archie shouted. 'I'll go get us a drink.'

The apartment had the same air of hopelessness as Ray's, though unlike Ray, the owners had made no attempt at homeliness—ripped upholstery on the couch and chairs, discoloured carpet which may have once been beige, mould-stained walls, bare except for a giant painting of a black swastika on a red background along one wall.

Eva positioned herself in a corner behind a group of scruffy, hairy-faced guys in dirty jeans who looked like extras from a Mad Max movie. In the middle of the room four women in jeans and midriff tops were dancing manically to the tribal beat of the music, wiggling their hips and butts to an appreciative male audience. Bare midriffs rotated and wobbled, belly button jewels glinted in the light.

Eva's mind went back to her teenage years, to parties in a farmer's barn or in the house of a school friend whose parents were away, which she'd sneaked out to while her mother was on the late cleaning shift. Music, dope, dancing, sex, glorious escape for one night until the bleak, claustrophobic reality of her life seeped back in with the breaking dawn the next day.

She smiled, soaking in a bath of warm nostalgia. These were her people. Her tribe. This could have been her apartment and her party if she hadn't met Charlie. And it could have been Charlie's as well, if he hadn't had the relentless drive to slough off the past like dead skin and create a new self. She tried to imagine his reaction if he were here now. He would have refused to come inside the house, probably wouldn't have got out of the car. He thought he'd escaped his past. But did you ever really escape?

One of the men in the group spied her and moved back beside her. Shaved head, torn, sleeveless t-shirt, forearms like tree trunks, every inch covered in tattoos. Reeking of after-shave, dope and alcohol.

'Hullo, lovely, where did you spring from?'

Eva smiled. 'A cloud of fairy dust.'

He grinned. 'And I'm the big bad goblin.'

'Pleased to meet you, big bad goblin.'

Archie appeared at her side, and handed her a can of bourbon and Coke.

'And this is the handsome prince, come to save me from the big bad goblin,' Eva said.

'Pity about that,' the man said, eyeing Archie. 'If you need rescuing from the handsome prince, I'll be here.'

'What was that all about?' Archie said as he steered her by the elbow through the living room, down a hallway, and onto a back deck, which overlooked a small, overgrown courtyard. A couple stood near the rubbish bin, lips locked, hands frantically exploring each other, obviously not concerned about the pungent ambience.

'Nothing that a handsome prince has to worry about,' she said. She took a swig of her drink. Archie leaned forward and gave her a soft, full kiss on the lips that made her tingle all over, then dug into his jeans pocket and held out his hand. In it were two small pink tablets. 'Want some candy?'

She shook her head. She'd taken the odd ecstasy pill as a teenager, but she had no desire to do so now. Mixing it with coke was probably not a good idea.

'Seriously?' Archie said. 'You strike me as a party animal.'

'I'm already high enough.'

'Yeah, what on?'

'Coke.' She regretted it as soon as she said it. It immediately set her apart and she wanted to blend in.

Archie raised his eyebrows. 'Whoa! Do you have a sugar daddy?'

'Something like that.' To change the subject she said, 'Do you want to go inside and dance?"

Archie popped two of the pills, put the other two back in his pocket and she led him back into the living room. They stood on the fringes of the dancing girls, Archie shuffling unenthusiastically until Eva could stand it no longer and launched herself into the group of girls.

She stomped and swayed her hips and threw out her chest to the accompaniment of shouts and whistles. The other girls made way for her, grinning and high-fiving her. She was aware of only her body and the beat of the music, they were as one, and the beat was the heartbeat of life and the universe and God, and this was all she ever needed and wanted, to feel at one with God.

Then Archie joined her, bumping her hips, grabbing her by the waist and swinging her round. He put his hand down the front of her dress and rolled the nipples of both breasts between his fingers until they were erect.

Then he slipped the straps of her dress off her shoulders and rolled it down to her waist, and there she was dancing topless. She felt free and uninhibited, like the first time she'd swum topless. A chorus of whistles and cheers went up. Hands reached out, grasping and groping her breasts but she didn't care. She was no longer Mrs Charles Dennehy, but Eva Stewart, daughter of Gerald, gambler, wife deserter and breaker of promises, and Coral Stewart, struggling single mother and pill popper, whose life was a parody of her firmly held belief that the meek would inherit the earth. And it was right that she, Eva, was dancing topless, drunk and high, in a room full of strangers. They loved her and that was all that mattered.

A couple of the other girls, obviously wanting their share of attention, also threw off their midriff tops and jiggled their breasts at the crowd.

'Show us your pussy!' yelled a raucous voice amid another chorus of cheers. One of the topless girls, a chunky blonde, wriggled out of her jeans, throwing them into the crowd, and continued dancing in a pair of white see-through knickers.

'She's no natural blonde!' someone called out.

The other topless girl, petite with bright red dyed hair and tattooed arms, peeled herself out of her jeans to reveal a skimpy g-string and small, perfectly shaped buttocks like bap rolls.

A chant started up. 'Take 'em off! Take 'em off!'

Archie rolled Eva's dress right down to her feet and she stepped gracefully out of it and now she was just in her G-string, suspender belt, stockings and heels. Hands were all over her body, rough, pinching and probing. And then somehow the big, bad goblin had pushed his way in and was dancing close to her. As quick as a breath he stuck his hand down the front of her g-string and began to finger her. Her pussy tingled, then Archie appeared, pushed the big bad goblin aside and grabbed her hand.

'Come on,' he said roughly.

He dragged her out of the room to a chorus of cries of 'Come back! Show us yer pussy!' He led her to the back porch, down the stairs to the courtyard and over to the corner in front of the garbage bins.

The other couple had disappeared. He slammed his mouth on top of hers, his hand in her g-string and fingers probing inside her, then as one they tumbled to the ground, Eva underneath him. The grass was cold and damp and prickly on her back. Archie unzipped his jeans, pulled them down and yanked her g-string down to her ankles. He climbed on top and they bucked together to a hard, fierce rhythm as Eva frantically stroked her slippery nub. The brutal beat of the music blaring out from inside was for them, an accompaniment to their performance. Eva cried out as she climaxed and Archie followed, juddering on top of her.

He hauled himself off her, pulled his jeans up and zipped them up. He looked down at her as she lay spreadeagled on the grass, her g-string bunched at her ankles. She was still wearing her high heeled sandals, but her stockings had come unhooked from her suspender belt and had slid down her legs.

'You're one hell of a sexy chick,' he said. 'Want another drink?'

She felt tired and heavy-limbed, the cocaine buzz was wearing off. It was time to go; one more drink for the road. 'Thanks.'

She scrambled up, shivering, suddenly realising how cold it was, yanked up her g-string and stockings then remembered her dress was inside. She followed Archie back up the stairs and into the living room, where half a dozen girls were now dancing in just their knickers, swivelling and jiggling in a striptease parody.

'I'll be back,' Archie said. Eva looked around for her dress and found it on the floor next to the couch, occupied by a bunch of girls who stared at her, glassy-eyed and giggling. Eva picked up the dress. It was wet, someone had spilled a drink on it. She hoped it was a drink. She slipped it on over her head. It was clammy against her skin, making her shiver again.

'You look much hotter with it off.' The big bad goblin was beside her again, beer in hand, and a wolfish gleam in his eyes. He slid his arm around her waist and put his mouth to her ear. 'How about we finish off what we started before your boyfriend rudely interrupted us?'

Eva was about to fob him off when she realised she didn't have her evening bag. She cast her mind back—it was hanging on its long chain over her shoulder when she'd started dancing. It must have fallen off in the melee.

'Have you seen my evening bag?' she said. 'Black diamante with a long chain.'

'I haven't and you probably won't either. Someone's probably hocking it as we speak.' He cupped her breast in his other hand and circled her nipple with his thumb through her dress. 'Don't worry about it, it'll turn up. Or not.'

Eva pulled his hand off her breast and wriggled out of his grasp. 'Sorry, but I have to find it.'

'Prick teasing bitch,' he yelled at her retreating back.

She pushed her way through the mass of bodies, eyes on the floor, ignoring the lewd comments and groping hands. She bumped into Archie bearing two cans of bourbon and coke. He held one out to her and she shook her head, pushing straight past him. She searched the whole apartment, interrupting two girls groping each other in the bathroom and a group of men smoking a bong in one of the bedrooms. Her queries were met with a blank stare or a shrug—they were all too off their faces to notice or care.

She let out a half sob. It wasn't so much the hundred dollars in her bag she was concerned about as her credit cards and keys to get into the house.

Archie was beside her again, still holding her drink, brow creased in annoyance. 'What's up?'

'Nothing.' She could cancel her credit cards. Getting into the house without her keys was the problem.

'Is there a phone in this house?'

'I don't fucking know.'

This heaving mass of flesh was closing in on her. It was stifling. 'I'm going home. Thanks for bringing me.'

'Hey, what's your phone number?' Archie yelled after her as she made for the front door, but she pretended not to hear him. Once out on the street, she took a deep breath, filling her lungs with fresh air. Fresher than inside, anyhow.

She looked around, hoping Archie hadn't decided to follow her. There was no sign of him; anyway, there were plenty of other willing candidates if he wanted another fuck. In the dim pool of streetlights she could just make out a phone box a couple of blocks away. She started down the footpath towards it.

The wind was biting, cold for a spring night, and she broke out in a spasm of shivering. Her shawl was also in her evening bag, though it was flimsy and wouldn't have provided much protection against the cold. Fashion before comfort was usually her motto; but she didn't care about that now.

She slipped off her sandals, unfastened her stockings from her suspender belt, and stuffed them into her sandals. The concrete path was rough under her bare feet as she walked gingerly along, her sandals swinging from her hands. Her crotch was damp, matching her dress. What she would give to be in 2015 with a mobile phone. Cars sped by, faces in their windows looking back at her. If anyone had stopped to offer her a lift, she would have accepted it, despite the dangers. But no-one did, and after an eternity, she reached the phone box and went inside.

Please God, don't let this phone be vandalised. The phone box smelt of stale urine, and on the shelf below the phone was a Yellow Pages phone book with ripped pages coming loose, and a pile of cigarette butts beside it. She picked up the receiver and heard the dial tone. *Thank-you God. Even though I don't believe in you.* She made a reverse charge call to Helga's number.

Please Helga, be at home. The second prayer of the night. She checked her watch. Eleven thirty. If Helga wasn't out partying, she'd be in bed.

'Hello?'

It was Sol's voice, annoyed and wary at this late call.

'Will you accept a reverse charge call from Eva Dennehy?' said the operator.

Silence. 'Yes.'

'Go ahead, please.'

'Hi, Sol, sorry to call so late. Is Helga there?'

'She's at her sister's in Melbourne, she's due back tomorrow.'

Shit. Eva remembered Helga mentioning a visit to her sister. She'd planned to ask Helga to phone for a taxi to pick her up and take her back to Helga's house for the night and then drop her home in the morning at nine o'clock when Vera their cleaner arrived, so she could let Eva in. Asking Sol to do so wasn't even an option. The last thing Eva wanted to do was turn up on her own doorstep at this time of night begging Charlie to let her in. And who knew if he would even be home?

'What's going on, Eva?'

'Nothing. Sorry to disturb you.'

She hung up. What now? There was no-one else she could ask for help. Frances and Diana had continued to maintain their distance from her and desperate as she was, turning up on either doorstep in the middle of the night dressed like a hooker with her tale of a stolen handbag would do nothing to revive their friendship. The last thing she wanted to do was the only course of action left.

She left the phone box and continued walking, scanning the road for taxis. She'd hailed four occupied taxis and walked another two blocks, past shadowed apartments, an enclave of neon-lit shops and a noisy pub, when a taxi finally pulled over.

She opened the door and slid in. The odour of onions overpowered the floral air freshener. The driver looked as if he'd eaten a lot of hamburgers in his life. His eyes met hers in the rear view mirror.

'Where to?'

She gave him her address.

'How are you paying?' The driver had obviously noticed her lack of handbag.

'I can get money once I'm home.'

'Listen lady, if I had a dollar for every time I'd heard that story I wouldn't be driving this shitbox on wheels, that's for sure.'

'I'm sorry but it's true. I had my handbag stolen earlier tonight and this is the only way I can get home.'

He swivelled his head around and looked her up and down, dishevelled and bare-foot with her shoes in her hands. 'And you live at Point Piper?'

'Look, I'm Eva Dennehy, Charles Dennehy's wife. Surely you've heard of him?' She tried to curtail the note of desperation in her voice. 'I can't prove it, because I haven't got any ID on me.'

He continued to stare at her. She whipped her wig off and fluffed her hair out into its usual bob. Recognition dawned on the driver's face. 'Yeah, I do know you. You're the one who got done for driving under the influence of cocaine.'

'That's right.'

'That's different, then, you're a celebrity.' His tone was heavy with sarcasm, but he pulled out into the traffic.

'Maybe you could pay me in coke.'

He caught her eye and grinned at her in the rear view mirror, pleased with his joke. He then went into a spiel about a woman he'd read about who'd been addicted to coke and ended up with a collapsed nose. She'd died on the operating table while undergoing plastic surgery to reconstruct it. Eva swallowed her irritation and looked out the window.

Her home was in complete darkness, except for the usual light over the security gate. Her key to the security gate was in her handbag, along with the front door key. She knew in her bones that Charlie wouldn't be there, was probably in bed with Veronika right at this moment.

'I haven't got my key, so I'll call my husband on the security intercom,' she said as she opened the car door. She felt him watching her as she pressed the button and said into the speaker, 'Charlie, are you there?' She repeated it a couple of times. No reply.

She opened the car door and poked her head in. 'He's not answering. I was sure he'd be at home.'

The driver sighed. 'Listen, lady, I mean Mrs Dennehy—'

Eva interrupted. 'Can you trust me to pay you tomorrow? I promise I'll pay you cash first thing, I can come to the depot or whatever is convenient for you. I'll pay you double for the inconvenience.'

The driver paused as if considering the worth of the double pay option, then shrugged. 'I should have known better than to trust a woman, and a rich one at that. I'll be at the depot in the city at nine am tomorrow. If you're not there on the dot with the money, I'll file a report with police and you'll be charged with fare evasion.'

'Thanks, I appreciate that.'

'What are you doing to do now?'

'I don't know.'

She didn't fancy hanging around the gate in the dark waiting for Charlie to come home. He could be hours yet.

'Is there a friend's house I can take you to?' the driver asked.

She thought of Ray—he'd be overjoyed to give her the money for the cab fare and a bed for the night. But his band played at a number of clubs and he was more than likely doing a gig tonight.

'I have a friend who lives at Ashfield, but he may not be home.'

The driver drummed his fingers on the steering wheel. 'Time is money for me, as I'm sure you don't have a clue about. I don't have time to be driving you all over the city.'

There was only one other person in the world who'd be glad to see her now. It was that, or find a park bench for the rest of the night.

'Can you drop me at the Downtown Club in the city?'

CHAPTER TWENTY-FOUR

'CAN I talk to Sniper? He's a friend of mine,' Eva told the cashier at the front door of Downtown, whose heavy-handed eye makeup made her look like a raccoon.

The cashier studied her with nonchalance. Did she look as if she'd just had a roll in the grass? She was still bare-legged but she'd put her heels back on, stuffing her stockings into her G-String. She tugged at her dress, pulling it down over her thighs and brushed an imaginary hair from her forehead, momentarily forgetting she was wearing a wig.

'Sniper has a friend?' the cashier said. 'You gotta be kidding me.'

'Is he in?'

'He's working the bar. One of the guys didn't turn up for work.'

Sniper on the bar. That would set a new benchmark for customer service.

'Could he spare just a moment? Tell him it's Eva, it's urgent.'

'Just a minute.' The girl took the cover charge from a couple who had just walked in and gave them change. 'Why don't you just pay your ten dollars and you can go in and find him yourself?'

Eva wasn't going to admit she had no money. The cashier would tell Sniper, and there was a good chance he'd refuse to see her, just to be perverse.

'I'd rather not because I only want to see him for a couple of minutes.'

The cashier opened her mouth.

'Look, I was serious when I said I was a friend. If Sniper knew you'd refused to tell him I was here, he'd be very angry.'

The cashier's expression changed. An angry Sniper was not a welcome thought. She picked up the receiver of the phone on her desk and dialled a number. 'Can you tell Sniper that an Eva is here to see him? Says it's urgent.'

She waited, put the receiver down and jerked her thumb in the direction of the stairs. 'You can go up.'

It was well after midnight, the band had packed up, but the club was still humming. Ray Charles boomed out from the jukebox. At the bar, two and three deep, Sniper and two other attendants were flat out. He looked almost respectable in a white long sleeved shirt with his hair tied back in a ponytail.

Eva joined the queue at the bar in front of Sniper and watched him as he pulled beers, made spirits and poured wines, with the clean, quick expertise of experience. She knew he'd seen her there and when it was her turn, she leaned forward so that her cleavage was staring him in the face and put on a seductive smile. 'How about I wait in your room for you and we can have some fun when you've finished here? '

Eva could almost see the wheels turning in his head. Did she have an ulterior motive for fronting up and suggesting sex when she was the one being blackmailed into it? But then his face broadened into a grin and he fished around in the pocket of his trousers and pulled out a bunch of keys. He slid a big square key off the keyring and handed it to her.

Eva flashed him another smile, took the key and made her way through the back exit to Sniper's bedsit. Whatever doubts Sniper had about her invitation had obviously been overcome by his desire to fuck her. Men really did think with their dicks, and thank God for that.

Eva unlocked the door and walked into a suffocating cloud of stale cigarette smoke, which immediately turned her fuzzy head into a full blown headache. A quick look around confirmed she was alone. Sweat-stained sheets were thrown back on the bed with a pile of clothes on top. On a small table beside it was an ashtray overflowing with cigarette butts. The table in the kitchen was stacked with empty beer bottles and cans of spirit mixers. The detritus of another party.

She went into the bathroom and looked in the cracked mirror. Her lipstick and mascara were smudged and there was a streak of dirt across her cheek. She took off her wig. Her head was sweaty and she didn't need it here. She ripped off a piece of toilet paper from the roll beside the toilet and wiped her face clean. She still looked like shit. Her nose was dripping, so she tore off another piece of toilet paper and wiped it. Cocaine downers were the pits—alcohol was the only thing that helped. Or more coke. Did Sniper have a stash somewhere here?

No time to look for it now. She was going to take this opportunity to search for more evidence to link Sniper and Tommy to Charlie, or all of them to the McCarthys. It occurred to her that perhaps Pete or one of his colleagues had already forced their way into this place and searched it. But she had to do something; waiting for him to dig up something was driving her crazy.

She went into the kitchen and opened drawers and cupboards. Nothing out of the ordinary—a few pieces of mismatched crockery and cutlery, tinned food, instant coffee and tea bags. Basic cooking utensils, battered frypan, toaster and jug. She went through the rubbish bin under the sink, which yielded nothing more than empty fast food wrappings, used teabags, banana peels and an empty baked beans tin. In the small, rust-stained fridge was an open carton of milk, half a bottle of orange juice and a sliver of mouldy cheese.

In the bathroom she checked the shower and behind the toilet. What was she looking for? Another piece of paper with numbers on it? That was a fluke, not likely to happen again. That made her think of pockets. Search the pockets in the clothes strewn on the bed. She went into the living room. Tommy stood there, pointing a gun at her.

Eva screamed.

'Don't bother screaming, no-one can hear you,' Tommy said.

Eva's heart was beating so hard she could scarcely breathe. She opened her mouth to speak. Nothing came out.

'So, Mrs Dennehy, to what do we owe the pleasure of this visit?' Cold, unblinking stare, steady hand, gun aimed right at her chest. His grandfatherly aura must have been a figment of her imagination.

Eva swallowed. 'I'm waiting for Sniper. He gave me the key.'

'And you thought you'd do a little exploring while you were waiting?'

Eva looked him in the eye. 'I was looking for some coke.'

'A plausible story, but I don't buy it.'

'It's the truth.'

'Whatever you're looking for, you won't find it here. That's a job better left to your private dick.'

No point in denying it. Pete hadn't been as careful in his investigations as he thought.

'I've been hearing rumours of your private dick getting the dirt on me and Sniper. And your husband.' He shook his head, making tut-tut noises. 'Disloyalty in a woman is so unattractive. I thought you were better than that, Mrs Dennehy, but underneath your glamorous exterior you're just a calculating slut, like every other woman. With the exception of my wife, of course.'

Eva held his gaze and said nothing, not wanting to give him the satisfaction of a reaction.

'I'll give you a warning, and consider yourself lucky to get it. Call your private dick off, before things get so hot he gets himself fried to a crisp, like those doughnuts he's so fond of. And it's not only me and Sniper you need to worry about, it's Mr McCarthy himself. He's a very private person, and he gets very upset if he finds out that someone's been poking around in his affairs. And upsetting Mr McCarthy can have fatal consequences.'

He waited as if expecting a response, but when it wasn't forthcoming, he turned and strode out.

•••

Her head was pulsing and her mouth was dry and gritty. Nausea was rising from her gut. She threw back the sheets, raced to the bathroom and just made it in time, retching and spewing into the toilet. She rinsed her mouth, avoided looking at herself in the mirror. Just another hangover. She'd made inroads into Sniper's bourbon as she waited for him to finish at the bar, drowning out the menace of Tommy's warning.

She returned to the bed, where Sniper was bunched in a heap on his side, facing away from her. The sheet had slipped off his back, exposing a narrow yet muscular canvas for an intricate network of tattoos she'd noticed before but never looked at closely. A jungle vine with a snake peering through it. A soldier with a rifle, eyes dark and menacing. A Chinaman in a coolie hat. Words: Fuck the world. Courage. Mateship. Death. Vietnam 6 RAR 1966 - 1968.

She could only faintly recall the night, a blur of sweat and greasy skin, fingers, mouths and tongues, Sniper exhorting her to 'tell me you're a dirty whore!' Making her repeat it so many times she was screaming it at the end. Falling into a deep sleep almost straight afterwards and being woken up, it seemed, just a couple of minutes later, though it was obviously longer, and doing it all again. She was too drunk to resist and why would she anyway? This was the price she paid for a bed.

She picked up her watch from the floor. Ten o'clock. She was supposed to be at the cab company an hour ago with her payment. The driver had probably already lodged the report with the police. So what? Evading a fare was kindergarten stuff compared to what she'd been through. Too bad about the cab driver not getting his money, but that was the risk he'd taken.

She pulled on her g-string and her dress and tiptoed around to Sniper's side of the bed. She watched him for a couple of minutes to make sure he was genuinely asleep, then picked up his jeans from the floor and slipped his wallet out of the pocket. It was fat with fifty dollar bills. She slid one out; he wouldn't miss it. She only needed enough for the cab ride home. Vera would be there cleaning and would let her in.

●●●

There was a note on the kitchen bench. 'Eva please call me straight away. I've reported you as missing to the police.'

Why the hell did he do that? All part of the concerned husband act and the grand plan to make her look like the culpable party in the inevitable marriage breakdown.

Vera was watching her reading the note. 'Mr Dennehy is very worried about you.'

'I'm sure.'

Vera had registered no surprise at Eva's appearance when she opened the front door to her, her broad Filipino face creased in smiles, welcoming Eva in as if it were her own home. In the ten years that Vera had been cleaning for them, she had been unfailingly cheerful and unflappable.

'He was calling the police when I arrived.' She was still hovering. 'Thanks, Vera,' Eva said brusquely. Vera hurried away with her dusting rag.

Eva went into the bedroom, shut the door so Vera couldn't eavesdrop, picked up the phone and dialled the number of Charlie's office.

'It's Eva,' she said in response to Ainsley's usual greeting. 'Can you give a message to Charlie that I'm home?'

'Mr Dennehy instructed that if you rang I was to put you straight through,' she said. Then Charlie was on the line.

'Eva, where have you been?' His voice was strained.

'What the fuck do you care?'

'What's that supposed to mean?'

'It means exactly what I said. Do you care where I've been and what I'm doing? Or is it just that your obedient little wife is not toeing the line anymore? That's really it, isn't it?'

'I can't discuss this now.'

'Of course not. We don't want anyone in the Dennehy Corporation to think that Charles Dennehy can't control his wife.'

'I'll see you tonight,' Charlie said and hung up.

Eva slammed the receiver down and sank on to the bed. Her head was still sore and she was trembling uncontrollably—from anger or fear she didn't know. Or desire. She craved a hit of coke, wanted it so badly she could feel the numbness in her nose and taste its bitterness in her throat. But it would be risky while Vera was still in the house. And she had another phone call to make.

Just as she was about to lift the receiver, the phone rang. 'Eva, it's Pete Homer.'

'Pete! I was just about to ring you.'

'I have some news.'

'I have some news too. What's yours?'

Her words were almost drowned out by the roar of what sounded like a bus.

'Where are you ringing from?' she asked.

'A public phone box down the road. I have a suspicion my office phone line is being tapped. I've pulled it apart and can't find anything, but I don't want to take any risks.'

'What's the news?'

'I've found records, or least my computer hacker friend has found them, of your husband and a man called Solomon Berman, depositing large amounts of money via an intermediary into a bank account in Liechtenstein, which, as you may know, is where a lot of illegal money is hidden. The account is not in their own names, of course, they've created a shelf company, which is why it's taken so long to find it.'

So her suspicions about Sol being involved were right. The bastard. How dare he look down on her with his eat-my-shit attitude when all the time he was peddling drugs?

'Are you there, Eva?'

'Yes. So what does that have to do with the numbers in Sniper's wallet?'

'That's the bank account used by Sniper and Tommy to deposit money they owe Charlie. It's also an offshore bank account and the money is then transferred to Charlie and Solomon's account. It's a very sophisticated system where money is constantly being shuffled from one account to another under all sorts of company names to prevent authorities tracking them. I'm guessing that Charlie's mate Andrew Thomason may have been instrumental in helping them set it all up.'

'And the money that Tommy and Sniper transfer to Charlie's account—I assume that's for drugs?'

'It's not evident from the financial transactions alone, but as I also have photos of Charlie in Melbourne with Nick D'Angelo, one of McCarthy's henchmen, on two occasions—in a motor cycle sales yard and outside Nick's house, it's a fair assumption that the money has come from drugs. We can leave it up to the police to get the rest of the evidence.'

'The police?"

Pete was breathing heavily. 'Eva, I'm pretty sure there's someone tailing me, and last night the phone rang at home and a man threatened me with death if I didn't stop poking around, as he put it. For my own safety, I need to hand that information to the police, as soon as possible.'

'Can you give me a copy of it?'

'Absolutely not—you'd be endangering your own life by having it. I can keep a copy to show you and then I'll shred it. I've got to go out on another job now. Can you call around tomorrow morning at ten o'clock?'

'I'll be there.'

'And what was your news?'

'I guess you already know it.' She told him about Tommy's warning.

'Why were you speaking to Tommy?'

'It's a long story. I'll tell you tomorrow.'

CHAPTER TWENTY-FIVE

THE steaming water, so hot it was painful, pounded her body as she stood under the shower, scrubbing away all traces of Archie and Sniper, as if doing so would obliterate them from her memory as well.

With Pete taking his information to the police, her plan to threaten Charlie with going to the police if he left her, had just blown up in her face. Why the hell couldn't Pete have been more careful? If Tommy knew about his investigations, chances were that Charlie did too. And Sol. The warning he'd given her at the cocktail party about sticking to what she was good at now took on an ominous portent.

There was only one course of action left—she had to play her hand now. Confront Charlie about Veronika, his plans to leave her and his illegal pursuits. Threaten to go to the police with her information, saying nothing about Pete's plans to do so. Better still, threaten to tip off the media. They didn't need evidence to start slinging mud.

She turned off the shower, stepped out and wrapped her shining pink body in a large, fluffy towel. She was still shaky and nauseous. This was some hangover. The coke hidden in the castor sugar jar still called out to her in honeyed tones, but she didn't dare succumb. She had to have her wits about her to confront Charlie. She lay on the bed in her towel and closed her eyes, just for a short nap.

She woke up with a start and looked at the bedside clock. Four o'clock. Shit, she'd slept for over four hours. Not that it had done her any good, she still felt heavy-limbed and woolly-headed. The front door slammed. Charlie was home early, for once. Footsteps trod down the hallway. He stood in the doorway of the bedroom looking down at her.

'Sorry to wake you. You must be tired after your big night out.'

She sat up. 'I'm sorry if I worried you, I lost my handbag—'

'I'm not interested in your feeble excuses. I've just come home to tell you I'm leaving you.'

'What?' It came out as a whisper.

'I'm leaving you. This can hardly be a surprise. I don't know what's going on with you, but I can no longer trust you or rely on you. You need to see a shrink.'

'I'm not crazy!' She sprang up from the bed, securing the towel around her. 'Anyway you can't leave me. I have incriminating information about you. About your association with the McCarthys and your off shore bank accounts. If you leave me I'll take it to the police.'

There was no surprise in his stony expression. 'Go ahead. I know you've got a private dick on my tail. Whatever information you have is hardly incriminating because it's completely untrue. It's just further evidence that you've lost your mind.'

He went over to the wardrobe, took out a suitcase and began to methodically pluck clothes from hangers and shelves and pack them neatly in the suitcase.

'I'm as sane as you are. I'm on to your tricks of trying to make me look like the bad guy, so you can run off with that smarmy Italian bitch and play happy families with her.'

Charlie continued to pack as if she hadn't spoken. She strode over to him and slapped his face. 'Don't fucking ignore me! The least you can do is talk to me, you owe me that.'

He whirled around and grabbed her by the shoulders. 'I owe you nothing! And there's nothing to talk about, get that into your drug-fuddled head.'

'Get your hands off me!' she hissed.

Charlie dropped his hands.

'You'll change your mind after I go to the police. But by then it will be too late. And I can guarantee they'll take my evidence a lot more seriously than you do.'

'You do whatever you want. It has no impact on me.'

He resumed his packing, taking his sky blue Ralph Lauren polo shirt from its hanger and folding it. The one she'd bought him on their Caribbean holiday because it made him look younger. No doubt Veronika would like it too.

Was his nonchalance about her going to the police just an act? Was he calling her bluff, thinking she wouldn't do it? Perhaps he had friends in high places and was confident of their protection. Or the friends were involved as well.

Charlie went into the ensuite and returned with his toiletries bag. He stuffed it into the side pocket of his suitcase. The snap of the locks as he closed it was like a punch to her chest. He was really leaving her.

He picked up the suitcase. 'My lawyers will be in touch. I want you out in two weeks.'

Tears streamed down her face and turned into sobs. 'You can't throw me out. This is my house as much as yours.' She followed him down the hallway. 'Can't we at least talk about this?'

The towel had fallen off and she was standing there naked, snivelling, bubbles blowing out of her nose. She was pathetic, she knew it, but she couldn't help herself. He turned and looked at her with such contempt she instinctively cowered.

'Look at yourself, Eva! You're addicted to cocaine, you're on your way to becoming an alcoholic, you go out at night to God knows what sort of places and don't even bother coming home, and to top it off you've hired a private detective to try and dig up some dirt on me. Why would I want to be married to a woman like that?'

Then he was gone with a final, irrevocable slam of the front door.

●●●

The phone rang just as she was heading out the front door. She wasn't going to answer it, but rushed back at the last minute and picked up the receiver. It might be Charlie, changing his mind and prepared to talk to her, though her rational mind knew she was delusional to even think it.

'Mrs Dennehy, this is Sergeant Watson from Marrickville Police station. An evening bag was found in the front yard of an address in Barclay Rd, Sydenham. It has two credit cards in it in the name Eva Dennehy. I presume the bag is yours?'

'Yes, it was stolen. I've cancelled the credit cards.'

'Was there money in the bag as well?'

'A hundred dollars.'

'There's none in there now, whoever stole it obviously just wanted the cash. You can come in and pick it up any time you like.'

The cab driver was tooting his horn out the front. She hurried out, slamming the front door and security gate shut and slid into the back seat, giving the driver the address of Pete's office.

A classical piano piece burbled through the taxi's sound system but it failed to soothe her. She felt wrung out, as if she'd been through a rapid speed washing machine cycle. She'd tried to repair the ravages of the previous night, plastering on the make-up and putting 'tired eye' drops in her eyes, but she still looked exactly how she felt. When had the bags appeared under her eyes and her skin become so blotchy?

The events of the night flashed through her mind in a disjointed kaleidoscope. Getting high, donning a cocktail dress and stilettos. Arriving in the city and stepping out of the taxi feeling like a celebrity arriving at the Academy Awards, turning heads as she entered The Express, a cocktail and wine bar frequented by professionals, who pretended they were there to talk business but were really looking for sex without strings.

She was sick of grunge, she needed some class; smooth, shiny, buffed men who smelled of after-shave and talked about the stock market and real estate, even it was just an illusion, because the sex was the same.

She'd joined a table of lawyers as Nancy. She was wearing her jet black wig which didn't suit her complexion, but who cared? They certainly didn't. Ben, with whom she went home (a lawyer with six pack abs, that was a real find) was only interested in the parts of her body below her shoulders and they'd fucked in several positions before his girlfriend rang and said she was coming around. Eva was relieved, as she didn't want to spend the night in his soulless timber and glass apartment—it was like having sex in a department store.

She used his phone to call a cab and as she was leaving, Ben shoved a couple of fifty dollar notes in her hand. She looked at them and then at him.

'For your ride home,' he said.

She threw the notes back at him and slapped his face. 'How dare you! I'm not a prostitute and I don't need your money.' Then she stormed out the door.

Eva smiled now as she recalled him standing there, stunned, with his hand to his face. It was a decent slap and would come up as a bright red mark, which would need all his lawyerly gift of the gab to explain away to his girlfriend.

The driver let Eva off outside Pete's building, with instructions to pick her up again in half an hour. She called in at the cafe on the ground floor to buy a coffee to take up with her. The coffee she'd had at Pete's last time was too insipid for her taste. She needed a decent shot of caffeine—she'd hardly slept after she got home, the comedown from coke making her restless and agitated.

She ordered a double shot espresso, and glanced at the newspapers on top of the magazine rack. The headline of the Sun Herald leapt out at her. 'Millionaire's wife in another drug scandal.'

There was a photo of her and Charlie standing together at the opening of Dennehy Towers, both smiling into the camera, Charlie with his arm around her waist. Underneath it she read:

'Eva Dennehy,the wife of mining millionaire Charles Dennehy, is believed to have attended a party on Wednesday night in Sydenham, which was rife with illegal drugs. Police attended the premises just after midnight and arrested a number of people in possession of cannabis, amphetamines and ecstasy. Although Mrs Dennehy was not present at the time of the arrests, her handbag was found on the front lawn containing credit cards but no cash.

Mrs Dennehy was convicted in Sydney Central Local Court last month for Driving under the influence of a dangerous drug, cocaine, and is believed to be seeking admission to the Hope Valley Rehabilitation Centre, founded by her husband five years ago.'

She had to read the words several times before they sank in. Her mind and body were numb. The report could have been about a complete stranger. She'd already failed to stop Charlie from leaving her; she was immune to further disasters. She didn't even care about the blatant lie of her seeking admission to the rehab clinic. It was typical of the tabloids; they couldn't resist the irony of it. Any excuse to kick her when she was down. She didn't even know why she was still keeping her appointment with Pete, apart from a curiosity to see the incriminating evidence herself.

She took her coffee and went up in the lift to the first floor. As she entered Pete's office, Barbara was just putting down the receiver of the phone. Her face was taut with worry.

'Mrs Dennehy, sorry, Mrs Deakin, I haven't had time to ring you. Pete hasn't turned up this morning, and he knew he had an appointment with you. I've rung his home a number of times, but he's not answering, so I've just rung Helen, his ex-wife, who lives in the next suburb, and asked her if she could pop around to his home.'

A glacial chill struck Eva right to her core and she repressed the immediate unthinkable thought. Barbara's eyes filled with tears. 'Maybe he's had a heart attack or a stroke and he's there all alone,' she gulped. 'He's a sitting duck, but he doesn't seem to care. He loves his food and alcohol more than he cares about his health.'

Eva patted Barbara's hand. 'Try not to worry. You've done all you can. There might be a perfectly simple explanation.'

They were hollow words that rang false to Eva even as she said them. If only there were a simple explanation.

'Do you happen to know if he went to see the police yesterday?'

Barbara looked surprised. 'I don't know. He was out on a job all day yesterday, so he may have. Did he tell you he was going to the police?'

'He said he might,' Eva said. Then to forestall any further questioning, she said, 'Do you want me to stay for a while?'

Barbara shook her head, took a tissue from the box on her desk and blew her nose. 'I'm sure you've got better things to do than hang around here. I'll just wait here for Helen's call.'

CHAPTER TWENTY-SIX

EVA left, with Barbara promising to call her the minute she had any news. When the cab returned to pick her up, she asked the driver to take her to Marrickville Police Station. She retrieved her evening bag, thankfully not having to wait too long to identify it and sign the necessary paperwork, then returned home, a round trip of almost an hour. She breathed a sigh of relief when the cab driver told her the fare—she had just enough cash to cover it.

As she alighted from the cab, cameras flashed and several reporters appeared out of nowhere thrusting microphones at her.

'Mrs Dennehy, do you have any comment to make about the party at Sydenham? Were you taking drugs there? When are you going into rehab? Is it true that you and your husband have separated?'

'No fucking comment,' she said loudly, and pushing her way through them, she unlocked the security gate, ran down the front path, unlocked the front door and slammed it behind her. Let them get a headline out of that one—Millionaire's Wife Swears at Reporters.

The phone rang continuously, but she didn't answer it, surmising it would only be journalists, but listening to any answering machine messages in case it was Barbara with news of Pete. She was sinking into the black hole; even while it made her want to curl up and die, its familiarity was comforting. Several times she went to the kitchen and pulled the jar of castor sugar down from the top shelf. She was running low, only had enough for a couple more snorts. Maybe she should just finish it all off now and start again with a clean slate.

But something made her put it back. ‘Save it,’ a voice in her head said. Instead she went into the cellar, grabbed a bottle of champagne, uncorked it and poured herself a glass. She gulped it down. The phone rang again and she ignored it until she heard Helga's voice. 'Eva what the hell were you doing in Sydenham? Unless the story's a complete load of bull, which is quite likely. Eva please pick up the phone, if you don't I'm coming right over and I'm going to buzz your security phone until you—'

Eva was at the phone, picking up the receiver. 'Helga, don’t come over, there are reporters hanging around.’

‘All the more reason for me to come and rescue you. I have a plan—you wait in the garage for me, and I’ll pull up at the top of the driveway. As soon as you see me, open the security gate, run up the driveway, jump in and off we go. If we happen to run over any reporters in the process, all the better.’

Eva wasn’t in the mood for an outing, but she knew Helga would refuse to take no for an answer. She sighed. ‘Okay, see you shortly.’

Eva placed a stopper in the champagne bottle and put it in the fridge. She locked the house, grabbed her handbag and slipped out the rear door of the house. As she passed the swimming pool, pristine and inviting in the spring sunshine, Harry was lounging on a recliner, eating his lunch. He'd spent the morning vacuuming the pool, trimming the surrounding palm trees and scrubbing the outdoor furniture.

'Hullo, Mrs D! Beautiful day, isn't it? Soon be pool party time.'

'Yes, it will.' Except she wouldn't be here. Veronika would be holding fort, parading around in a tiny bikini, being the perfect, charming hostess, and all the same people would be here that she, Eva, and Charlie always invited, because they were all his friends. And no-one would care that she'd been replaced by a younger, sleeker model. Except maybe Helga.

Eva waved to Harry and hurried on to discourage any further conversation. She opened the garage door, and retrieved the remote control for the security gate from the console of her car, which had languished in the garage since it came back from the repairers, waiting for her to get her licence back. Next to it, Charlie's 1955 Rolls Royce, which he never drove since it was only for show, shone with ponderous self-importance.

Helga's Lotus pulled up at the top of the driveway, engine purring. Eva pressed the remote control button and the security gate slid open. She pressed the button to close the garage door and raced up the driveway. Helga leaned over and opened the passenger door.

The reporters were already clustered around as Eva jumped in. One of them thrust a microphone at her. 'Mrs Dennehy, were you taking drugs at the party in Sydenham? What did your husband say about it?'

Helga backed out into the road, causing the reporters to jump out of the way, the security gate slid shut and she took off with a mighty roar.

'What fun! Just like James Bond!'

Eva looked behind her. 'You can slow down now, they're not interested in a car chase.'

'Darling, this car doesn't know the meaning of slow.'

The top was down, Madonna warbling out of the car's CD player, the breeze ruffling their hair.

'Where are we going?' Eva asked, as Helga turned into New South Head Road.

'When was the last time you went on a picnic?'

'A long time ago.'

Once, going on a picnic was the thing she and Charlie most liked to do on a Sunday. They'd take off for a day's cruising around the Harbour on Charlie's yacht The High C, anchor at one of the secluded beaches and feast on seafood salad, chocolate dipped strawberries and a bottle of wine. The combination of the food and alcohol, being in the outdoors and the relaxed ambience usually resulted in a lovemaking session in the bushes; the public arena and the risk of being discovered, small though it was, adding an extra frisson of excitement. But Charlie hadn't had a Sunday free for forever—not since she'd started her new life.

'I've got a picnic hamper in the back,' Helga said. 'I thought we'd find a quiet beach somewhere and gorge ourselves with food and drink and commune with nature. It'll do you the world of good.'

The prospect of a couple of hours of feeling the sun on her skin, breathing in the salty air and not thinking about Charlie leaving her or reporters or Pete's whereabouts, was suddenly the most enticing thing in the world. Helga always had the knack of knowing exactly what she needed.

Eva gave her a grateful smile. 'Sounds wonderful. Thanks.'

Helga turned off to Vaucluse Road then down Queens Avenue, where luckily, she found a space in the small parking area. They unloaded the picnic hamper and a cold bag, carrying one each, and negotiated the steep rocky path down to the beach. Once there, they took off their shoes and walked along the hard sand, weaving in and out of clumps of rock.

A woman and a toddler paddled in the shallows, and a young couple lay on a towel on the sand, arms and legs entwined around each other. Eva looked away, banishing the memories from her mind.

They stopped at a shady spot under a clump of pandanus palms. Helga took out a picnic rug from the hamper and spread it out on the ground. They were surrounded by bushland. The ocean, glistening in shades of blue and aqua, stretched out to the Harbour Bridge and the Opera House on the horizon. The only sounds were the symphony of chirping crickets and screeching seagulls.

Helga laid out some crusty bread, cold meats, pate and cheese, opened a bottle of sauvignon blanc and poured them both a generous glass.

'Just being out in nature makes me feel fabulous,' she said. 'Almost as good as sex. She raised her glass. 'To nature.'

They clinked glasses and sipped. Eva realised she hadn't eaten for hours and made herself a ham and mustard sandwich.

'You have to set me straight on that newspaper report,' Helga said. 'Were you really at a party at Sydenham?'

Eva thought of denying it, but how would she explain why her handbag was found there?

'A friend knew someone having a party there, so I went along.'

'What friend was this?'

'You wouldn't know him.'

'Him. Okay, I get the picture. But Sydenham?' She shook her head. 'What's going on with you and Charlie?'

It was pointless denying it, Helga would find out soon enough. 'Charlie has moved out. But it's only temporary to give ourselves time apart. We'll work things out.'

Saying the words out loud gave them credibility—she almost believed them herself. And she didn't mention that he'd ordered her to leave, because she had no intention of doing so.

'Really? In my experience, when people say they're taking time apart, it's usually the beginning of the end.'

'In this case, it's not true,' Eva snapped.

'Where does Veronika fit into all of this?'

'She thinks she's got the better of me, but she's wrong. I've invested everything in this marriage, Charlie's not going to dispense with me as if I were one of his tarts.'

Helga spread some pate on a crust of bread. 'Tell me again how you met Charlie.'

'I've told you the story.'

'But I want to hear it again.'

'Why?'

'It's romantic.'

Eva looked at Helga with suspicion. Romance and Helga were mutually exclusive.

Helga waved her crust of bread at her. 'Fire away.'

‘My boss had asked me to drop off some papers to a client. I didn’t see the red light in time and ran into the back of Charlie’s car.’

‘Where was the client’s office?’

‘In St Ives. What’s this about?’

Helga pointed the butter knife at her. ‘If I remember correctly, you told me you worked in Coogee and you ran into the back of Charlie's car in St Ives. An hour’s drive on a good day. A long way to go to deliver papers to a client.'

'What are you getting at?'

'I'm always interested in how couples meet. That random chance that they both happen to be in the same place at the same time. Or sometimes, not so random.'

'What's that supposed to mean?'

'I think your story's just what you said it is—a story. I think you planned the whole thing. Somehow you found out where Charlie lived and you followed him when he left home and deliberately ran into the back of his car as a way of meeting him, so you could work your charms on him. You had to engineer it because you would never have had the opportunity to meet him socially.'

In her previous life Eva had always wondered if Helga suspected the truth about her meeting Charlie. The same way as she'd wondered if Helga had guessed the truth about Charlie's death.

'So what? It's not a crime.'

'Don't get me wrong, honey. I'm not condemning you. I'm in awe of the planning that went into it. How could you be so sure he'd fall for you?'

'How do you think? The usual—flattery, admiration, vulnerability and weave in some mystery and playing hard to get. And sex, of course. You just have to know the right quantities and ratio.'

'Granted that would work for most, but Charlie's not just any man. He'd been married twice before, not to mention his playboy reputation, so he'd had a lot of experience with the games women play.'

'I did my research,' Eva said. 'It wasn't hard. There's a lot of public information about him. I knew he'd be an ideal candidate because it was five years since his second divorce and I figured he'd be thinking it was about time he married again. Men like him need to be married, like they need the mansions and the fancy cars. Both his previous wives had been outspoken and assertive, so I figured he'd be looking for a woman who was more pliant, who was happy to just be Mrs Charles Dennehy, to take care of home and hearth and leave the limelight for him. And I was right.'

'If I was wearing a hat, I'd take it off to you,' Helga said. 'You've played the role to perfection.'

'It's not a role, it's who I am.' She finished her wine and Helga refilled their glasses. 'I admit it was difficult when we were first married, I knew I was being evaluated and judged—people either thought I was a calculating gold-digger or a girl from the wrong side of the tracks who was way out of her depth. I had to prove to them, and to myself, that I was up to the task.'

'You certainly did that.'

'There was more to it than just meeting Charlie and reeling him in. I knew that someone like him would require his wife to be not only beautiful and charming, but also at ease within his social circle. She had to be intelligent, have an appreciation of the arts and able to hold a conversation on any subject. So I studied.'

'You went to university?'

Eva shook her head. 'I nursed my mother through cancer for the last eighteen months of her life. I had plenty of spare time, apart from my nursemaid duties, so I'd go to the local library and arm myself with books on art, music, literature, history, politics. I even studied sports and forced myself to watch it on TV, so I could impress men with my knowledge.'

'But you hadn't met Charlie then.'

'No. At that time I had no-one specific in mind. I just knew that once Mum died, I was going to do my damndest to make a new life for myself. I looked around at all the girls I went to high school with—they were either living with their no-hoper boyfriends and a tribe of kids, on the dole smoking dope all day, or in some dead-end factory job. There was no way I was going to end up like that and a wealthy husband was my ticket out of that life. It was only later when I was doing my research that I decided Charlie would be the ideal candidate.'

Helga shook her head. 'I have to hand it to you, Eva. You are one hell of a determined woman.'

'But I made one crucial mistake,' Eva said. 'I fell in love with him. That wasn't part of the plan.'

'You really think it was a mistake?'

Eva gave a bitter laugh. 'Listen to you, oh rational one! According to your logic I shouldn't have allowed myself to fall in love with him at all.'

'On the contrary. Falling in love with the man you were planning to marry regardless seems a very sensible thing to do.'

‘Perhaps—if he could keep his dick in his pants. If I didn't love Charlie, it wouldn't hurt so much that he's unfaithful. I can't help my jealousy—this shrill, demanding, needy woman takes over my mind and I can't stop her. And the difference now is that he's in love with Veronika, so even if I wanted to, I couldn't ignore it. He's probably with her right now, fucking her brains out.'

She put her head in her hands, rubbed the tears out of her eyes and looked up. 'If he leaves me, I have nothing. Not even myself.'

If I'm no longer Eva Dennehy, wife, lover and companion to Charles Dennehy, who am I?

'How will you persuade him to come back?'

'I'm working on it.'

Although her plans had gone up in smoke, all was not completely lost. If the police acted on Pete's information and Charlie was charged, that might scare Veronika off. She might think twice about having a criminal as a husband and the father of her child. And where would that leave her, Eva? Would Charlie have her back if Veronika wasn't on the scene? And if he went to jail, what would happen to his business, to all his wealth? Would she be left with nothing?

Then there was the matter of Sol. Helga would be affected as well if Sol went to jail. How much did she know? Eva tried to think of a way she could broach the subject, to find out what Helga knew without giving away her own involvement.

She was aware that Helga was saying something.

'—which I know you'll completely ignore, is that if Charlie is determined to divorce you and start a new life with Veronika, sooner or later you have to accept it.

You can't make him stay and you can't make him love you.'

'That smacks of giving up. And I'm not ready to give up.'

'There's a fine line between perseverance and stubbornness.' Helga downed her wine. 'No more for me, seeing as I'm the chauffeur. It's gone straight to my bladder.'

She peered into the bushland behind them. 'Don't fancy going in there, there could be snakes. I'll go for a wander.'

She got up and headed off down the beach, rounded an outcrop of rock and disappeared from view. She'd left her handbag beside the picnic hamper. Eva picked it up. It was large, almost the size of a tote bag, dark brown Louis Vuitton with gold trimmings. She undid the clasp and looked inside.

In the main compartment was Helga's purse, a packet of tissues, a small cosmetic bag, a bottle of spring water and a muesli bar. Eva took out the purse and opened it. Credit cards, several notes, bulging coin compartment. She counted the notes. Four hundred and thirty-five dollars. She slipped out two fifty dollar notes and a handful of two dollar coins and put them into her own purse. She wanted to take more but didn't dare. Helga might not miss a hundred dollars, perhaps would think she'd miscounted or spent more than she thought. Even if she did miss it, would she immediately suspect Eva?

In any case, she had no choice but to take it. All her credit cards were at their limit and she'd spent the last of her cash advance on the taxi ride home from Pete's office. Since Charlie had cut off her access to his bank accounts, the only way she could get money was to ask him. And that was one thing she refused to do right at this moment; even if she knew where he'd gone.

Keeping one eye out for Helga's return, Eva rummaged around in the inside pockets of the handbag in case she had more money stashed away. Tampons, condoms, address book and pen, more tissues. In the largest zip-up pocket her hand gripped something hard. She knew instantly what it was. Gingerly she took it out. A revolver, silver with black handle, smaller and more compact than the one she'd found under Charlie's couch.

Why in hell would Helga be carrying a gun in her handbag? Was she up to her neck in this drug trafficking operation as well? There was a world of difference between knowing it was going on and being a part of it, and it was hard to believe that Helga's loyalty to Sol would extend to becoming involved in something so sordid and risky. Maybe she was just collateral fallout—perhaps Sol had been threatened and she was carrying the gun for her own self-protection.

Eva searched all the pockets again. No bullets. She opened the latch on the revolver. Six chambers, all loaded. Her heartbeat went into overdrive. Was Helga going to use the gun on her? Had she lured her to this beach under the pretence of a picnic to shoot her? Perhaps Sol had found out that Eva had obtained evidence of his and Charlie's activities and had instructed Helga to shoot her. Or perhaps Charlie had told Helga to shoot her—very convenient for him to have her out of the way.

Eva's hand shook as she closed the latch and slid the revolver back into the pocket of Helga's handbag. She zipped up the handbag and placed it back beside the picnic hamper. There was no sign of Helga yet. Eva jumped to her feet, slipped on her shoes, picked up her own handbag, and raced along the beach back to the rocky path. She looked back, just making out a flash of colour as Helga came into view.

Eva scrambled up the path, tripping over several times in her haste, stubbing her toe and scraping her knee. She raced through the car park and down Queen’s Avenue. It was only when she reached busy Vaucluse Road that she dared look behind her. No sign of Helga. She continued running, legs heavy, gasping for breath, hailing taxis as she went. None stopped. She reached a bus stop just as a bus pulled up, joined the queue and got on. It was going in the wrong direction, but she didn’t care.

At least she was safe.

CHAPTER TWENTY-SEVEN

A COUPLE of reporters were still loitering outside her front gate when the cab driver pulled up. She'd got off the bus at the first stop and walked to the nearest taxi rank. Thank God she had the money she'd stolen from Helga. She paid the driver and as she got out, the two reporters, one male and one female, pounced on her.

'Mrs Dennehy,' said the male, 'Can you comment on the party at Sydenham? Why did you go there?'

He was young, clean-cut, supercilious. Eva rounded on him.

'Who says I was there?'

'Your handbag—'

'In case you haven't noticed, my handbag is not me. And I'm sick of you lot hanging around making up stories about me. If you don't go right now I'm going to phone your editor and lodge a formal complaint that you've been harassing me.'

He held up his hands. 'Okay, no need to get upset, I'm just doing my job.'

She heard the click and whirr of a camera as the female reporter took several shots. Eva immediately saw the photo in her mind's eye and how it would be misconstrued—she leaning towards the reporter, he backing away with his hands up, as if she were about to attack him. She didn't even want to think about the accompanying caption.

The girl gave Eva a cheeky grin and grabbed her colleague's arm. 'Come on, Matt, let's go. We've got what we wanted.'

Eva turned and walked in the front gate. She heard a car's engine start up down the street and roar off. Once inside the house, she collapsed on the living room couch, weak and shaking from the after-effects of the shock of finding the gun in Helga's handbag and her anger at the reporters.

The house was like a mausoleum now that she knew Charlie wasn't coming home; cavernous and lonely, still echoing with the ghost of Dodie. She turned on the TV for the illusion of company.

She was at the bar fixing herself a scotch and soda when she heard, 'And coming up in the news tonight, a man's body was discovered in an alleyway at Newtown early this morning. He had been shot in the head. More in the six o'clock news.'

She heard the sound of shattering glass and looked down to see that she'd dropped her drink on the floor, fragments of glass swimming in a puddle of scotch. She cleaned it up, poured herself another, perched on the couch and waited. After an eternity six o'clock arrived. She gripped her glass as the news theme music gave way to a chic female newsreader.

After the leading story about a public spat between the prime minister and the leader of the opposition, a scene appeared of an alleyway between two dingy shops, cordoned off by crime scene tape.

'A man's body was discovered in an alleyway at Newtown early this morning. The man was identified as forty-four-year-old Peter James Homer, a private investigator from Manly.'

The scene changed to a stretcher with a blanket-covered body on it being loaded by two paramedics into an ambulance.

'He had been shot in the head. Police are appealing for witnesses to the incident to contact their local police station or Crimestoppers on— '

She stared blankly at the TV as the news she'd dreaded sank in. Newtown. A fair distance from his Pete's home, and a suburb with a large criminal element. Had he been lured there by someone pretending to have information? Or maybe he'd been killed somewhere else and his body dumped there. The time of death hadn't been publicised, but Eva knew with every instinct she possessed that it was before he'd had a chance to go to the police. The world had tilted, things were spiralling out of control. Now she knew why she'd kept that last stash of coke.

•••

Within seconds of inhalation, her head was clear and the familiar burst of energy surged through her. But it was energy born of anger, pulsing inside her with a life force of its own, as if there were a wild animal trapped inside her. Charlie had had a hand in Pete's death, she was sure of it. Maybe Sol, maybe even Helga. There was no-one left in the world she could trust.

She went into Charlie's study, extended the footrest of the couch and pulled the lever underneath it. The compartment slid into view and she opened it. Empty. Of course he'd taken his gun with him—no criminal worth his salt would be without one.

She got up and opened the top drawer of his desk. In it was a tray containing several bunches of keys, which she'd seen numerous times before. None of them were labelled—they could have been keys to drug storage warehouses, illegal casinos, former girlfriends' apartments, for all she knew.

Stuck to the back of the drawer with Blu-Tac was another bunch of keys. She pulled them out. The key tag was labelled number five, with no address, but she knew what they were. The keys to Charlie's apartment at Potts Point, where he was living when they met. He owned the whole block and rented them all out except for number five, which he kept vacant for the use of out of town business colleagues. There were two empty blobs of Blu-Tac on the back of the drawer where the other two sets of keys usually hung. She knew with a dead certainty that's where he was, shacked up with Veronika.

She took the keys, stuffed them in her jacket pocket and called for a taxi. It was eight o'clock, there was a good chance Charlie would be out, wining and dining Veronika. She could see them now, heads bowed towards one another as they planned their future together, Veronika smug as a Siamese cat, with her sleek skin and slanted eyes.

The cab arrived, Eva got in and gave the driver the address. As they drove along New South Head Road, she gazed up at the sky. The stars were bursting with brilliance; they seemed so close she could almost reach out and touch them. Was Pete up there somewhere? Of course not, that was just a story her mother told her as a child. When you died, you went up to heaven and became a star, shining down on all your loved ones, looking out for them until it was their turn to join you. *If you're up there, Pete, please don't get mad at me. Just keep on shining.*

'I beg your pardon?' the cab driver said.

Eva wasn't aware she'd spoken out loud. 'It's a lovely night, isn't it?'

The driver, an older man with a wizened face, needed no further encouragement to chat. 'Indeed it is. Are you going out to dinner?'

Eva looked down at her jeans, jacket and sandshoes. People went out to dinner in all sorts of outfits these days.

'Yes, I am. I'm meeting my husband and we're going out for dinner at our favourite restaurant, then we'll hire a gondola for a moonlight glide around the harbour and have a nightcap at one of the bars downtown.'

'You're very lucky to have such a romantic husband. The other night the wife and I went to—'

They chatted away until he pulled up outside the apartment block at the end of a cul-de-sac. A large neon sign announced it was Trendsetters. 'Five star Serviced Apartments. Urban living. Ocean views.'

She paid the driver, checking to make sure she had enough money to get home. 'Have a lovely night,' he said with a wink as she alighted.

The apartment block was seventies-style brick, but inside every unit had undergone a complete renovation. Eva used the swipe key to open the main doors, then again in the lift to the first floor.

Number five was at the end of the corridor on the right. Eva put her ear to the door. No sound from within. She rapped on the front door, body tensed, ready to duck into the garbage shute alcove down the corridor if she heard any movement from inside.

Silence. She rapped a second time and waited. Holding her breath, she inserted her key and unlocked the door. She opened it a little way and peered in. A short hallway opened out to a spacious dining and living area. No-one there. Eva slipped inside and locked the door behind her, making as little noise as possible. Just in case.

She hadn't been back here since her marriage, but it was exactly as she remembered it. Furnished in the style of a Home Beautiful magazine; even the sunglasses and folded newspaper on the dining table and the high heeled sandals on the floor near the couch looked like photograph props. The aura was one of a temporary stay—a business trip or a city holiday. It had seemed that way to Eva even when Charlie had lived here.

The curtains over the French doors were closed, hiding the wide balcony that boasted harbour and ocean views. She and Charlie had spent many mornings there having breakfast, bacon and eggs he'd cooked himself, when she stayed overnight.

No time for memories. Eva crept into each room, making certain there was no-one home. The stainless steel and marble kitchen gleamed like a TV ad for cleaning products. The two bedrooms, each with its own ensuite, were elegantly, yet comfortably fitted and furnished. The second bedroom showed no signs of habitation.

Eva entered the master bedroom, the room where she and Charlie had spent their first night together. The quilt cover was pulled up crookedly and the pillows piled haphazardly, as if making the bed was a last minute thing done before dashing out the door. A light, musky aroma hung in the air. *Her* perfume.

The first task was to find Charlie's revolver. His briefcase was beside the bed. She opened it and rifled through it. Nothing except business papers; Sydney city council development proposals. His suitcase stood in the corner of the bedroom next to a larger leopard skin case. Both empty.

She went into the walk-in wardrobe and rummaged through Charlie's clothes, then Veronika's as well, out of curiosity. Veronika liked smooth, flowing garments in purples, reds and browns. Eva felt a stab of envy. She loved those colours but they didn't suit her complexion.

In the corner of the wardrobe was Charlie's sports bag. Eva hauled it out. The odour of liniment wafted out as she opened it. There was a tube at the bottom of the bag, underneath a pair of shorts, singlet, socks, joggers, boxing gloves, hand wraps and mouthguard. So his devotion to Veronika didn't extend to giving up boxing—all the more reason to keep fit, to be able to match her energy in bed.

The photos of the two of them in bed that Pete had sent her flashed into her mind. She picked up the bag and threw it hard back into the wardrobe, where it hit the back wall with a satisfying thump.

She slid the wardrobe door closed and went into the ensuite. On one side of the shelf above the basin, Charlie's deodorant and shaving gear were neatly stacked. On the other side sprawled a jumble of creams, lotions and make-up. A hair straightener was plugged into the wall. So Veronika was the messy type. She smiled with grim satisfaction. How long would it take Charlie to get fed up with that?

She checked the cupboard under the basin and behind the toilet. Nothing. Surely Charlie hadn't taken it with him—a risky thing to do, if he was just out for dinner. It had to be somewhere easily accessed if he needed it in a hurry. The bedroom was the logical place. She searched Charlie's clothes again, including his trouser and coat pockets. There was one coat she hadn't seen before—a dark blue Burberry. Had Veronika given it to him?

There was nothing in any of the outer pockets, but when she slipped her hand into the top of the silk inner lining, she felt an opening in the fabric. She slid her hand down and closed her fingers around hard metal. She pulled out the revolver and ran her fingers over it, feeling its smoothness, its grooves and indentations, as if exploring a lover's familiar body. It had lost its menacing aura; it was her friend, her personal body guard.

She opened the cylinder. Empty. She slid her hand down the inner lining on the other side of the coat and pulled out the box of bullets. She opened the cylinder and slid in three bullets. *What the hell, put them all in.* She slid the other three in, closed the cylinder and threw the empty box on the floor. Of course she wasn't going to use the gun. It was just to give her control. People usually did what you wanted when you were pointing a gun at them.

Now all she had to do was wait. She went into the kitchen. You couldn't see into it from the front door and she could spring out and surprise Charlie and Veronika as soon as they walked in.

The beast roaring inside her was making her heart race and her nerve ends twitch. *Slow down. Breathe.* She looked around to distract herself. A coffee plunger with a sludge of coffee dregs in it stood on the kitchen bench. She looked in the pantry. A jar of coffee beans, a packet of herbal tea bags and a box of crackers. In the fridge was half a bottle of milk, a block of Edam cheese, a bottle of chilli sauce and an avocado. As she thought—Veronika wasn't into cooking.

An hour and a half later, she heard the scratching sound of the key turning in the door. She leapt to attention. Footsteps shuffled on the carpet, the door closed with a bang.

'Would you like a coffee, darling?'

Veronika's sultry tones.

'I'd love one, sweet pea. I've got some papers to go through before bed.' Charlie's voice sent her heart into a tailspin.

She stepped out of the kitchen and willing her hands not to shake, she pointed the gun straight at Charlie's chest.

Veronika screamed. 'What the fuck, Eva?' Charlie said.

'Shut up,' Eva said to Veronika. 'Or I'll shut you up.' Veronika shut her mouth, hands clutching her evening bag. Her hair was out over her shoulders and she wore a simple knee-length red dress that hinted at rather than defined her curves. Even frightened out of her wits, she oozed sensuality, and in that moment Eva hated her more than she had ever hated anyone in her life.

'How did you get in?' Charlie said. His voice was calm. If he was afraid, he was hiding it well.

'You killed Pete Homer, didn't you?'

'I don't know what you're talking about.' Oh, he was good. But she'd seen the subtle change of expression.

'Don't lie to me!' she screamed. She held his gaze, the gun steady in her hand. She knew he was trying to calculate the chances of her using it.

'I'm telling you the truth, I didn't kill him.'

'You had someone do your dirty work for you.'

He said nothing.

'Didn't you?' she screamed, tightening her grip on the gun.

'Why are you asking me? You're so sure you know the answer.'

Veronika looked at Charlie, eyes wide. 'What are you talking about?'

'Nothing that concerns you,' Charlie said. He put out his hand. 'Give me the gun, Eva.'

'So Veronika knows nothing about your unsavoury associations.' Eva gave Veronika a sly smile. 'Charlie's far from the fine upstanding citizen you think he is. If you knew the truth, you'd pack your bags pronto. And don't even think about having a baby.'

She gave a satisfied smile at the look on Veronika's face, shocked that Eva would know about her plans for a baby. Eva looked at Charlie. 'Will I tell her the truth?'

'There is no truth.' He held out his hand again. 'Give me the gun, Eva. If you kill me you'll spend the rest of your life in prison.'

'I'm not giving you the fucking gun, you filthy liar. You told me you were leaving me because I'd changed and you couldn't live with me any longer. But the truth is you left me for her.' She spat out the last sentence, giving Veronika a venomous look.

'Even if I hadn't met Veronika, I would have still left you. I think you know that, but you don't want to admit it.'

'Don't tell me what I know, you condescending prick. God knows you don't deserve it, but I'm giving you a choice. Come back to me or I'll go to the police.'

'With what?'

'With the evidence I have of your little sideline business. You've stopped Pete from doing it but you won't stop me.'

Veronika's knuckles were white from gripping her bag and she was looking from Charlie to Eva with bewilderment.

'Better still, I'll tell Veronika as well. Then you'll have no-one to run to.'

'Tell me what?' Veronika said, her voice shaking.

Eva aimed the gun at her. 'I told you to shut up!'

Veronika gave a whimper and shrank back.

Eva looked at Charlie. 'Well? What's your answer?'

Charlie shook his head. 'I'm not coming back, Eva. By all means go to the police, but they'll laugh at you. I don't have a sideline business, as you call it, and there's no evidence that I have.'

'That's where you're wrong,' Eva said. Pete had photocopied his findings to show to her, but she'd been so shocked at his disappearance that she hadn't thought to ask Barbara for it. In any case, Barbara probably wouldn't have given it to her without Pete's permission.

'I assure you I'm not. There is no evidence.'

The certainty in his voice stopped her. Was he telling her that Pete's office had been done over and the photocopied evidence destroyed? Her stomach knotted as she realised the truth of it. These were professional criminals—of course they would have destroyed every bit of evidence they could find. She could bluff and say she'd obtained a copy before they'd cleaned the office out, but if Charlie called her bluff, she had nothing.

'As for Veronika,' he continued, 'I doubt that she'll believe the ravings of a paranoid, hysterical drug user.'

'Is that so?' Eva turned her gaze to Veronika. 'Charlie and his partner in crime Sol have a very profitable drug running business and before he was so conveniently killed, Pete Homer had obtained evidence of them transferring large amounts of cash to a foreign bank account, using company names to hide their identity. He'd also obtained photos of Charlie with a member of one of the most notorious crime gangs in the country and I happen to know he's in cahoots with two of Sydney's top drug dealers.'

Veronika looked at Charlie, her face rumpled as if about to burst into tears. 'Tell me that's not true,' she whispered.

'Of course it's not true,' Charlie said. 'She's made the whole lot up. It's her idea of revenge for me leaving her.'

'Revenge?' Eva said, as if the idea had just occurred to her. 'How about this for revenge? Come back to me or I'll kill you.'

For the first time since he'd entered the room, a shadow of fear passed across Charlie's face. He took a step forward. 'Please Eva, I beg you—'

'Stop right there,' Eva commanded. 'Do you love her?'

Charlie spread his hands in a placating gesture. 'I'll answer your questions if you put the gun down. We can work things out without it.'

'Just tell me the truth or I'll shoot you.' She marvelled at her own voice—so steely calm.

Silence. Veronika took one hand off her bag, reached for Charlie's hand and gripped it.

'All right, I love her.'

Charlie leapt forward. Eva pulled the hammer back and pressed the trigger. The crack was deafening, her arm shot up in the air. Charlie stopped in his tracks, clutching his shoulder. Veronika gave a piercing scream. 'Charlie!'

Eva aimed for Charlie's chest and pressed the trigger again. Charlie rocked on his feet, then slumped back against the couch and slid to the floor, a stain of red spreading across his shirtfront.

Veronika was still screaming, it was making her head hurt. This woman she hated was just a pathetic creature, like herself. They were both pathetic, united in their love for this man who was lying dead on the floor.

The wild animal inside her had died as well. Shrivelled to nothing. Eva was exhausted, trembling from head to toe, as if her bones had collapsed and couldn't hold her flesh together. She slid on to the floor, cradling the gun in her lap. She didn't know how long it was before she heard the sirens.

CHAPTER TWENTY-EIGHT

September 2016

'IT'S good of you to drop in, Bishop. I'm in need of some company.'

Father O'Halloran ushered in the bulky, ruddy-faced man whose presence filled his tiny living room. 'Would you like a cup of tea?'

The Bishop made a show of looking at his watch. 'It's almost four. I think we could have something stronger, don't you?'

'Of course. Have a seat, I'll get us a Scotch.'

Father O'Halloran went to a small cabinet and took out a bottle of Johnnie Walker black label Scotch he kept especially for the Bishop's visits. He went into the kitchen and returned with two glasses of Scotch and soda on ice. He sat opposite the Bishop in a worn recliner. They raised their glasses in a silent toast.

'You look tired, Mick,' the Bishop said.

Father O'Halloran smiled. 'It's been a long sixty-nine years. I'm looking forward to retirement at the end of the year.'

'You said you were in need of company. Is something troubling you?'

'Nothing apart from the usual. It's just nice to talk to someone about things other than the floral arrangements for the Sunday services, hospital visits and funerals—worthy though that all is, of course.'

The Bishop placed his drink on the side table and leaned back into the couch, trying in vain to derive some comfort from its unyielding hardness. 'So how's our celebrity murderess going?'

'I believe the correct term these days is murderer for both sexes. Never let it be thought that our female murderers are of a lesser status than the males. And to answer your question, she seems to be going well. Of course it's early days—she's only been out two months and she's still adjusting. Twenty years is a long time to be locked away from the world, and life is vastly different now.'

'You've seen her often?'

'I've visited her on a few occasions. She's in a small flat in Auburn, very dingy, a far cry from what she was used to before. But it was all the parole people could find for her.'

'Better than a prison cell, I'm sure.'

'Indeed.'

The Bishop leaned forward, his hands hanging between his legs like slabs of raw meat.

'An extraordinary outcome, you'd have to agree.'

Father O'Halloran sighed. 'Yes and no. Yes, because she was given the opportunity to live her life again and atone her sins, and instead she commits the same sin again. And in a much more spectacular fashion than the first time. And no, because this is human nature. At best, unpredictable; at worst, repeatedly submitting to temptation and unable or unwilling to accept the grace of God.'

'But you have to admit, Mick, that this is the most notable incident of lack of penance you've encountered since you've started this—whatever you call it. Witchcraft.'

'I object to that term. I believe my gift comes from God.'

The Bishop made a noise between a snort and a 'Hmmph,' downed his Scotch and held out his glass for more. When Father O'Halloran returned from the kitchen with his refill, he said, 'You know I've only condoned this for all these years because if I told the Cardinal he'd send me for psychological testing and then put me out for early retirement. '

And because you can't stop me doing it anyway, Father O' Halloran thought. Out loud he said, 'Come on, Bishop, you know you love listening to all the stories of how people have used or abused their opportunities for redemption.'

The Bishop permitted himself a half smile. 'I do admit that. You should write your memoir—a pity no-one would believe it. Now, about Mrs Dennehy. Do you believe she's atoned for her sins now?'

Father O'Halloran took a large swig of his Scotch. He rarely drank alcohol, but this case had got under his skin as well. 'She has paid her due in man's court of law, but as for her spiritual atonement, that's between her and God.'

'Surely she feels remorse for murdering her husband a second time.'

'That's true, but I think in some way she feels redeemed this time around. In her previous life, she killed her husband but was never punished for it and carried around the burden of guilt for twenty years. We've both seen the effects of guilt; it eats away at your body and your soul. The longer you carry it around, the worse it gets. It sends many stark raving mad. Now she still has that burden for the rest of her life, but serving twenty years in prison has gone some way to satisfying her need for punishment.'

'And she's had to endure the judgments of society at large and being put under the media microscope,' the Bishop said. 'What did they call her? That's right, the White Widow. Just today I read an article in The Herald about prison sentences. The Shadow Attorney General was trotting out the usual hard line about how violent criminals should serve their full sentences and Mrs Dennehy was given as an example.'

Father O'Halloran shook his head. 'In her case, keeping her in prison for the rest of her life would serve no rehabilitative purpose whatever. It was a crime passionnel, as the French call it, it's not something she would ever do to anyone else. And as for all the media hype, she's borne it all with admirable grace. She told me, "Father, I've been through hell, nothing anyone has said about me could hurt me."'

'What are her plans now?'

'She did a Bachelor of Arts degree in prison, English and history—she got Honours too. Says she did it out of boredom but also to prove to herself that she could. I don't know what she's got planned for the future, but she's a very determined woman, so I'm sure she'll be successful in whatever she decides to do.'

The Bishop drained his glass again and placed it on the side table. 'I'd love another, but I'd better not, as I'm driving. Don't want to see myself in tomorrow's headlines. So I take it that when you retire, your gift, as you call it, will retire with you?'

'I've already retired it.'

The Bishop raised his eyebrows. 'Oh?'

'I've been doing this for a long time, ever since I discovered in my first posting that I could send people back in time to undo their sins. And over the years, as you know, there have been some spectacular results. Criminals who've made good in their second lives and become fine upstanding citizens, men who've kept their families together instead of straying, and so on.

'And then there have been the failures, those who went on to commit the very same sins they had before—the philanderers who just couldn't help themselves, the businessmen who succumbed yet again to bribery and corruption. Or exchanging one sin for another—the drug addicts who became alcoholics, the promiscuous who channelled their sexual impulses into greed or selfishness. Admittedly, none fell from grace as spectacularly as our Mrs Dennehy. And it was she who caused me to really sit back and reflect.'

'How so?'

'You're aware she was under the influence of cocaine when she killed her husband?'

'Of course, it was splashed all over the headlines at the time.'

'I asked her if she'd have killed him if she hadn't taken it and she looked me straight in the eye and said, 'Yes.' So of course I asked her why. Why did she commit the same crime when the whole purpose of travelling back in time was to prevent it? And she said, "Father, some things are just meant to happen, and nothing or no-one, not even God, can prevent them."'

'What are you saying, Mick? That some people are incapable of redemption? That no matter how many chances they're given, they're destined to keep sinning?'

Father O'Halloran clasped his hands together in a steeple. 'I don't believe there's a person on this earth who's not capable of redemption, if they're willing to do the work. But I've always had ambivalent feelings about my powers. On the one hand if God had, as I believed, bestowed them upon me, then it was my duty and responsibility to use them.

‘But it also seemed to me that I was interfering with the will of God by doing so. It takes a tremendous amount of energy—physical, mental and spiritual—to transport someone back in time, with the consequence that I can only do one a month. It has always seemed unfair to me that only some people get a chance to redeem themselves, while others who are just as worthy miss out.'

'But if it's God's will that you use your powers, then is it not also his will that some miss out?'

'You could interpret it that way. But I'll tell you another thing. I kept a record of the results of every single time travel I executed, and on balance, more people failed to undo their sins than succeeded. So looking at the bigger picture, it hasn't done humanity any good. And it also proves—as if we need any proof—that we humans are by nature spiritually and morally weak.

‘So when Mrs Dennehy, who is admittedly calculating and self-centred but is not, I believe, an evil person at heart, tells me that nothing could have stopped her from killing her husband, I think it's time for an old, tired man to bow out gracefully.'

The Bishop glared at Father O'Halloran. 'Cynicism doesn't become you, Mick. Maybe it's a good thing you're retiring.'

Not cynicism, realism. But Father O'Halloran didn't say so aloud—the Bishop had a tendency to become argumentative after a couple of drinks.

The Bishop heaved himself to his feet. 'Time for me to go before I overstay my welcome. Thank-you for your hospitality. I'll miss our little chats.'

At the front door he turned. 'By the way, those records you have of your time travellers—I'd love to have a read of them some time.'

Father O'Halloran gave a wry smile. 'Sorry, Bishop, I shredded them. There's no evidence whatsoever that any of this happened at all. It's all just a figment of your imagination.'

The Bishop shot him a look as if he didn't quite believe him, gave another 'Hmmph' and left. Father O'Halloran watched his stout figure ambling to his car parked on the kerbside. It was true that he'd shredded the records—only yesterday in fact. He didn't want them getting into the wrong hands after he died. As the Bishop said, no-one would believe them anyway, but all those who'd participated—and there'd been hundreds over the years—deserved their privacy.

He checked his diary for the next day. A meeting with the parish committee in the morning and a social visit to Eva Dennehy in the afternoon. He looked forward to his visits with her. She was still a good-looking woman despite twenty years in prison; the fine bone structure of her face and the liveliness of her eyes drew your attention away from the pouches under them and the sagging skin under her jaw.

He was certainly not immune to feminine charms, and he could see why Charles Dennehy, experienced playboy though he was, had fallen for her. Flirting was as natural to her as breathing, and she emanated that irresistible blend of little-girl innocence and bad-girl seductiveness.

An uncharitable thought flashed through his mind. *Just as well you're not rich, or she'd make a play for you.* Whenever he felt himself succumbing to her flattery, he reminded himself that this woman was a murderer. Twice over.

But it didn't stop him from enjoying being thoroughly trounced by her in a game of Scrabble.

CHAPTER TWENTY-NINE

'YOU don't have to keep visiting me, Father,' Eva said. 'I'm sure God is far from happy with me, but I don't intend to start going to Mass anytime soon.'

Father O'Halloran smiled. 'I'm aware of that. But everyone needs friends and that's what I'm offering you—the hand of friendship.'

Eva poured the boiling water over the Darjeeling tea leaves in the teapot. It was hard to maintain standards in a place like this, but she did her best. She'd spent most of her first social security payment after her release from prison on a bone china crockery set to use for guests. But so far her only visitor had been Father O'Halloran.

'That's very kind of you.' She set the teapot and cups and saucers on the scratched, rickety table, a charity shop special, opened the rust-stained fridge door and took out a plate of tiny custard tarts and sponge fingers. 'Although I know you only come for the food.'

'I should be thankful my other parishioners don't bake as well as you, or I'd be heart attack material.'

Eva poured the tea, lifted her cup and inhaled the aroma before taking a sip. Prison taught you to appreciate the simple pleasures, like a decent cup of tea. Which was the strongest thing she drank these days. Alcohol was off limits while she was on parole, but in any case she had no desire to drink.

'As for friends,' she said, 'I've learnt to enjoy my own company. I didn't want to get too close to anyone in prison.'

The only person who'd tried to stay in contact after she went to prison was Helga, who'd rung the women's correctional centre many times to get permission to visit her, but Eva had refused to see her. A year later she received a letter from Helga saying that Sol had retired and they were sailing around the world in a chartered yacht. Over the ensuing years, as the gangland wars in Melbourne hotted up and many of the main players, including the McCarthy family, were killed by rivals, Eva wondered if Sol had seen it coming and escaped before the heat was turned on to him. Charlie's name never came up, and the Dennehy Corporation was bought out by a Japanese consortium.

Five years into her sentence, Eva happened to read a small paragraph in the daily newspaper that Solomon Berman, lawyer and property developer and former associate of murdered businessman Charles Dennehy had drowned off a Samoan island, leaving behind a wife, a son from a previous marriage and two grandchildren.

Drowned or murdered? Eva suspected the latter. Did the fact that Helga's life had been spared mean that she'd played no part in Sol's and Charlie's criminal activities? Or did she still keep a gun in her handbag, afraid that retribution would one day catch up with her? Eva felt a pang of sadness, and in that moment realised how much she had missed her friend. Helga would be distraught at Sol's death, but she was a survivor. She'd get on with her life, undoubtedly console herself with a new lover.

'I'm sure you won't be lacking in male friendships,' Father O'Halloran said. 'I hope you don't mind me saying you're still a very attractive woman. '

'Thank-you. You've aged pretty well yourself. That's what comes of being a priest, I guess. No sins of the flesh.' She flashed him a coquettish smile. 'But as for men, I've had two lifetimes of them. More than enough for any woman.'

'Present company excepted,' she added. She offered the plate of cakes to Father O'Halloran. 'If anyone had told me that at the age of sixty I'd be spending my time drinking tea and playing board games with a priest, I'd have told them they were mad.'

As she was setting up the Scrabble game, she said casually, 'The time travel, you've done that for other people, haven't you?'

Father O'Halloran took out seven face down tiles from the box and set them up with precise deliberation on the tile stand. 'You were the last; I'm retiring very soon. And that's all I'm saying on the matter. If you mention time travel again I'll deny it happened and no-one will believe you anyway. '

'I'm going to mention it one last time, because I want you to know something. On the surface of it, it looks as if I made a mess of it. I murdered Charlie a second time. But my life this time around has been infinitely better. Not because I paid the price of twenty years in jail for it—I could easily have come out just as torn up by guilt as when I'd gone in. But because I've realised what a useless emotion guilt is, acknowledged it not only in my head but deep in my heart.' She struck her chest in emphasis. 'It serves no purpose except to make you suffer and to make you look better in the eyes of other people. If you're seen as suffering from guilt about your crime, people are more disposed to feel sympathy towards you. And I'm sorry if this offends you, Father, but religion is responsible for so much guilt. If there were no suffering, you wouldn't be in business. So it's in your interest that people succumb to guilt.'

She pursed her lips and jutted her chin out. 'But I don't care one iota what people think of me. I refuse to let my guilt control me. It's always there, lurking in the background, but that's where it stays. That was my mistake in my first life, I allowed the guilt to get the better of me and eat me away, even to the extent of visions of Charlie haunting me every night. Do I miss him? Of course I do. Every day. There will never be another Charlie in my life. But there are no guarantees in life. He could just as easily have died of a heart attack, a genuine one, and I'd still be mourning him today.'

She looked at the tiles she'd assembled on her tile stand and a smile played around her lips. 'Let the game begin!'

•••

She won the Scrabble game yet again—how could she not? She'd had twenty years' practice. After Father O'Halloran left, she showered and changed into a simple black and white cocktail dress, stockings and white heels. Earlier in the week she'd taken a bus over to the affluent North Shore and spent hours scouring the charity shops until she'd found the Lisa Ho dress and Gucci sandals. The sandals were not her first choice; with their large buckles and thick straps, they were too clunky for her taste, but she had to make do. If the rest of her looked good, Henry wouldn't notice her shoes.

She put her hair up into a bun, fastening it with a tortoiseshell comb and allowing a couple of tendrils to fall down to frame her face. She applied her make-up artfully. Less was more when you got to this age. She checked the time. Four thirty. Twenty minutes until the bus, which stopped at the corner. She was meeting

Henry for coffee at Rosehill, a nearby suburb. He didn't drink either, which was a bonus.

She'd lied to Father O'Halloran about having no further interest in relationships. She hadn't met Henry yet, though she'd seen a photo of him, which he enclosed in the letter he sent her in prison. She'd received truckloads of letters, which she subsequently discovered happened to all celebrity prisoners.

Most were from men wanting to start a regular correspondence with a view to meeting in person. Some even skipped this step and proposed marriage right away. The letters ranged from crazy and downright obscene to needy and lonely, and she wondered at the perverse mentality of men wanting to meet a woman who'd murdered her husband. Did they want to hear the gory details? Or did they think they were the one who could restore her faith in men? Maybe it was the pure thrill of it, that they could boast to their friends that they were on intimate terms with the White Widow.

One of the letters she received was from Ray, shortly after her incarceration. 'So sorry to hear about your circumstances, I always thought your husband must have been a bastard. I still love you Eva, and what you've done hasn't changed that at all. Can I come and see you? '

Eva didn't bother replying. Ray sent more letters, each one a detailed account of his boring life and his troublesome kids, and ending with, 'I love you, Eva. Please let me come and see you.' After six months he gave up and she never heard from him again.

Henry's letter, which she received five years before her release, was the only one she replied to. It stood out in its simplicity and honesty. And he had money, though she was yet to confirm if this was true, and if so, how much. He was a retired engineer from the North Shore and owned a number of investment properties. His wife had died two years previously, he had two adult children, and liked golfing, sailing and travelling.

'I'm writing because I thought you might be bored and welcome some intelligent conversation, albeit by letter. I'm enclosing a photo so you can see I'm a normal person.'

In the photo he was standing on a beach in jeans and t-shirt holding an ice-cream cone. Tall and ungainly-looking with a paunch, thinning hair and thick spectacles. Not her type at all. But that was fine, she didn't want to fall in love. And a homely man was less likely to stray and end up wanting a divorce.

They wrote to each other regularly until the day she got out. Henry was well-read and in their letters they discussed art, literature, history, the politics of the day—anything except Eva's day to day life in prison, which she refused to talk about. He sent her books he thought would be useful for her studies. What Henry lacked in looks he made up for in sincerity. And perseverance. They talked on the phone occasionally, but it was strained. Eva was so conscious of her surroundings—other prisoners constantly walking past the phone, sometimes blatantly listening—that she found it hard to relax. If she wasn't forthcoming or had to end the conversation abruptly, he understood.

After a while he asked if he could visit her in prison, but she refused. She wanted to be in control when they met in person, not in the visitors' room with its hard plastic chairs and flickering fluorescent lights, being watched by cameras and screws.

On her release from prison, Henry was champing at the bit to meet her, but she kept him at bay for the first few weeks.

'Please be patient for a little longer,' she begged him over the phone. ‘I need some time to adjust to my new life.’

'But I can help you with that.'

'I know you can, and I'm looking forward to you helping me.' Warmth with just the right amount of flirtation.

And now, finally, the time was right. She'd taken playing hard to get to its extreme, and Henry had passed the test with flying colours. She felt strong and self-confident.

She locked the front door behind her, squared her shoulders and stepped out into the grey, smoggy afternoon and the roar of traffic. Through an open window she heard the woman in the apartment next door screaming at her child over the blare of the TV.

If all went well with Henry, she'd be out of here before too long.

THE END

Thank-you for buying Murder Undone. I hope you enjoyed it.

I would appreciate it very much if you would take a few minutes to leave an honest review on Amazon or whichever site you bought it from. Reviews help other readers to decide whether they will enjoy the book, as well as helping it to gain more visibility and ultimately, more sales.

Nothing is more rewarding for me than people reading and enjoying my books.

Get my e-book of four short crime stories On The Edge by
becoming a subscriber to Storey-Lines.
Go to http://storey-lines.com for your free copy now.

ACKNOWLEDGMENTS

As usual, this book is a result of input from many others; I have a fantastic team of assistants and cheerleaders.

Thank-you to fellow authors Andrew Patterson and Garry Rodgers, and my daughter Emma Hoiberg for their help with my research into poisons and police and legal procedures. I'm indebted to my beta readers Aaron Parker, Pam Mariko and Alison Quigley for all the time and energy they put into reading the manuscript and providing valuable feedback and constructive criticism.

Judy Bullard has once again come up with a brilliant cover design and my thanks also to Jo Robinson for her prompt and efficient service with my proofreading.

My family is always in the background cheering me on and I couldn't have written this book without the love and support of my partner Aaron Parker, who is not only one of my beta readers, but also helps me brainstorm ideas, answers questions about everything from sports cars to guns and is my on-the-spot technical support person.

OTHER BOOKS BY ROBIN STOREY

For books in the Noir Nights crime/suspense series and Robin's stand-alone novels, please visit Storey-Lines http://storey-lines.com or find Robin Storey on Amazon or IngramSpark.

E-books are available at all major e-book retailers.

ABOUT THE AUTHOR

Robin Storey is an indie author who lives on the picturesque Sunshine Coast in Queensland, Australia. She's a former freelance writer who is hooked on writing novels – it's the most challenging, but also the most satisfying thing she's done.

Robin is a certified book nerd and recharges her creative batteries by getting out into nature – hiking and chilling out at the beach.

Robin would love to connect with you on the following social media sites:

Facebook
https://www.facebook.com/RobinStoreywriter

Twitter https://twitter.com/RobinStorey1

Goodreads
http://www.goodreads.com/author/show/7057008.Robin_Storey

Robin Storey

www.ingramcontent.com/pod-product-compliance
Lightning Source LLC
Chambersburg PA
CBHW030626110726
47901CB00002B/338

* 9 7 8 0 9 8 7 5 3 6 6 8 6 *